I0583963

THE REBELLIOUS SISTER

THE REBELLIOUS SISTER

UNSTOPPABLE LIV BEAUFONT™ BOOK 1

SARAH NOFFKE
MICHAEL ANDERLE

DISRUPTIVE IMAGINATION

The Rebellious Sister (this book) is a work of fiction.

All of the characters, organizations, and events portrayed in this novel
are either products of the author's imagination or are used fictitiously.
Sometimes both.

Copyright © 2019 NM Sarah Noffke & Michael Anderle
Cover copyright © LMBPN Publishing
A Michael Anderle Production

LMBPN Publishing supports the right to free expression and the value of
copyright. The purpose of copyright is to encourage writers and artists
to produce the creative works that enrich our culture.

The distribution of this book without permission is a theft of the
author's intellectual property. If you would like permission to use
material from the book (other than for review purposes), please contact
support@lmbpn.com. Thank you for your support of the author's rights.

LMBPN Publishing
PMB 196, 2540 South Maryland Pkwy
Las Vegas, NV 89109

First US Edition, February 2019
Version 1.03, March 2021
eBook ISBN: 978-1-68500-375-3
Print ISBN: 978-1-64202-135-6

Thanks to the JIT Readers

John Ashmore
Misty Roa
Daniel Weigert
Keith Verret
Angel LaVey
Peter Manis
Crystal Wren
Kelly O'Donnell
Jeff Eaton
Micky Cocker
Terry Easom
Larry Omans

If I've missed anyone, please let me know!

Editor
The Skyhunter Editing Team

For Kathy.
Thank you for giving me my first fantasy book.
Since then, the world has been a better place.

CHAPTER ONE

In every person's life, there is that rare and distinct moment when they doubt their loyalties. Ian Beaufont was living in that moment, an internal battle waging itself on his insides. He was much closer to finding out *the* truth, yet the closer he got, the more he felt like an avalanche was about to befall him.

At the threshold to the cottage he shared with his sister, Ian checked over his shoulder. The Pacific Ocean crashed against the shore on the other side of the house. The night had swallowed the cottage, making it blend into the dark sky and hillside. Maybe if he wasn't so tired, he'd venture down the stairs and stroll along the beach later that night. The gentle beating of the ocean on the sand always put him at ease, which was why he and Reese had chosen this place away from headquarters. No one knew they had it, and it would stay that way for as long as they needed to uncover *the* truth.

Ian held up his hand in front of the seemingly ordinary deadbolt on the cottage door. Touching nothing, he twirled his hand a half inch to the right, two inches to the left and then reversed in a full circle as if he were unlocking a safe, muttering an incantation as he did. A moment later the door creaked opened, granting him admission to his home.

Before Ian was even over the threshold, he began pulling off his scarf and long traveling jacket. The winds were mild that night in Southern California, but they'd been punishing an hour ago in London.

"Reese, I'm home," Ian called, squinting in the dark for a place to lay his jacket. It felt like ages since he'd been home, but maybe that was because he'd missed it so much. This was the only place where he knew what was going on.

Ian directed his hand to the chandelier that hung over the great table in the middle of the room, but strangely, nothing happened. It wasn't like he had to worry that a bulb was burned out. Those things never mattered for magicians.

"Reese?" Ian called again to the quiet house. "What's going on with the lights?"

He peered at the chandelier, catching the ambient light that traveled through the bank of windows that faced the ocean, then spotted the open bottle of red wine on the table. He lifted it, surprised by how light it was. He didn't have to read the label to know it was a bottle of Opus One, Reese's favorite.

Ian sighed. "You got started without me? I thought we said no drinking until after we debriefed?"

No answer came from the back bedrooms like he'd expected.

She'd probably drunk herself to sleep, and he couldn't

blame her. It was hard for Reese to stay behind while he was off on missions, but that was her role as councilor.

Ian brought the half-empty bottle to his nose and sniffed, welcoming the aroma of dark fruit and spice. Those familiar scents hit him at once, but there was something else—a subtle note of oleander. One wouldn't even have noticed it if one wasn't acquainted with the poison.

Ian dropped the bottle, his heart suddenly racing. He didn't even look back as it toppled to the table and rolled onto the floor, spilling its contents over the polished tile.

He burst into the back bedroom, wishing a damn light worked somewhere. Every attempt he made to ignite one was futile. When he pushed the door open to Reese's bedroom, he froze. His heart tightened in his chest, his resolve nearly breaking. His sister looked like a statue that had fallen over, collapsed elegantly on the hearth in front of her fireplace. The coals were still red but slowly dying.

Ian rushed to her, pressing his hands to her neck, but he was unsurprised to find no pulse. She'd drunk half the bottle. There was no recovering from that much poison. There was no magic he could do to save his sister. She was gone forever.

Behind him, the door creaked. Ian stiffened. He wasn't alone. He'd felt it all night, but only now realized the sinister implications. Ian had defeated leagues of enemies. He had single-handedly brought down a sea monster the size of a battlecruiser. He was the strongest warrior the House of Seven had raised in centuries. However, if someone had gotten this far then he knew his options were limited.

Gently lowering Reese's head back down, Ian rose to face the open door.

It was hard to make out the figure in the doorway but the familiar shape of the man's eyes and rattling of his breath gave him away.

"This was you? How did you find us?" he asked, his doubts falling away to allow the picture he'd been trying to construct for quite some time to form.

"Ian, you can't hide anything from me. I know you've gotten too close. You've forgotten your place," the man said, his voice a raspy whisper that seemed to travel great distances to reach his ears.

Ian's fingers twitched by his side, but without making more than the slightest movement, he knew something was wrong with his magic. Somehow it had been disabled. Only one organization was powerful enough to disrupt a magician's magic like this. Ian had no time to deal with the disappointment. He'd been right to follow the leads, but it had also been dangerous, as he and Reese had known. For her, it had been deadly.

Ian sprang forward, picking up the side table next to the hearth and throwing it in the direction of the other magician. The table crashed against the doorframe where the man had been; he had disappeared and reappeared a few feet away. From that distance, Ian could see his face more clearly: the ancient wrinkles and the eyes he'd always mistaken as kind.

"You can't get away with this," Ian said, scanning the room for options. Without magic, he was…normal, and his options were few. He hadn't believed this day would come.

Ironically it had, and against the one man he never thought would be his adversary.

"We already have, poor Ian," the man said. "You should have left things alone."

Ian felt behind him for the fireplace poker, but when he had it in his hand, the would-be weapon flew from his fingers, landing on the far side of the room.

The man shook his head. "You know I think of you as a son."

Ian grimaced, pain in his heart making it hard to breathe. He pointed at his dead sister. "And was she like your daughter?"

The magician's face remained indifferent. "I didn't like killing her, nor will I like doing the same to you. But I promise, just like with your sister, I'll make it as painless as I can."

The magician raised his withered hand and instantly Ian felt the constriction in his throat. His feet rose off the ground and he kicked, trying to fight but sadly knowing it was useless. All his life, he'd felt the magic flowing in his blood, and, in the moments before his death, he felt its absence. What had ended his sister and would soon be his own demise was magic so powerful and encompassing that there was no way to fight it. He closed his eyes as his breath ran out, his vision turning black as he was lowered gently to the ground.

The old magician was careful to lay Ian beside his sister, making them look like they'd just fallen asleep on an awkward place on the floor. He had thought so fondly of the two. Had expected great things of them. But their loyalties, in the end, had been misplaced. They had put everything in danger, and so there had been no choice but to end them.

From the pocket of his blue silk robes, the magician pulled a single red flake the size and color of a rose petal. He let it fall from his fingertips and it caught a draft and drifted down, landing gently on the floor beside the bodies.

"What's done is done," the magician said, and strode for the unlocked door. When he was safely across the front step and back into the salty air, he spoke a single incantation and the small cottage erupted into violent flames that would burn everything inside.

CHAPTER TWO

"Open up already!" Liv Beaufont yelled, banging on the door. She pulled back her foot, ready to kick the crummy old thing when John's voice called from the other side.

"If you break it, you buy it," he warned, referring to the door.

She stomped, furious that he always seemed to know what she was going to do before she did it.

"Well, then open the door and take your meds, old man" she said, reaching into her pocket and retrieving the pill bottle John had left at the repair shop.

"They hurt my stomach," he replied.

"But they keep that tiny, cold heart of yours beating," Liv stated.

"I'll see you at work in the morning," John said stubbornly. "I'm going to bed right now."

Liv's fist slammed against the wall beside the door, her frustration at the cantankerous old man making her head simmer.

"If you keep this up, people are going to start thinking you care about the senile old man," Plato said, strolling out of Liv's open door down the hallway. The mostly white cat had four black spots across his body, making him resemble a cow, which was why the neighborhood kids mooed at him when he strolled by. Plato handled their teasing by ignoring them and later peeing on their scooters and bikes parked in front of the building.

"I don't care about John," Liv argued. "It's just that our apartments share air ducts, and if he dies in his, it will take forever to get the stink out of my place."

Plato gave her a look that said, "I'm not buying that."

Liv tucked a strand of blonde hair behind her ear, thinking.

"You're not tall enough to reach the fire escape," Plato said, as if he knew where her brain was going.

"Yeah, yeah, I get that my height is once again a disadvantage." She often joked that she was still growing, but the truth was that at age twenty-two, there was zero chance she was going to get any taller.

Liv looked down at her ripped jeans and grease-covered t-shirt, searching for options.

The last time John hadn't taken his medicine, he was in the hospital for a week. Liv could run his repair shop on her own, but not very well. The customers preferred to talk to him and didn't buy that she could repair things as well as he could. However, he'd taught her everything she knew, and her eyes were a whole hell of a lot better than his.

It was because of John that Liv had a job, although it didn't provide quite enough to survive on. He knew that, which was why he discounted her rent for the studio apartment next door. A place like that in West Hollywood should go for a lot more, but John pretended that he was giving her a competitive rate.

"Can I suggest that you try that *one* thing," Plato said, a hint in his voice.

Liv cut her eyes at the feline. "You know that I'm not strong enough. I keep trying."

"You fixed the microwave yesterday using magic," Plato stated.

Liv turned around suddenly to ensure they weren't being overheard by one of the kids playing downstairs or anyone else in the hallway. The old building creaked and moaned constantly, which usually covered Plato's voice, or so he told her.

"That was a fluke," she hissed. "I don't know how that happened."

"It's like a muscle, Liv. The more you use it, the stronger it will get."

She shook her head. "No, that's not how it works. You know I'm limited. They have me blocked."

"And yet, you were able to use your magic yesterday," Plato said, a knowing tone in his voice.

He would know. Plato was the smartest creature Liv had ever met. She'd been blessed with his presence since that first day, when she found herself on the streets with nowhere to go and no money to her name. It was like the cat had been sent to her as a guide as she started her life all over. Five years later and he was still her best friend, really one of her *only* friends.

Taking a deep breath, Liv held her hand up, trying to

remember the incantation for unlocking. The words, like all her memories of magic, were trapped somewhere in her mind. She flicked her wrist and muttered words she'd heard her mother say long ago. The lock jiggled.

Elated, Liv tried the door handle, but to her dismay, found it still locked.

"Damn it," she complained, stomping in the direction of her room. A moment later she reappeared holding the small sheath of tools John had given her. She pulled one of the hooked picks from the set and went to work on the door lock.

Behind her, Plato sighed. "You gave up awfully fast."

Liv blew her hair out of her face since both her hands were busy working on the lock. "I'm using my time efficiently. Tinkering is what I'm good at, not using that hocus pocus stuff," she said quietly.

Plato's ear twitched, catching a noise approaching. "The giant is coming," he announced.

Liv straightened as Rory thundered up the stairs. She pressed her tools behind her back and pretended to be casually studying the peeling ceiling.

The giant, who was almost seven feet tall, halted at the suspicious sight of Liv standing in front of John's door and Plato nonchalantly licking himself like a normal cat would.

"Hello," Liv said, trying to keep her voice light. "What brings you to our neck of the woods? Here to see John?'"

Rory eyed her and shook his head. "No, I'm here to see... Well, it doesn't matter."

It was Liv's turn to eye the giant suspiciously. He didn't live in the building, but he was always calling on the residents toward the end of the month. Most wouldn't notice, but Liv was excellent at correlating details. Today was September 30th, and the last time she'd seen Rory here was the end of August. He'd been in John's shop throughout the month, but that was because he was constantly dropping off electronics he'd "found" that John could resell. Liv wasn't sure what John traded for the electronics. Hopefully nothing much.

"Well, good luck with whatever you're doing here," Liv said dismissively.

The giant, who she sensed had magic blood, looked down at the cat and then at her. He shook his large head, making his curly brown hair sway. Rory had bright green eyes and large lips, and rarely smiled. Liv had studied giants when she was a child, and knew they weren't prone to overly jolly dispositions. They were also extremely powerful, wielding a branch of magic that couldn't be controlled by the House of Seven. That made Rory both dangerous and also powerful. And although Liv preferred not to interact with magical beings, she made an exception for Rory in case she ever needed his help. Liv didn't know if he knew who or what she was, but she hoped that he didn't.

Rory opened his mouth like he was about to say something, but then, thinking better of it, he closed it again. When he strode past Liv and Plato, the dusty floor creaked as though it were in pain. Rory knocked on Ms. Madden's door on the far side of the hallway. A moment later, the old woman opened the door and let the giant in without a word.

"What do you suppose *he's* up to?" Liv asked, looking down at Plato.

"I'm not sure. He's probably wondering the same about you," Plato offered.

She ducked, going back to work on the lock. A few seconds later she heard the victorious click that signaled she'd unlocked the door. She pressed the door back and peered into the dirty apartment. Old carburetors and parts from three different fans littered the dining room table.

"Don't be naked, John," Liv called. "I'm coming in."

Pickles, John's Jack Russell terrier, looked up from his place on the sofa when Liv and Plato strolled in. He bounded off the couch at the sight of Liv, jumping on her leg, begging to be petted.

Plato leapt onto the table, scowling at the dog. "You're such a hooker. Always looking for attention."

"Shhh," Liv warned, peering around.

"Don't worry, John can't hear me," Plato said. "He isn't here."

"What?" Liv asked, whipping around and striding for the bedroom. It was empty. "Where'd the old fart go?"

Plato nodded in the direction of the open window, where the stained curtains were dancing in the wind. "I'm guessing he's up there, star-gazing."

"Damn it," Liv grumbled, moving for the window. "And after all my efforts. I could have just gone up to the roof all along."

Liv shimmied out the window, pulling her legs over the wall one at a time. The rusty fire escape creaked when she started the climb to the rooftop. Plato disappeared and reappeared in the open window to her apartment some ten yards away. He looked rather bored with the chase.

Liv was unsurprised to find John standing on the roof,

looking out at the neighborhood. She sighed loudly when she stepped onto the rooftop.

"Seriously, old man, do you want me to push you off this building?"

He snickered, taking a handkerchief from his pocket and blowing his large nose. His thinning gray hair swayed in the breeze. He was wearing pajama bottoms but still had on the work shirt he'd worn earlier, which was streaked with grease and dirt. "You came all the way up here to bring me my meds, and I don't think you're going to try and kill me after all that."

She shrugged. "Not today I won't. Tomorrow is a new day, though."

Liv pulled the bottle of pills out of her jeans pocket and held them up. "Take these or I'm going to start singing."

"Liv, I told you I don't like how they make me feel."

As loudly and as horribly as she could, she started singing John's favorite song, *Ave Maria*.

Immediately he clapped his hands to his ears, the wrinkles on his long face deepening.

"Fine, fine!" he yelled over her awful warbling. "I'll take the dumb pills."

Liv smiled victoriously and handed him the bottle. "See, that's not so hard, is it?"

He opened the bottle and took out one of the small white pills, swallowing it dry. "But as you say, tomorrow is a new day."

"And it's also a day when you're going to stay up on your meds, or I'll develop the bad habit of humming at work," she said, singing the song again under her breath.

He shook his head. "One of these days I'm going to fire you."

Liv smiled. "You've been threatening that for years. It doesn't scare me anymore."

John strode past Liv to the fire escape. "Well, one of these days I just might surprise you. Don't stay up here too long. I want you opening the shop tomorrow."

Liv saluted formally. "Aye aye, Captain."

She heard John greet Pickles when he was farther down the fire escape, probably about to climb back through his open window. Looking at the orange and pink sunset, Liv realized why John had gone up to the roof. He kept thinking he could fix his ailing heart with beauty or something. She'd told him there was no magic cure for heart disease, although she knew that wasn't entirely true. Tomorrow she'd talk him into calling his doctor to change his medicine to something that didn't upset his stomach. Tonight, she'd relax after a long and tiring day.

Behind her, she heard the whooshing of air and tensed. It was a distinct sound, one she hadn't heard in over five years.

Liv's hand flexed by her side. If she was quick, she could pull one of her tools from her back pocket. She nearly laughed at the ridiculous notion. Someone with magic was standing at her back, which meant she was absolutely screwed in defending herself.

After all these years, they'd finally found her. There would be no running. No more hiding. It was time she faced her past.

Tentatively, Liv spun and was surprised by who she found staring back at her.

14

CHAPTER THREE

Liv let out a gasp. Doubt and confusion welled up in her. She tensed. Although she knew the face in front of her, for a moment her mind had trouble placing it, like she was suddenly in a strange dream, the kind full of strangers.

Her mouth opened, but the name for the person didn't roll out. Instead, it bounced around in her head as if she were trying to determine if she in fact had it correct.

The figure was taller than she remembered, but maybe it was only the lights and shadows playing tricks on her. His jawline was definitely more distinct than in her memories. And those eyes! They were like those of her father's ghost staring back at her, full of passion and warmth and carrying that trademark Beaufont cerulean blue.

"C-C-Clark," she finally said, uncertainty heavy in her voice. "How did you find me?"

Liv took a step backward. Her older brother was wearing a dark traveling cloak of fine dragonhide over what looked to be a very uncomfortable suit. His blond hair was parted down the middle like how he'd always worn it.

He tilted his head back and to the side, something he'd always done when he grew impatient. "Olivia, we've known where you were from the beginning. You were naïve to think the House wasn't always keeping an eye on you." Clark looked around at the dilapidated rooftop and similar old buildings in the distance. "What remained a mystery to us was why you chose *this* spot."

Liv folded her arms across her chest. "Because it has character and *real* people."

He sighed. "Non-magical people, you mean."

"They are still people, not that the House of Seven treats them that way. Or anyone else, really."

They'd been in each other's presence for about a minute, and they were back to the same argument. Five years had changed nothing.

"Olivia, I'm here because I need you to come back," Clark said and pressed his lips together, realizing the severity of his request.

She gave nothing away, only scowled and said, "My name is 'Liv.'"

He shook his head. "Your name is Olivia Beaufont, and you belong at the House of Seven. You always have. The council members have tolerated your need to rebel, but they won't for much longer."

"They locked my magic," she argued. "Why do they care what I'm doing as long as I'm not creating trouble for them?"

The old anger she associated with her brother flared in his eyes. "You had no right to make those allegations.

They've overlooked it, though. Chalked it up to you being young."

Liv laughed. Clark was barely a year older than her, but he had always treated her like she was so much younger than him, and didn't understand the ways of the magical world.

"Did they ever find out who murdered our parents?" Liv asked, but she already knew the answer because it was plainly written on her brother's face.

He shook his head.

"Then I was right," she asserted. "The House of Seven didn't do enough to find out what happened to them. They dismissed the whole thing as a magical accident."

"It *was* an accident," Clark corrected.

"Two extraordinary magicians simply fall off the side of a mountain to their deaths? Really? You're still buying that?"

He shook his head more forcefully this time, but his hair didn't move. He loved his damn hair gel. "Olivia, you just never wanted to believe they could make a mistake. They were powerful, but they were still human. And unfortunately, humans make bad decisions. The conditions weren't right to go up the Matterhorn. They fell and died. That was what happened."

For five years, she'd been trying to make sense of her parents' death. They'd had no reason to be in the Swiss Alps, especially together. They weren't ones to take risks. And yet, they'd done something that the House of Seven had deemed unadvisable. The case was shut after minimal investigation. Liv had protested. She'd created so much ruckus at the House of Seven that they were happy to see her leave when she did, and she hadn't really looked back after all these years.

What was back there for her, anyway? And even her siblings weren't convinced that there had been any foul play. She hadn't ever fit in there. Without her parents, she felt like a true loner, so she abdicated her role in the House of Seven, and with it, her magic. It had felt like the right thing to do at the time. Magic had only ever led to trouble as far as she was concerned. Well, the type of magic the House of Seven protected, anyway.

"I *thought* I smelled something fishy," Plato called from behind Liv. She didn't turn around, but instead waited until the feline sidled up next to her.

Looking down at him, she said, "He smells fishy?"

"I smelled human magic," Plato answered.

She nodded, returning her gaze to Clark. He was glaring skeptically at Plato.

"Where did you get him?" he asked, nodding in Plato's direction.

Liv rolled her eyes and rubbed her hands on her arms. The chill was starting to come on as the sun set at their backs. "I didn't get him anywhere. That's not how relationships work, but you wouldn't know that. The House just acquires those they want to serve them."

Clark's jaw flexed. "That's not how it works. We protect."

Liv nodded dismissively. There was no point in going back through all this. It was always the same.

"Clark, what are you doing here?" she asked after a long silence.

"It's Ian and Reese," he explained, referring to their

older brother and sister. They were powerful, having taken on their father and mother's role of Warrior and Councilor when they'd died...or been murdered.

"Oh, do they have a fancy family reunion they require me to attend?" Liv asked. "Tell them that I would, but I don't have a thing to wear." She looked down at her baggy jeans, faded t-shirt, and boots.

"No," Clark said impatiently, running his hand over his hair. "Olivia, they're dead."

Liv opened her mouth, but she had no response. It hit her in the chest, making her feel she might stumble back a few feet. She hadn't seen her older brother and sister in a long time, but that didn't make the announcement of their death any easier. And the implications of their deaths nearly knocked her to the ground. When she felt Plato rub against her leg, she straightened, bringing her chin up from her chest where it had fallen without her realizing it.

"I wanted to tell you this from the start, but how could I begin with that after not seeing you for so long?"

"How did it happen?" Liv asked.

"I found them," Clark explained.

"You?"

"Well, what was left of them," Clark said tensely. "I had to use a spell to identify them. They were in the old family cottage when a fire broke out."

"What? Why couldn't they get away?"

Clark shook his head. "I think they were drunk. Reese was probably practicing one of her potions or homemade spells. Things are confusing in the magical world right now. You have to understand that magic is at risk. Things like this keep happening."

"Magic has never been at risk," Liv argued. "It is magic that puts *us* in danger."

"Regardless of how you feel about magic, you know there's no stopping it. We can only contain and control it. That's what the House of Seven does."

"That's what the House of Seven says they do," Liv stated, pressing her hands to her hips. "They write laws that benefit magicians."

"Damn it, Olivia!" Clark yelled loud enough to disrupt a flock of pigeons on an electrical wire. As they flew off, Plato followed them with his eyes. "It's about justice."

"Justice is never about the law. It's about doing the right thing, which I don't remember being what the House of Seven does. Not if it contradicts their needs," Liv fired back. "And damn it, my name is *Liv*."

Clark shook his head. "Regardless of your views, you know what this means." He gulped, a rare sensitivity rising in his eyes. "Ian and Reese are dead. That makes us the next two eligible Beaufont children. I'm the next odd-numbered child, making me our family's Councilor for the House. And you…"

That would make me a Warrior, Liv thought, the true implications of this strange ordeal making her head cloud with frustration. She was the next even-numbered child in the Beaufont family.

"But I abdicated," she said in answer to the question hanging in the air.

Clark nodded. "But due to the circumstances, the House of Seven is giving you a chance to take back your role."

"What about Sophia?" Liv asked, referring to their

younger sister. She was the younger of twins, but Jamison didn't survive long after birth. "She's an even-numbered Beaufont child," Liv reasoned.

Clark's gaze dropped with disappointment. "And she's eight years old, not eligible for the role of Warrior for twelve years."

"You know I've never wanted this," Liv stated bitterly.

Clark nodded sympathetically. "I know, but you can't ignore who you are forever. Your family needs you. The House of Seven needs you."

"Is the House of Seven still serving their own needs, without concern for real justice?"

"It's not like that," Clark answered.

"And if I don't take the position?" Liv asked.

Clark thought for a moment and shrugged. "I'm not sure. No family member has defaulted when called in a millennium. I really didn't think *you* would. I mean, you only ran away before because you could. Because Ian and Reese took on the responsibilities for the family. But now that we need you, will you walk away?"

Liv looked automatically at Plato, a question in her eyes.

"I'm not sure," the cat said contemplatively.

Clark threw up his hands in automatic frustration. "You're seeking the counsel of this lynx?"

Liv had never thought of Plato as a lynx, but now that she heard the term, the teachings from her upbringing flew back to her. Plato was magical. She'd known that from the beginning, but she'd also trusted him.

"Yes, I'm seeking his counsel. He's the only one here not colored by the House of Seven," Liv answered.

"He's a lynx," Clark argued. "They only care about themselves. More so than any magician."

Liv didn't think that was true, but she decided not to argue. "He's not full of bullshit, which I can't say for anyone else."

Plato's green eyes shifted to the side before connecting with Liv's. "There's no harm in going to the House of Seven to listen to their offer. You don't have to agree to it here, but you shouldn't turn it down without knowing all the implications. And you *can* do things on your terms. It's important to remember that."

Clark ground his teeth, his eyes close to rolling back in his head. "There are still certain rules and customs."

Liv pretended like she hadn't heard him as she nodded. "Yeah, I think you're right. I'll see what they have to say and do it my own way."

Clark shook his head, but still seemed relieved by this answer. "Fine. We should go immediately."

"I've got to work in the morning," Liv told him, noticing how dark it had become.

"Yes, but if you remember, the House of Seven meets at night," Clark reminded her. He softly snapped his fingers, and a mostly green ball materialized in the air in front of them. There was only a tiny sliver of yellow, like a tiny piece of pie at the top of the orb. That was the way the House told time, and it was based on their priorities. "They are due to meet very soon," Clark explained, glancing at the time orb.

"Okay then, but I have to be back for work tomorrow morning," Liv stated. "And I should fetch a jacket from my apartment before we go."

Clark looked her over. "I was thinking you should fetch more than just a jacket."

"Dress code is one of the many customs of the House I won't be observing," Liv snapped. "I'll go like this or not at all."

Clark seemed to resist for a moment but then shook his head. He extended a hand, and Liv's black hoodie materialized in his fingers. "Okay, fine, but know that they'll be scrutinizing you. I'm only trying to help."

She took the hoodie, enjoying its soft warmth. "Well, lead the way, then. I'm sure they've changed the route to the blasted place since the last time I was there."

Clark extended a hand and a bright portal opened on the rooftop, shimmering with nearly blinding blues and greens. "We have to take the back route. This will lead to the Santa Monica entrance."

Liv looked down at Plato. "You ready for this?"

"Wait, the lynx is going?" Clark asked, holding out an arm.

"Of course he is," she said. "And his name is Plato. Is this a problem?"

Clark thought for a moment, then dropped his hand and shook his head. "I guess not."

Liv gave Plato a wink as they stepped through the portal together.

CHAPTER FOUR

It had been so long since Liv had traveled through a portal that she had forgotten the weird sensation it created in the pit of her stomach. She used to tell her father that the feeling was unnatural, and he always replied the same way: "Nothing is more natural than portal magic. Once you believe that, it won't be so strange."

As she sank to her knees, overwhelmed by nausea, she couldn't disagree more with him. Hunched over and tasting something acidic in her mouth, Liv tried to remember to breathe. She forgot her surroundings until a hand clapped her shoulder softly, encouraging her to get up.

"Are you all right?" Clark asked, pulling her to a standing position.

"She hasn't assimilated yet," Plato said in his usually casual voice.

"I know that, but I'm checking to ensure she's okay," Clark told the feline. "There's something I can give her if she's experiencing portal sickness."

"That only bandages the problem," Plato countered. "She has to adapt."

Clark didn't respond, but the frustrated sigh that fell out of his mouth explained how he felt about the cat's unsolicited advice.

Liv shook her head and blinked at her surroundings, realizing what Plato meant. She wasn't going to feel any better until she took in her environment using her senses.

The rushing of the Pacific Ocean on the beach in the far distance was barely audible over the drum music and loud voices. They were on the boardwalk in Santa Monica, a short distance from the pier where the neon lights of the Ferris wheel and roller coaster could be seen glowing as they moved.

Around them tourists and locals jostled by on bikes, skateboards, scooters, or on foot. No one paid her any attention, probably assuming she'd just stumbled drunkenly out of the pub beside them. The ocean breeze felt refreshing on Liv's face as she took a deep breath—which she instantly regretted when the smell of pot and fried food assaulted her olfactory senses. She exhaled through her mouth and nodded at Clark, who was looking at her as if she were a fragile doll that might shatter.

"I'm fine," she said, shrugging off his hand on her shoulder and turning around to more carefully take in their surroundings. Since it was after sunset, the happening places in Santa Monica were just getting started with party-goers. Liv thought she'd be sick again as a gang of hipsters cruised past them on rent-a-scooters, nearly knocking them over.

"Get in the bike lane, dipshits," Liv yelled at the pack. They chortled and sped up.

"Looks like you're back to your old self," Plato observed.

"Seriously, they have their very own lane, but they can't be bothered to use it," Liv complained.

Clark shook his head. "They're just tourists who don't know any better."

He still had too much patience for dumbasses, Liv realized. Some things never change.

Liv looked around. "So, the entrance to the House?"

Clark grabbed her arm and pulled her down the boardwalk. "It's closer to the Venice side."

"Oh, that's a risky place for the entrance," Liv observed. "Aren't the hoity-toity magicians afraid one of the bums is going to rub their germs on them during the commute?"

"They are usually concealed," Clark explained. "As I mentioned, magic has been at risk. We've been taking extra precautions."

"Which is why the entrance is in Venice instead of Beverly Hills like it used to be," Liv said mostly to herself.

"There are still three entrances to the House, but the others are only for House royals," Clark explained.

"That would be you now, wouldn't it?" Liv asked. Since Reese's death, that would have automatically made Clark the Councilor for the Beaufont family.

He nodded, surprise springing to his face for a moment. "Yes, I guess it would be. It's just, I'm not used to it. Everything has been very sudden."

Liv paused, making the group behind them veer around

her. Clark turned at once and looked at her, irritation on his face at first. Then, reading her expression, he softened.

"I'm sorry," Liv said. "With you popping up randomly to see me and the strangeness of this all, I forgot to say it. I'm sorry about Ian and Reese. You must be devastated."

Clark nodded, then shook his head. "I am. It's hard, but we haven't been close. Not in a long time. Not since Mom and Dad died…and then you left. We've all sort of done our own thing, but yes, I miss them very much."

Ian had always been the pillar of the family, strong and clever. Reese was the eccentric one who dared to dabble in experimental magic. They were their parents' children and resembled them in many ways. In contrast, Clark was calculating and practical. Their mother said he had been born with a crease between his eyes, as if even as an infant, he was trying to figure out the most efficient solution. Then there was Liv. She was the outcast; the one who was skeptical and constantly getting in trouble for talking out of turn.

A moment later Clark came back to himself, shaking away the grief. "The entrance is right down here. Just a bit farther."

A moment later and he stopped in front of a doorway on the busy thoroughfare.

"This is it?" Liv asked, wondering if he was joking, although that would be a bit out of character. They stood in front of a black single door with a hand-painted sign that read "Closed." Around the door was a black and red checkered frame, and above it, a neon sign flashed "Palm Readings."

The building, which was narrow and seemingly

connected to the ones around it, had one window on the second story covered by a set of paisley drapes, with various shadows moving behind it.

"Yes, this is it," Clark said, rubbing his hands together as if he were cold, although the dragonhide cloak should have prevented that, as it held many protective properties.

"Did the House lose its fortune gambling or something?" Liv asked.

Clark cracked a smile. "No, but remember what I said about magic being at risk? Blending in is more important than ever."

"Yes, but I'd think a less trafficked area would be safer," Liv observed.

"You'll remember that the ocean is a source of energy for the House, which is important," Clark explained. "And no one notices much here, with everything going on. We're much more susceptible to scrutiny in areas where people don't come and go frequently."

Liv looked at the colorful shops selling postcards and t-shirts or bars filled with hippies with thick beards and surfers in tank tops. Across the way, a musician sat on a bucket playing a harmonica. Beside him a woman danced, wiggling her bare midriff to the music. Liv turned back to the Palm Reading shop. This place definitely fit into the strangeness that was Venice beach.

"So what do we do?" Liv asked her brother.

He held up his hand. "It's a Palm Reading place, so let it read your palm." Clark stepped up and pressed his hand to the front of the door under the sign that read "Closed." A moment later the golden handle glowed faintly and the door clicked open, sending a strange musty smell through the air. Clark pushed the door open, disappearing into the blackness. "Just do as I did and you should be fine. This door will automatically shut behind me."

Liv was about to protest, but Clark was gone. She hiccupped on a ragged breath. "How does he know it will work? I abdicated."

"You have the blood of the Seven," Plato, who sat by her feet, said calmly. "It will work."

Liv sighed. "Yeah, and if it doesn't, I can forget this mess and get back to normal life."

She stepped up to the door and held her breath. This was it. After all these years of declaring she never would, she was about to step across the threshold into the world she'd wanted nothing to do with for so long. She didn't feel an instinct telling her to embrace this challenge or run from it. All she felt was the steady ticking in her heart.

"There is no right or wrong path," Plato told her.

Liv dropped her raised hand. "Huh?"

"You're wondering if this is right or wrong, but I suspect your path will find you whether you willingly walk through this door or you don't," he clarified.

Liv grumbled, "I'm not sure I like your sage wisdom right now. It feels too much like a riddle." Something occurred to her, and she abruptly looked down at the cat. "How will *you* get in?"

His green eyes shone in the dark, reflecting the neon lights of the sign above. "You shouldn't worry about me."

"But the House will have wards to keep intruders like you from entering!"

"I'm sure they do," Plato stated confidently. "Now, go on. You don't want to keep them waiting."

Liv laughed. "I think they can wait a little longer. Actually, I'm starving. Want to grab a hotdog?" She indicated to a street vendor down the way selling sweaty hotdogs and mushy buns that had been in the humid sea air too long.

Plato sniffed. "You don't want whatever they're passing off as hotdogs. However, the fish tacos over there are up to standards." He nodded in the direction of a food truck.

Liv grimaced. "Why people ruin tacos by putting fish in them, I'll never know. I think I'd rather have one of those slices of pizza the size of my face."

The door opened abruptly and Clark peeked through. "Are you coming?"

Liv sighed. "Yeah, yeah," she sang, looking back down at Plato. "Pizza the size of my face straight after this. Oh, and an ice-cold beer."

"Fish tacos," he repeated.

Liv stepped up to the door, wiping her sweating palms on her jeans. She could only imagine the myriad of germs on the door from all the dirty magicians who had pressed their hands to it. She tried to forget that and stuck her hand on the weathered surface.

Under her fingertips, the door rattled slightly. She was sure she only felt it, and no one could see the tremor that seemed to spasm out in all directions. For an instant, she was certain it hadn't worked and she'd been rejected entry, then the door popped open dramatically—not like when it had creaked open and Clark had entered. This time it swung back, revealing blackness before her.

That musty smell tickled her nose again, reminding her of playing with Clark in the library during her childhood. Practicing braiding her mother's hair on Sunday mornings.

Skipping into the kitchen for an afternoon tart. It brought to mind everything she'd been trying all these years to forget. Liv felt the ticking of her heart, like it was a motor propelling her forward. She took a step and entered the blackness.

CHAPTER FIVE

The door shut with a loud bang behind Liv, and for a moment, she was blind. She squinted in the darkness, feeling helpless and hating it. And then firelight flickered down a long corridor, making her squint from the sudden brightness.

Liv didn't remember that the entry into the House of Seven was arched with intricate symbols adorning the walls or that the various archways were elegantly carved in beautiful mahogany. They rose to the ceiling, which had to be over thirty feet tall. The gold-flecked paint on the walls looked like it belonged in a thousand-year-old church, yet she knew from that musty smell she was standing in the House of Seven.

Why don't I remember this? she wondered, studying the tiled floor under her feet. It was a mosaic of sea glass in a conglomeration of soft greens and blues.

Down the long corridor, seemingly a million miles away, was Clark, looking impatient. He kept glaring over his shoulder at something in the next room and waving her forward.

Liv didn't hurry but instead took a tentative step, running her fingers along the walls. As she did, sparks radiated from her fingertips, lighting up the symbols, which she couldn't read. She yanked her hand back, worried she'd be shocked.

"It's the ancient language of the founding families," Plato said from Liv's side.

She startled, pulling her hand away. "You made it through?"

He gave her a smug look that said, "Of course I did" and returned his attention to the wall.

"Can you read any of the symbols?" he asked.

Liv squinted at a set of lines in front of her that were joined by a thick squiggle. "No, I don't think so. Why have I never seen this entrance or these symbols before?"

Plato strolled several feet past Liv before turning back to her. "I believe you *have* been through here, but the entrance to the House of Seven would have appeared different to you before. Now that you're a Royal, a certain magic has been unlocked within you. The language of the founders, for instance, can only be read by a Councilor or a Warrior."

Liv looked at the wall of symbols and then at Plato. "But you can see the symbols? And the corridor as a grand entrance?"

Again, the cat gave her an annoyed look. "Certain restrictions don't apply to me."

Hence why Plato was in the House of the Seven, Liv

thought. "When I was a child, this entrance was shorter and dark. Plain."

"That was how you saw it," Plato corrected. "Things rarely change in our environment. When we see things differently, it is usually we who have changed."

"But I *haven't* changed," Liv argued. "I haven't accepted the Warrior role, and my magic hasn't been unlocked."

"Yes, but it is still your birthright," Plato replied. "Therefore, you see all of this as a Warrior would until you turn down your position."

Suddenly Liv didn't want to decline—not if it meant the corridor would be cast in blackness again. She'd never been enticed by magic, unlike others in her family—like Clark and Reese. However, this magic felt different. It felt ancient and worth protecting. She ran her hand over the wall again, relishing the way the symbols lit up and danced as she touched them.

"Why do they do that?" she asked.

"The language of the Founders lies dormant, begging to be read," Plato explained.

"But you said Councilors and Warriors could read it."

"Just because they can doesn't mean they do." Plato's tail swayed in the air as he continued down the corridor. "Men are capable of doing acrobatics and other incredible physical acts, but that doesn't mean they do."

"So the ancient language wants to be read, like a living, breathing thing that wants attention?" Liv asked.

"The language was constructed to hold magic," Plato answered. "And as much as you might have reservations about it, magic is very much alive."

Liv stared at the massive wall of symbols before her,

entranced. There was so much information here, and she didn't understand any of it. What was the language of the Founders trying to say? She felt like the messages were humming in her head, tempting her to understand.

"Okay, I really have to insist that you come along now," Clark said from a few feet away.

Liv hadn't noticed him approaching.

"I know the entrance hall is mesmerizing the first time you see it as a Royal, but we can't keep them waiting," Clark continued. His hands were on his hips, and that impatient look was still on his face.

"So you see them too?" Liv asked, reaching toward the symbols again.

"Yes," Clark breathed. "They are beautiful."

"Can you read them?" she asked, making Plato turn around and look at them with a curious expression on his face.

Clark's brow creased. "Read them? I don't think anyone can. The language has been lost for ages."

"How is that possible?" Liv asked. "Councilors and Warriors should be able to read it."

Clark gave Plato a disgusted look. "Don't listen to everything the lynx says. We are able to see the ancient language, that's it. Its meaning was locked away long ago in order to protect the magic it holds."

Something in Plato's expression made Liv think that wasn't entirely true, but who should she believe on these matters? Her brother, raised and educated in the House of Seven, or Plato, who she really knew nothing about other than that he liked to eat the plain corn chips when she got nachos, insisting she peel the toppings off them.

"The Seven are waiting for you," Clark said, holding out his arm to Liv. "Shall we?"

It was such an odd gesture for him to make to her, but then standing here in the House of Seven with him was also completely bizarre. Her list of unexpected things was growing.

"Isn't it just the Six if we're not there?" Liv asked, rejecting his offered arm and marching forward.

"Ha-ha, Olivia," Clark said with no humor in his voice. "The Seven refers to the pact that was made between the families. We are simply the servants chosen by the House."

"Servants? You're totally not selling this Warrior business," Liv said, her eyes on the sparkling walls. "And your listening skills are horrible. My name is Liv. Olivia was someone else. Call me that again and I'll put you in a headlock."

A minute smile cracked Clark's face. "You'll have to get a stepstool first."

"Oh, look who has told their first joke?" Liv said as they neared the end of the hallway. "It's about damn time."

Clark strode forward, halting in front of Liv where the hallway split. It continued into darkness, although small wisps of light could be seen in the distance. To the left was a door the size of a small house, and to the right was a mirrored door. It appeared like the surface of water, rippling with distortions. Liv wanted to step around Clark for a closer look but he held his hand out, sensing her curiosity.

"You must pass through the Wall of Reflection to enter the Chamber of the Tree," Clark informed her in a tight whisper. "At first it's a bit jarring, but remember that what you experience, no one else sees. Only you. Also, it's important to know that it's not real, although it will feel like it is."

"Wait, I have to walk through that mirrored door to get to the Seven?" Liv asked, making a complete turn. She remembered the massive door, or rather, what was on the other side of it—the cold dark hallway that had seemed to be a part of her nightmares when she was a child. She never wanted to venture down there again, but the mirrored door was like the entrance. She hadn't seen it before.

"Yes, all Royals are expected to pass through the Wall of Reflection every day when we meet," Clark explained. "It's supposed to be a purifying technique, so we shed our baggage and bring only our best intentions for protecting magic."

"That sounds like something a dumb vegan would do," Liv said dryly. "Do we have to do a juice cleanse afterward and meditate?"

The impatience on Clark's face flared. "Liv, this is serious. Just remember that whatever you see in the mirror is for your eyes only. Deal with it as best you can and then walk through the door. I'll be on the other side waiting for you."

He pivoted sharply and regarded the mirrored door with a focused look for a moment before striding forward. As if he were stepping into a pool of water, the reflective surface swallowed him gradually until he was gone.

Liv looked down at Plato and gulped. "What the hell have I gotten myself into?"

CHAPTER SIX

L iv's reflection blinked at her. She looked the same as she always did, although she felt entirely different. Her blonde hair was windswept from being on the beach, and the lack of sleep was starting to show in her tired eyes. Liv pushed her wavy hair behind her ears and offered her reflection a forced smile.

"Okay, just walk through that mirrored surface," Liv told herself. "I can do this. How hard can it be?"

She started forward but halted, looking at Plato. "Are you going through too? *Can* you?"

He nodded. "This isn't the same obstacle for me, but yes, I'll be there."

Liv eyed him skeptically. "One of these days you're going to tell me how you do all this voodoo."

The feline sauntered forward. Just before he entered the mirrored door, he looked back at her. "We both know that would spoil the magic for you. Better to keep up the veil."

Liv laughed as Plato disappeared. "Damn cat thinks he knows everything."

Alone in the corridor, Liv suddenly felt vulnerable. A shiver ran up her spine and she spun, thinking someone was watching her. The large door at her back was still shut, but the dark area to the side was as open as ever, like a large cave mouth waiting to swallow her. Liv stepped back, looking toward the golden entryway. It was empty, but she could have sworn she'd seen movement there out of the corner of her eye.

Shaking off the strangeness, Liv prepared herself again. If she kept the Seven waiting any longer, Clark was going to have a hissy fit and probably stomp around wearing that impatient look. She giggled to herself, feeling strangely fond of her older brother. Maybe she'd missed him these last five years, although there'd been little time to reminisce. For so long she was just trying to survive. Still, she was never telling Clark that she had missed him. That would only lead to his head getting even bigger. Then he'd need even more hair gel to corral his blond locks.

Smiling to herself, Liv stepped into the mirrored surface. It was like walking into a warm bath, but what surrounded her wasn't water. It felt like moist air whipping against her face.

Liv's vision blurred. She tried to blink, but that made her eyes sear with pain. Figures stood around her, their forms wavy. Liv's eyes burned, tears rolling down her face. She rubbed, but nothing seemed to fix her vision.

"You're blind," a voice intoned in her mind.

The figures began to move closer, chanting softly, "You're blind. You're blind. You're blind."

Fear rose in Liv's chest as her vision receded. She couldn't imagine not seeing again, but the more she tried to force her eyes to work, the more they burned with a pain that was becoming unbearable.

"You're blind," the figures chanted, their voices growing louder in her mind.

She clapped her hands to her ears, reeling from a sensory overload she'd never before experienced. She was going blind while her hearing was simultaneously amplified. It made no sense.

"You're blind!" the group yelled, nearly making her double over from pain and fear.

"No! No! No!" Liv screamed, rushing forward and slipping, falling to her hands and knees.

Her vision suddenly cleared and the voices were gone. She lifted her head and realized at once that she'd entered the Chamber of the Tree.

CHAPTER SEVEN

For a minute Liv felt like she'd fallen into the wrong room, then she saw Clark looking down at her from a high table, where six others sat around him. His expression accurately expressed his embarrassment. Even in the darkened space, she could see his cherry-red cheeks and low angle of his eyes as he stared away from the others, who were looking between him and his sister.

Liv stood abruptly, stumbling back on her shoes as she stared at the figures in front of her. There were six magicians standing before the council in a half-circle, each on a circular blue light. They had turned to gawk at Liv as she continued to back away until she felt the mirrored door behind her.

The Warriors were all dressed differently, although each wore the finest of fabrics. Some wore silk robes or sophisticated suits, others traveling cloaks with shimmering designs. She didn't recognize most of the faces, although old memories flickered to the surface as she studied them.

A magician sitting in the half-circle of Councilors at the high table at the back cleared his throat. His long white beard and the matching hair on his head didn't contrast with his pale skin. Adler Sinclair was one of the few who Liv recognized. He was the longest-standing Councilor the Seven had ever had, but his age wasn't why he had a face full of white hair. Adler, as an albino, had always looked as he did now.

"Welcome, Olivia Beaufont," Adler greeted her, his voice low and raspy. "Did you have difficulty coming through the Door of Reflection?"

Liv felt the strange warmth of the door behind her like it was trying to suck her back through. She straightened and took a step forward. It was then that she noticed the solid white tiger standing next to her. Reflexively, she shrank away from the creature, wondering what it was doing there. She recalled that there were many strange pets in the House of Seven, where the families all resided with their own. However, she'd never seen anything as majestic as the tiger staring at her. It was massive, almost as tall as she was.

"I-I-I'm fine," Liv stuttered, still gazing at the all-white tiger.

"What did you see in the Door of Reflection?" Adler asked from the council table.

Liv pulled her gaze away from the tiger, but strangely found herself still looking at the face of the all-white magician. She caught Clark's eyes next to Adler and they seemed to say, "No, don't answer that."

"I don't recall," Liv responded, taking another step forward.

It was then that she noticed that the chamber was shaped like a half-dome, which matched the half-circle of the council table and the one where the Warriors stoically stood around. On the far wall, behind the council, was a picture of a giant tree. Its trunk was gold, and each of the seven branches swept overhead and forked in two. One part of each branch glowed blue, while the other was bright green. Liv squinted and noticed that the branches were labeled with the family names of the Seven: DeVries, Ludwig, Beaufont, Sinclair, Mantovani, Takahashi, and Rosario. Each colored portion was labeled with the name of the Councilor or Warrior. The last one had the green portion of the branch lit up, and under it was Clark's name. However, the other part of the branch was pale gray, with no name.

Liv's chin rose as she noticed the twinkling gold lights that cascaded over the tree and above them on the domed ceiling. She instantly knew what the lights represented. Her father had told her about the Chamber of the Tree but had made all this sound romantic and fantastical rather than intimidating.

"The ceiling of the Chamber of the Tree is filled with the lights of all the registered magicians," her father had told her one night as he prepared to tuck her into bed. "They shine down on the Councilors and Warriors, reminding us of our mission: to protect and serve them."

Liv was overwhelmed by the number of twinkling lights. Were there a thousand? Ten thousand? It was impossible to tell.

"Olivia Beaufont," Adler began, "you know why you've been called here today, correct?"

Liv caught a flicker to her left but kept herself from looking in that direction. She would have recognized the flick of Plato's tail anywhere, even though he was hiding in a dark shadow.

"My brother, Ian, the eldest even-numbered child in the Beaufont family, has passed," Liv said, finding her voice low and aching.

"That's correct," Adler said, his voice lacking remorse. "Which means you're next in line to take the role of Warrior for your family. Are you prepared to do that?"

Liv tried to clear her throat, but she couldn't get whatever was in it out. "I think so, but—"

"The role of Warrior is not something anyone should take on lightly," a woman with her black hair pulled into a high bun beside Adler said. Bianca Mantovani. She wasn't much older than Liv. They used to play together, but the high collar of her dress and smug expression made her appear a decade older than Liv.

"I agree," a young Japanese man said. He sat on the other side of Bianca. "Do you know what is expected of you as a Warrior? You have been out of the House of Seven for many years, is that right?"

Liv looked up at the family tree and found the man's name: Haro Takahashi. She stepped forward. "I grew up here. I know that Warriors carry out the tasks the council assigns. You all rule over the affairs of the magical community, and the Warriors go into the field, working cases."

Liv couldn't believe how even her voice sounded. It didn't even have a hint of bitterness as she plainly described the strange system the House of Seven had used for centuries to "objectively" divide the work.

"A Warrior does more than work cases," Decar Sinclair said, sweeping around to face Liv straight on. He was younger than his brother Adler but had the same albino coloring, his piercing light eyes seeming to glow in the darkened room. Unlike Adler, he had no beard, but his straight white hair cascaded down his back in a long braid. "As Warriors, we are expected to face danger in order to protect magic. A Warrior must be strong, expertly trained, and above all else, courageous."

Adler nodded at his brother before directing his gaze to Liv. "We understand that you've been away for a while and your education neglected. We are prepared to have you trained, but you will be expected to work cases simultaneously."

"But she's not ready," Clark protested, earning the attention of everyone in the room. Well, everyone but the white tiger, who had settled down and was resting his head on his giant paws. Clark leaned back, blushing from all the eyes on him. "My sister hasn't had her magic in five years. She'll need time to get used to it."

Adler gave a small, insensitive smile. "Your sister made the choice to abdicate her role with the House of Seven. We as a group have met on the matter, and feel that giving her a second chance is beyond kind. If she's going to take on this role, she'll do it as anyone from a family of the Seven would: seamlessly and with the urgency that it deserves. Magical disasters and crimes will not halt for her to train, and therefore we can't delay any longer in filling this role."

"But you will put her in serious danger if you thrust her out there without training," Clark countered, his face growing redder. "She doesn't even know how to control her magic. That takes time."

Bianca leaned forward, peering over the table at Liv. "You did always struggle with your magic if I remember correctly. Your training might take longer than most."

Liv wanted to remind Bianca that she had peed the bed until she was twelve, but this didn't seem like the time to do that.

"The length of Ms. Beaufont's training is not our concern," Adler stated. "If you are to accept the role the Seven have generously offered you, you will train while working as a Warrior. Otherwise, we will have to resort to other methods to fill your position."

"Other methods?" Clark asked, leaning forward and looking down the table at the older magician.

"Sophia isn't old enough," Liv interjected. "You can't put an eight-year-old in the role of Warrior."

Around her, the Warriors and Councilors laughed. A man with short black hair and a chiseled goatee shook his head from the bench. "Adler is referring to replacing your family in the Seven. It hasn't been done in a little while but—"

Clark stood up at once, shaking. "You can't do that! The Beaufonts were some of the first. We were Founders."

Adler shook his head as though he was dismayed by this but could do nothing. "It's true. Your family, as well as mine and the Takahashis, have been part of the Seven from the beginning. We do not take replacing a family lightly, but it has been done in cases such as these. It's important to remember, young Mr. Beaufont, that we serve the magical community and not ourselves, and we can't do that properly when we are short a Warrior."

Liv wanted to laugh. It was such a crock of bullshit. The Seven were constantly overlooking rules that didn't favor their families or friends, but all of a sudden they were going to stand on some spotty principle of servitude? The Sinclair brothers probably wanted Liv to decline. Then they could boot Clark and her out and be one of the last two remaining Founders.

Liv looked to the side, briefly catching Plato's expression. He appeared as impassive as ever, but there was a new fire in his eyes—one that infected her at once.

"I'll do it!" Liv declared, and everyone turned to face her.

Clark was visibly shaking. He opened his mouth to protest, but she held up her hand and stepped forward. "I'll take the role of Warrior, which is mine by birthright, and I will train at the same time, as soon as you unlock my magic."

The smug look on Adler's face disappeared as he sat back in his seat. "We will arrange for your training once you receive your magic."

"I don't want to be trained here at the House of Seven," Liv argued.

Around the room, muttering broke out. Clark's eyes looked like they were about to burst out of his head. He still stood, but he was now leaning over the table, his hands resting on its surface.

"It is customary that Warriors train here," Bianca stated, her face pinched.

"But it isn't required," Liv said definitively. She might

not have been good with her magic, but she'd read the books her mother had given her, trying to prepare her for her potential future as a Warrior. She knew that Warriors could choose their own method of training. It could be tailor-made to fit the specific person or customized by family tradition. It was only Councilors who had to undergo a specific education, which Clark would have passed years ago.

"She's correct," a young man just in front of her said. He wore a solid black suit and a curious expression. She looked at the spot where he stood and followed it to the family tree. Stefan Ludwig.

"And you want to seek out your own training, thinking it is better than what we can offer you?" Decar Sinclair asked.

"I think it's none of your concern," Liv retorted boldly. "If I agree to both train and work cases as a Warrior, you have no room for objection."

They all stirred uneasily. Clark had never looked so furious with Liv. Still, she kept her chin up and didn't falter, although the white tiger had risen to his feet and was closer than before.

Adler looked down the table at a few befuddled Councilors but quieted them with a wave of his hand. "I think that if Ms. Beaufont wants to handle her own training, we should fully support her." He sounded almost giddy.

Decar agreed at once, his light eyes dancing with evil delight. "Yes. To each Warrior, their own."

Liv wanted to yell at them all, declare that she knew what she was doing. However, that wasn't true. She didn't know where she'd get trained, but she knew it couldn't be here in the House of Seven where she trusted no one. Instead, Liv strode to the empty circle between two Warriors and directly across from Clark. She stopped on top of the only unlit circle in the arc and looked at her peers. "Well, since that's settled, I'm ready for you to give me my magic back."

CHAPTER EIGHT

L iv looked at the Warriors, who all regarded her with both awe and mild irritation. She felt like a dwarf, standing in the half circle among the fierce, strong soldiers who towered around her. They were all dressed in traveling clothes, many of them bearing sheathed swords on their belt or across their backs. Some had pouches tied to their belts or other weapons strapped to them. Liv nearly laughed to herself, thinking of the sheathed tools she still had in her back pocket from picking John's lock on his door. She wasn't just out of her element, she was in a whole new world of weirdos. She tried to remind herself that she used to be one of these freaks before she chose to leave.

On the far side of the chamber, the white tiger regarded her with curiosity as he sauntered in her direction from behind the Warriors. For a moment, she considered that he might pounce and maul her when he neared. She didn't have time to worry about that, though, because the council stirred, doing something that she couldn't see.

"Councilors, prepare to unlock Olivia Beaufont's magic," Adler stated, not looking impressed by her display as she took her rightful spot.

Liv glanced down at the dimmed circle where she stood. It was hard to believe that only a few days ago, Ian had stood in this spot, ready to do whatever the council asked of him to "protect" magic. Before him, it had been her mother. A cold chill wrapped around Liv's throat, threatening to close her airway.

She hadn't allowed herself to think about her mother as a Warrior or how beautiful she always looked after returning from missions, her long, flowing blonde hair a gorgeous chaotic mess and her cheeks flushed from the night air. But even more memorable to Liv was the way her father's stressed face changed to relief when Guinevere Beaufont walked through the door, safe for another day. She was about to take her mother's place as a Warrior. Ian's place. Liv didn't feel like she was good enough to be here. It didn't feel like the role fit her, but she was damned if the Beaufont family would lose their standing in the Seven because of her.

This is for you, Mother, Liv thought, looking up at her brother. Clark seemed lost in thought as he punched several keys in front of him. When he was done, he gazed at Liv with anticipation.

"My codes have been entered," Clark said, his voice clear and loud.

Around him, other Councilors muttered confirmation that they'd done the same.

A decade prior, the House of the Seven had done something risky, at least by her parent's standards. They'd moved to magical tech, intertwining many of their security systems with technology fueled by magic. Her parents had said that it was dangerous to protect magicians using technology, which was why many had been resistant to register their magic when the change happened. Yet, Liv's parents, as well as all who opposed the advancement, had been outvoted.

Probably every member in that chamber where Liv stood had a cell phone that looked completely normal but had features unique to magicians. For instance, before Liv had left the House and was stripped of her magic and anything magical, her phone could find lost objects, call people whose numbers she didn't have, or appear in her hand simply by her intending it. And her phone never had to be charged, since it was powered by the ever-present source of magic. Liv had never been good at using all of the features, though, since it meant she had to have control over her magic. Many times her phone had ended up in someone else's hands when she summoned it, or it found the wrong lost object.

"All codes but one have been entered," Adler said, his light eyes cast low on the screen before him. He looked up at Liv, suddenly appearing much older with the lights above him creating shadows under his eyes. "Are you ready, Olivia Beaufont?"

Liv nodded, but then, catching the punishing glare from Clark, she said, "Yes, I am, Councilor Sinclair."

Adler's gaze flicked in the direction of his brother, who was next to Liv. They both appeared amused, but who could know why? For as long as Liv could remember, Adler had seemed to think he was in charge of the Seven, although the idea had always been that there was no real leader. Rather, there was a balance between Councilors and Warriors. Knowledge and strength. Strategy and courage. Consultants and soldiers.

"It has been five years since you've had your magic," a woman with softly flowing black curls said from the other side of Clark. Raina Ludwig. She had kind eyes and a thoughtful expression on her pale face. "You might go through a bit of shock when we unlock it, just as a warning."

Liv opened her mouth to thank the Councilor for the warning, but she was cut off.

"I'm certain Ms. Beaufont can handle the small bit of magic she'll be given," Bianca said, looking bored by all this.

Liv felt something stir next to her, and for a moment she thought Plato had dared to come out of the shadows for this. She nearly jumped backward when she realized the white tiger was near enough to touch. How had he sidled up next to her without her even noticing?

As if sensing her apprehension, the tiger looked up at her, his pale-greenish eyes communicating a message that strangely put her at ease. She reached out and stroked her hand over the top of his head, not realizing what she was doing until gasps from around the room paralyzed her. With her fingers still resting on the tiger's head, she mechanically looked at the others, who were gaping with their eyes wide.

Apparently, petting the pretty magical kitty is off limits, Liv thought, pulling her hand to her side. The tiger didn't growl or try to maul her. He simply brought his attention to where the Councilors were all regarding him with anticipation. When he simply blinked at them, they began to stir again, clicking on the devices before them and exchanging uncomfortable glances with one another.

Clark shook his head minutely at Liv, giving her a severe expression. Sensing an opportunity, Liv stretched her hand a few inches in the tiger's direction, teasing her brother. Clark's eyes bulged again, and he shook his head more dramatically.

Liv laughed to herself, pulling her hand back to her side. The tiger, which was nearly pressing against her now, hadn't taken his gaze off the Councilors.

"Okay, here we are," Adler said, recapturing everyone's attention. He looked down at the screen in front of him, which Liv couldn't see, as he read. "Olivia Beaufont, age twenty-two, second founding family of the House of Seven. You were born to Guinevere and Theodore Beaufont, the fourth of six children, making you eligible to be a Warrior. Your magic was locked five years ago on the fifteenth of August when you abdicated your place within your family."

That had been one week after her parents' death. It hadn't been easy to leave her siblings, but she hadn't thought twice about locking her magic. The tiger's tail swiped the floor behind them, sending a whooshing breeze over Liv's back.

"Do you consent to take back your magic, and with it, your role as one of seven Warriors in the House?" Adler asked. "This is not a position that you can walk away from once you consent unless you are taken by death or serious injury. Only once the next Beaufont child is of age are you eligible to step down. Do you understand the terms of this role? They are non-negotiable."

Liv's gaze flicked to Clark. His expression seemed to be saying a whole host of things, none of which Liv could decipher. Of course, he needed her to take the position as Warrior. Their family needed that. Maybe the Seven didn't need her, but the House couldn't operate with only six. It upset the balance.

Liv blocked all of that out and listened to that gentle ticking that was ever-present in her heart. It was constant, like her mother and father's love. In her mind's eye, she saw her mother and father the day before they failed to return, smiling at her with their unwavering love.

"We'll be back in the morning. Please take care of your sister," her mother had said to Liv, who was lying in her bed. "And make sure Clark doesn't stay up too late." Her mother rose from where she had been sitting and joined her husband, who was standing in the doorway. Liv's room had been dark, the only light coming from the hallway.

"Oh, and remember, Olivia, that no matter what, we love you," her father had said and pulled the door shut.

That was the last time she had seen them alive and all these years, she had known that she had let them down, but dealing with her grief had been the only thing she could handle. She'd fought for them when everyone said their deaths had been an accident—and now she was going to continue to fight for them, in a place where she could actually win. Without her magic, without the resources, she'd never find out the truth. All this time, she'd been running, but she was finally ready for the challenge she'd never thought she'd have the chance to embrace.

Liv lifted her chin, looking at each of the Councilors before gazing at her soon-to-be-fellow Warriors. "I understand the terms of my position and fully accept my role as a Warrior for the House of Seven."

CHAPTER NINE

The silence wrapped around Liv, making her want to fidget or whistle or do something to end it. All of the Councilors had their heads down, studying the screens in front of them. The Warriors stood as stoically as ever, their hands pinned behind their backs and their chins held high. It was Clark who broke the strangeness of the moment, looking at Liv in awe. Was he confusing his expressions? Wasn't he supposed to be giving her a frustrated glare? Maybe the strain of everything was finally getting to him.

"Is that correct?" a woman with spiky gray hair asked.

Liv studied the tree overhead, looking for the Councilor's name. Hester DeVries.

"It must be a mistake," Bianca said, but she didn't look convinced as she gazed between her screen and Adler.

He coughed, squinting at his screen. "Yes, I'd say so too. Probably a result of the magic being locked for so long. We generally only do that to criminals for such an extended period of time and they usually don't get their magic back, so we don't have much data on how it responds when released."

For two decades, the House of Seven had required all magicians to register their magic. Failure to do so resulted in fines and punishments, and in the end, delinquent magicians were forced to register their magic and then it was locked for good. Many rebellious magicians chose to fight to the death rather than comply. Once the House had the magician's magic registered, the person was under the House's control.

Liv looked at the thousands of sparkling lights overhead, all registered magicians whom the House "protected." Many times, Liv had heard her father complain about the plea for social order. It had never seemed right to him, but like many things the Councilors had voted on, he'd been outnumbered.

"I'm not so sure," Haro Takahashi stated, combing his hand over his chin. "That meter is exceptionally high for it to be a mistake."

"We'll just have to keep an eye on it," Adler suggested. "I suspect it will normalize in a day or so. Probably just a surge."

"Ummm...is there a problem with my magic?" Liv asked.

"Problem?" Adler asked, looking distracted. "Oh, no. We're sure it's nothing. Now, are you ready, Ms. Beaufont? In a moment, the Councilors will flip their switches, unlocking your magic."

Flip switches? Her magic was controlled like a light? That seemed a little lackluster. She sort of thought there should have been a ceremony with dancers and an orchestra and maybe some fireworks. Her stomach rumbled, and Liv remembered that she'd forgotten to eat dinner.

I'd settle for a steak dinner, if there's no celebratory ceremony, Liv thought. "I'm ready," she said, eyeing Clark and trying to decipher the confused expression on his face.

"Councilors, on my mark," Adler announced. "Three, two, *one.*"

In unison the Councilors flipped a switch on their consoles, making a series of clicking noises, then everyone in the domed room looked at Liv in anticipation. Her face flushed, not from magic but from embarrassment. What were they expecting to happen to her? Did a fancy gown appear on her small frame and her messy hair slick back into a more refined style, like the Warriors standing around her?

Liv glanced down at her stained jeans and the t-shirt under her hoodie. She still looked the same as she had moments prior, but more importantly, she didn't feel any different.

"Ummm, are we sure it work—" Liv's words cut off as a searing heat exploded in her chest. She clapped her hands to the site since it seemed like her heart was about to explode. It felt like the worst case of indigestion in the world. Was she having a heart attack? Something was definitely wrong. Liv stumbled backward, watching as the Warriors stared at her blankly. They didn't appear the least bit concerned by the horror-struck look on her face or the fact that she was moments away from falling over dead.

Even the white tiger seemed impassive to her plight. He'd risen from a sitting position, but was simply looking at her with a calm expression. The room spun, turning all of the figures into blurs and making her stomach twist with unease.

"Remember to breathe," a voice said from behind her in a low whisper.

Liv looked over her shoulder and made out Plato's faint outline in the shadows. She forced oxygen into her lungs, an act that had never felt so incredibly difficult before. The air was hot and made her chest feel constricted, but when she blew out the breath, she got a small bit of relief. The room stopped spinning. The dizziness subsided and Liv smiled a little, realizing that she had taken back control. For a moment, she'd really expected to pass out.

Liv lifted her chin and wiped the sweat off her forehead, and choked on her next breath. The assault that hit her chest next left her no choice but to fall straight back. Her head careened into something hard, and her insides seared like they were being boiled by her blood. With her last strength, Liv tried to push back up to her feet. The attempt was useless, although she managed to roll over on her stomach. Her vision was half-obstructed by the floor under her face, which felt as heavy as lead. The last thing she remembered seeing was the white tiger, staring down at her like he might feast on her body. Then everything went black.

"It was too much at once," a voice said too loudly. Didn't this person know that Liv was trying to sleep? She couldn't remember why she was asleep, but nothing felt more important right then than resting.

"It wasn't too much," a man argued. "She's just undisciplined and unpracticed."

Would they all shut up already? Liv couldn't push the need to sleep away, but their voices were a definite deterrent.

"I'm not sure *I* could have handled that surge," someone said in a muffled whisper nearby.

Liv noticed the cold floor under her. Her chest was raw and aching, as if it had been split open and freshly sewn back together. Reflexively, she clapped a hand to it and to her relief found it unscathed. A sudden cough made Liv's eyes fly open, and she bolted to a sitting position.

"See, she's completely fine," Adler said, his arms crossed over his chest. He hadn't moved from his place behind the bench, but Clark had crouched on the floor next to Liv. Many of the Warriors were out of formation, but none were close. The white tiger stood on the other side of Liv, looking down at her with an unreadable expression. *So he didn't eat me when I passed out,* she thought with relief.

"Are you all right?" Clark asked, thoughtfully rubbing Liv's back when she coughed again and doubled over.

She nodded, although that was completely untrue. She'd never felt more not all right in her life. For a moment, she firmly believed a giant snake was slithering around inside her, pushing through her organs as it navigated. Something was definitely different about her body, like she'd grown a foot.

"I need to get up," Liv heard herself say, although her voice strangely sounded different, although she wasn't sure how.

Clark gave her an uncertain look but assisted her to her feet.

Liv swayed, noticing the various faces around the room regarding her with quiet curiosity. *Nice. First I screamed incoherent things upon entering the chamber, and now they've all seen me pass out,* Liv thought, trying to hide the mortification on her face.

The dull ache on the back of her head reminded her that she'd hit the floor when she'd passed out. She kept herself from rubbing her head to check the bump that was most definitely rising from the surface.

Liv avoided eye contact with the Warriors, who were all standing too close to her. The circle on the ground where she'd been standing caught her attention. It wasn't dimmed like it had been before, but now was a light shade of blue. Liv's eyes traveled up the tree, and her mouth popped open when she noticed that the Beaufont branch was now lit with both green and blue. Under the blue part of the branch was the name "Olivia."

Her eyes continued to move upward to the ceiling, where the lights twinkled overhead. Somewhere above them was a new light that had been sparked when Liv's magic was unlocked.

The lights somehow looked unusual to Liv. Then she blinked at the domed room and realized that it appeared different than before as well. Absentmindedly, Liv pulled up her hand, studying the back of it. Everything looked different.

A flapping sound pulled her attention away from her body. Perched on the far corner of the bench, next to Lorenzo Rosario, the man with the chiseled goatee, was a large black crow. Liv felt something brush by her and looked down as the white tiger moved into the center of the half-circle where the Warriors normally stood. They were still out of formation, but ushered by the movement of the white tiger, they moved back into place, not giving Liv their full attention anymore.

The crow cawed loudly, making Liv slam her hands to the sides of her head harder than she intended. She was then overwhelmed by the assault she'd done to her ears in an attempt to block out the loud noise. Again she was astonished by how different noises sounded. They were amplified. Crisper. Carrying color and emotions she'd never noticed before.

"Yes, I daresay we've spent too much time on this," Adler murmured as if in reply to a complaint. "Ms. Beaufont, you've elected to do your own training, and you'll need to start that right away. The Seven will meet again tomorrow night. Do not be late, as you were today."

"I didn't realize I was late," Liv stated, her voice vibrating with new hostility. She wanted to cry and yell as if every emotion she'd ever felt was brimming to escape right then.

"You were," Adler said matter-of-factly. "You are dismissed for the night. We will see you tomorrow at nine. Do try to start your training. It's important."

Liv wanted to tell the old albino that he could shove his clock up his tight ass and take his training advice and wrap it up in his wiry beard and wear it as a hat. Instead, she allowed Clark to tug her toward the mirrored door.

"Oh, and Olivia?" Adler said at her back.

She turned around, noticing that all eyes were on her.

"It's nice to have you back," the old magician said with a disingenuous smile.

Liv didn't return the grin. She simply nodded and said, "Thanks, but note that my name is Liv, not Olivia."

At the conclusion of her statement, the name under her blue branch was erased. Many in the room released sounds of astonishment, and then, as if there were an invisible pen, the letters "L-i-v" were etched into place.

CHAPTER TEN

Liv had a bazillion questions when Clark pulled her back through the mirrored door, which thankfully didn't feel as strange as it had before. It simply felt like she was walking through a sopping-wet veil, but when she reached the other side, she was grateful to find herself completely dry.

"What was that about my magic?" Liv asked as Clark continued to tug on her arm. "Was it supposed to knock me out? Is there something wrong with me? Why were the Councilors all giving me those strange looks?"

Clark turned around when they were just in front of the large door across from the council room. "How did you do that?" He shook his head, his face pale and his breathing shallow.

"She held her breath," Plato said from his place by Liv's feet.

Liv shook her head at him. "I tried not to. There was just so much going on. I didn't mean to pass out."

Clark shook his head. "No, I meant changing your name on the Tree of Seven."

Liv thought for a moment and shrugged. "I'm not sure. I mean, I don't think it was me. I just told them what to call me."

Clark ground his fist into his forehead the way he used to do when they were kids and he was trying to figure out how to get them out of trouble. "It had to be you, but I don't get how you did it, especially without realizing it."

"Well, why don't you start with telling me what's up with my magic?" Liv asked. "Is there something wrong with it? Has it gone bad? Expired or something?"

Clark lowered his hand and pulled out the large door in a quick movement. The giant oak door creaked as it opened, making the group back up to make room for it to swing. "Like Adler said, the reading was probably off. They'll keep an eye on it and I'm sure it will normalize tomorrow."

When the door was open all the way, Liv found a sight she'd remembered. It was almost as fresh as her latest memories. The long corridor was lined with various doors that led to different suites. To the right, a long banister ran up the stairs that led to the other six stories. The hallway was filled with chandeliers dripping in sapphires and emeralds. Large paintings adorned the paneled walls. Liv remembered running down these hallways when she was on her way to and from lessons or hiding from Ian and Reese when they were trying to round them up at night for baths. Most days were spent in their family's suite, but when Liv got out, she and Clark kept running, giggling up the stairs to the attic on the seventh floor.

Clark held the door open and directed Liv into the hallway. She halted, though. Firstly, because she sensed something at her back, something she could have sworn she saw dart into the entryway. Second, because she saw no reason she should enter the rooming corridor. Liv backed up, giving Clark a skeptical glare.

"I don't trust Adler or any notion he has about my magic," Liv began. "If there's something going on, I want you to tell me. We need to be straight with each other from the beginning."

Clark sighed, continuing to hold the heavy door open. "It's nothing to worry about. And Adler is... Well, he means well. He just comes across as abrasive."

Liv shook her head, looking back briefly at the mirrored door. "As I said, I don't trust him, and you shouldn't either."

"Don't be so paranoid," Clark complained.

"Be straight with me from the beginning," Liv repeated. "What's going on with my magic?"

Clark motioned for Liv to step across the threshold. When she didn't, he rolled his eyes but seemed to relax slightly. "Fine. Your magic meter is a little high."

"High? Like from me having had my magic locked?" Liv asked.

Clark shook his head. "For any magician of your caliber. It's higher than any of the other Warriors'."

"Well, that must be a mistake," Liv stated, looking down at Plato for an answer.

The cat didn't appear concerned. He sat back and licked his rear end.

Clark agreed with a nod. "Like I said, it will normalize in a day or so. Probably just a spike."

"What about that white tiger? What was up with that?"

Clark gave her a tentative look and shook his head. "It's nothing. He just helps maintain the balance."

"Balance? Like between what and what?" Liv asked.

"I'll explain in time. Now, go ahead and get in here." He motioned to the open door.

"Why, do you want to show me your new knife collection or something?" Liv asked.

Clark grunted in frustration. "No, I'm showing you to your room. Our suite moved after... Well, you know..."

Liv stepped back into the hallway. She didn't care if the suite wasn't the one she had shared with her parents, she wasn't going there. "I'm not staying here at the House of Seven."

"This is where you belong now," Clark argued.

"Why, because I'm a Warrior?"

Clark took his hands off the door, and it rammed into his shoulder. "Because you're a Beaufont. This is where you've always belonged."

"I haven't belonged here in a long time. I'll do as the Seven command me. I'll fight for their supposed justice, but I refuse to stay here."

"What, are you going back to that shitty studio apartment?"

Liv's temper flared, and for a moment her vision was blanketed in red. She thought it was a trick of her eyes, but when she told herself to calm down, her head felt as though it released steam and suddenly her vision cleared.

This magic business was going to take some getting used to.

"I happen to like my apartment," Liv snapped, inhaling a measured breath and clenching her fists in an attempt to quell the fire burning deep within her.

"But your family is here, and now that you've returned…"

"Look, I can't stay at the House of Seven," Liv explained, trying to inject sympathy into her voice. "I'm back, but I'm not entirely *back*. I need to do things my way."

Clark hesitated before nodding. "Yeah, I should have expected as much. I was just hoping…" His voice trailed away as his eyes found Liv's clenched fists. "What about your training? How are you going to handle that? Do you want my help?"

Councilors had their own training. There wasn't much crossover between that and what Warriors were taught. Clark was trying to help. He kept trying to help, and Liv felt heartless because she just couldn't accept his assistance, as much as she might want to. She shook her head. "Don't worry about it. I'll figure something out."

"Are you sure you're not being stubborn just for stubborn's sake?" Clark asked, crossing his arms on his chest.

"Look, we see things differently," Liv stated. "That's allowed. I'm going to do what the Seven tell me to, but I don't have to stay here, and I don't have to accept their training."

"But I don't see what's wrong with it, Liv."

She thought for a moment. "You remember when we were little and I always used to sink your battleships?"

Clark's head twitched. He had obviously not been expecting the sudden strange question. "Yeah?"

"Why was that?" Liv asked.

Clark looked away before returning his gaze to her. "Because I always put them in the same location."

"Yes, exactly," Liv said victoriously. "The House has been doing everything the same way for a long time. They always put their battleships in the same place. I'm not a traditional kind of gal, though, and I think that to be a successful Warrior, I can't accept their same old ways of doing things."

"But magic's foundation is grounded in the traditions," Clark argued.

Liv gave him a consoling look as she backed away. "That's what they *want* you to believe."

Clark nearly rolled his eyes but stopped himself. "You don't have to be so paranoid about everything."

"And you don't have to accept everything they say without questioning it," Liv countered. "Being skeptical isn't against the law."

"Yes, but the more resistance you put up, the more others won't like you," Clark stated.

Liv nodded proudly. "I'm not here to make friends, Bro. I'm here to protect magic."

He smiled. Maybe it was the use of her old nickname for him, or that they'd easily fallen back into their usual roles—Liv the troublemaker and Clark the people-pleaser. Their parents had always said they were good for each other, but Liv knew that they never suspected the two would be Councilor and Warrior one day. There was no way their parents could have foreseen it because it would have meant so much death would have to have come first.

With a suddenly heavy heart, Liv offered Clark a sincere smile and turned to the entryway. Before she had gotten more than a few paces, she heard Clark retreat and the large door fall shut.

She took her time walking down the long corridor, watching the symbols dance as her fingertips grazed the wall. When she was almost to the entry, she halted, Plato beside her.

Without turning around, Liv turned her chin until it was even with her shoulder. "I know you're there," she said to the seemingly empty hallway. "Why don't you come out already and we get this over with."

CHAPTER ELEVEN

The firelight in the long corridor dimmed for a moment as if the torches were holding their breath, waiting in anticipation. Liv remained frozen, her back still to the hallway, her eyes looking over her shoulder. She heard a small shuffling noise in the distance, then it sounded only feet from her, and in an instant, it was far away again.

Liv looked down at Plato. "How long have you known she was there?"

The cat turned around, sat down, and regarded the empty hallway. "Since the moment you entered the House of Seven."

"The little sneak has been watching me that long?" Liv asked. "I thought I spied someone."

Copying Plato, Liv spun, her arms crossed on her chest and eyes scanning the empty hall.

"Maybe try a different approach, since 'let's get this over with' didn't work," Plato offered.

The flames flared slightly as Liv's annoyance built. "Okay, how about this?" she said in a whisper to Plato before spinning back around and striding for the exit again. "Oh, well. Too bad you won't show your face. See you later, you little sneak."

A blast of icy wind hit Liv in the face, whipping through her clothes and making it hard to progress. She stopped, threw her hand in front of her, and closed her fingers into a fist, sucking the air away all at once. Turning back to Plato, she gave him a curious expression.

He looked impressed. "Was harnessing that wind intended?"

She opened her hand, half-expecting the gale-force wind to whip her in the face again. When it didn't, she shrugged. "That was pure improv. I don't know where that came from."

"Magic is mostly instinct," Plato reasoned, returning his focus to the long, empty corridor. "But it appears that your little friend has her own tricks."

Liv corralled her tangled hair, getting her fingers stuck in several knots. "Okay, cute little display with the wind," she said in a loud voice. "You don't want me to leave, but you aren't willing to come out. You realize that's sort of annoying, right?"

Plato gave her a contemptuous look. "Try a little tact. It could go a long way."

Liv sighed. "Hey there, little buddy. Would you please come out and play?"

A red ball materialized in the middle of the gold hallway, contrasting brilliantly with the blue and green floor.

Liv's brow furrowed, and she stepped up next to Plato. "What am I supposed to do with *that*?"

"It's a ball," Plato said dryly. "Play with it."

Liv thought for a moment. "How?"

Plato's tamed expression flared into one of pure annoyance. "I don't know. Go kick it or something."

Liv laughed. "You don't know how to play either." She strolled forward and picked up the plastic, red ball. "For all your wisdom, dear Plato, you're as clueless as I am when it comes to having fun."

"I'm simply out of practice," he stated, his green eyes on a shadow that had just materialized. "Years of hanging out with you has done that to me."

"Well, no one is forcing you to keep me company," Liv teased. Not once had she ever worried that Plato would leave her side. He was the constant in her life. Always there when she woke up and always curled up next to her at the end of the day. She might not always know where he was, but she always knew he was close by.

Liv tossed the ball into the air, bouncing it on her fingertips. "You know what my least favorite game was as a kid?"

Plato yawned, lifting his paw to lick it. "The quiet game."

She shot him a cold stare. "No, I'm great at that game. It was Clark who always spoiled things when we tried to sneak down to the kitchen for a midnight treat." Liv bounced the ball on the floor. "Keep away was the worst game. Ian and Reece used to make us play, and I never won."

"Height-disadvantaged," Plato said simply.

Liv squatted to the ground and rolled the red ball forward. "All I ever wanted was a good game of back and forth."

The shadow shifted rapidly, and suddenly a little girl materialized on the other side of the ball, catching it. Her blonde ringlets framed her heart-shaped face and the Beaufont blue eyes. Liv didn't have to guess how old she was. Sophia had been three years old when Liv left the House of Seven, making her eight now.

"Me too," the little magician said, taking the ball in her small hands and holding it close to her chest.

Liv nodded, trying to pretend that this whole situation wasn't highly bizarre. In her world, children didn't hide as shadows or send a blast of wind at people they didn't want to leave. She reminded herself that this was her world now, with all its absurdities. Furthermore, this had always been her world, even if the last five years had changed everything for her.

Liv curled her fingers forward. "Go ahead then, toss me the ball. That's how back and forth works, right?"

Sophia nodded and threw the ball, launching it in Liv's direction with a force to impress. Liv's fingers burned from the impact when she caught it.

"So you're Sophia?" Liv asked, gently tossing the ball back to her sister. The little girl looked how she remembered, but also quite different with her full features and the baby fat having melted away.

"Do you remember me?" Sophia asked, catching the red ball.

"Of course I do," Liv said with a laugh. "Do you remember *me*?"

The little girl shook her head.

"You were young," Liv murmured, and remorse instantly crawled into her stomach. Sophia probably wouldn't remember their parents. What a blessing and a curse.

"You left," Sophia said simply, her small voice carrying a great weight to it.

"I know," Liv replied. "I just couldn't be here. It's hard to explain."

"But you're back?"

Liv tossed the ball to her sister again. "Sort of. I've taken the Warrior role, just until you're old enough."

"That's a long time," Sophia said, catching the ball and setting it by her feet. She wore a blue dress that hung to the floor and was tied in the back with a white satin bow. She looked like a little doll with her soft cheeks and button nose.

"Tell me about it," Liv agreed, taking several steps closer. She knelt, looking up at the young girl. "Are you okay, Sophia? Do you miss Ian and Reese?"

She nodded, chewing her bottom lip. "Are you going to be my sister now that they are gone?"

Liv thought for a moment. "I've always been your sister, even if I wasn't here. But yes, I'll come around and see you when I'm here. Maybe we can play ball, and you can teach me some games."

"Where are you going?" Sophia asked, pointing at the doorway down the hall.

Liv turned around. Only then did she realize that the corridor looked much different to her sister. It would have appeared as Liv had always seen it, with pale walls and a short walkway. "I'm going home."

"Can I go with you?"

Liv shook her head. "No, West Hollywood is for freaks and the lost and lonely. You belong here."

"But you told Clark that *you* didn't belong here," Sophia said, a stubbornness flaring on her face that took Liv back suddenly. She had a flash of her mother playfully challenging their father, as she did so often it became a nightly ritual.

"I guess I'm one of the lost and lonely," Liv stated, and added, "as well as a freak."

Sophia checked over her shoulder like she'd heard a noise. "Ian gave me something for you."

Liv felt herself tilt backward and nearly thought she'd tip over. "What? Why would he do that?"

Sophia shrugged, reaching into the deep pocket on the front of her dress. "He said that if anything ever happened to him, I should give it to you but not tell anyone about it."

She withdrew her closed hand from her pocket, holding it expectantly in the air. Liv placed her palm under the young girl's, and felt as something heavier than she expected dropped into her hand.

"Sophia!" Clark called from the far end of the hallway.

Liv's head jerked up and she yanked her hand to her side, looking at Clark with sudden trepidation.

His face softened when he recognized Sophia standing in front of Liv. "Oh, good, there you are. I've been looking for you everywhere," Clark said, striding toward them.

Sophia pointed up at Liv. "I just wanted to say hi."

Clark nodded. "Yes, I can see that. It's late though, Soph.

You should get up to bed. You can have more visits later. Unless…" He gave Liv an expectant look, hope in his eyes.

She shook her head at once. "I'll just be off. I have a lot to do."

Liv waved at her younger sister, the mysterious object clutched in her other hand as she backed toward the door.

CHAPTER TWELVE

The heat from the giant fireplace in Adler Sinclair's private study was almost too much. He pulled off the silk scarf and his robes, shedding clothing until only his undershirt and loose pants remained. Usually, he wouldn't have the fire burning so intensely, but his miniature dragon, Indikos, was molting and desired the extra warmth.

Adler's beloved creature lay on the hearth, his nose almost too close to the fire. His mouth gaped as he panted, and his old reddish skin peeled away from his body, making way for the shimmering new scales.

Decar eyed the process with mild interest as he fanned himself with a thick piece of parchment. "Really, we could have met in my quarters."

Adler shook his head, striding for the large desk beside the fireplace where the animal, who was about the size of a small dog, lay looking helpless. "No, I like to be with Indikos when he's renewing. The last time I wasn't, his old skin caught fire. It was such a waste. It's a very valuable potions ingredient."

Decar regarded the dragon, noticing how close it was to the fire and easily seeing how the skin could find its way into the flames.

"Besides, I have too much work to do to be anywhere else," Adler went on.

"I thought you said that things should slow down now that the Beaufonts' position is filled," Decar stated.

Adler nodded. "Things *will* settle down, but there's still much to oversee. This new Warrior...she's a bit of a challenge. I need to make arrangements for her."

Decar stood, pacing away from the leather sofa and farther from the fireplace. He opened the window on the far side of the room and stuck his head out for a moment. When he returned, his white hair was out of place, and his pale skin was red from the winter night. "Her magic? Do you think it was a surge?"

Adler nodded, looking down at the various papers strewn across his desk. He pushed them aside and picked up a tablet. Swiping through various screens, he came to the one on which he'd recorded Olivia Beaufont's magical statistics. Usually these things remained in the Chamber of the Tree, but Adler had found reason after reason to transfer the information to his personal devices, and now no one seemed to notice when he did.

"It can only be explained as a buildup of magic," Adler stated. "I have every reason to believe that it will normalize in a day or two."

"Was it wise to allow her to leave the House untrained

with that level of magic flowing through her?" Decar asked, his head half out the window again.

Adler's attention was mostly on the tablet in his hand. He squinted at it and looked up absentmindedly. "What? Yes, it's fine. The girl is not a concern for us."

"But you said her magic levels were unprecedented," Decar said, his light eyes flicking in the direction of the tablet, although from across the room he couldn't see much.

Adler switched off the tablet and buried it under the papers again. Warriors weren't given access to the same information as the Councilors, which was for the best. That allowed them to focus on their missions and left the Councilors the burden of information. This was the way the balance had been set up, and it had worked for centuries.

"The girl's magic is a momentary anomaly," Adler stated, his eyes swiveling to the dragon, still panting by the fire. Indikos' wings unfurled and beat for a moment, fanning the fire and sending a blast of heat and sparks through the large study.

Decar popped his head out the window again, and Adler shielded his face from the surge of heat. When Indikos settled his wings, Decar dared to pull his head back into the room. He studied the dragon with annoyance and then looked at his brother.

"How do you know this Olivia Beaufont won't be an issue?" Decar asked. "You remember how she was before?"

Adler picked through the papers on his desk, looking for a specific report. "She was only a child then and hurt by her parents' deaths. She made a few accusations, but in the end, she left without incident."

"But she's back now, and a Warrior," Decar stated. "She's in a position of power."

Adler released a strange smile, holding up the paper he'd been looking for. "Ms. Beaufont may be one of the Seven, but power is relative."

"What's that?" Decar asked, striding over to the desk to get a closer look.

Adler didn't say another word, simply handed the report to his brother.

Something sparked in Decar's eyes as he looked up. "You're going to assign her *this* case?" He laughed. "That will keep her busy for weeks, especially with you requiring that she train while working."

Adler nodded victoriously. He picked up another report and handed it over. "And when she's done with that, the Councilors will assign her this. This is what I wanted to work on tonight."

Decar took it and scanned the page, laughing again. "That's brilliant."

"It will keep her busy and out of harm's way," Adler said proudly. "See, I *told* you there was nothing to worry about."

"I wasn't really concerned about the girl," Decar stated. "She is untrained, unaccustomed to our lifestyle, and lacking a proper filter. I just didn't want her hampering things."

"And I told you not to worry, Brother," Adler said simply. "We were required to fill the open position of Warrior. I would have been happy to replace the Beaufonts, but this is almost better. Two amateurs have joined the Seven. We really couldn't have asked for more."

"So what do we do now?" Decar asked, taking out a handkerchief and wiping the sweat off his brow.

"'Do?'" Adler asked. "We don't need to *do* anything."

He glanced at his small dragon. Adler had acquired him during his travels in India from a merchant who didn't understand that the serpent's egg he had was nothing of the sort. Six months later, when Indikos hatched, Adler finally affirmed he was the owner of a rare miniature dragon, one with unique powers like the magician's. For a decade he'd been his most faithful companion, showing a devotion that most never knew. *If only everyone in the Seven showed such loyalty,* Adler often thought.

"So you suspect things will go undisturbed from here on out?" Decar asked skeptically. "Because you've had that presumption before."

The insinuation hung heavy in the air, but Adler dismissed it with a wave of his hand. He strode to a decanter of brandy beside the couch and poured two glasses. Handing the first to his brother, he kept the second for himself. "Don't worry, Decar. I believe the House of Seven has reached a new pinnacle. Gone are the days where we have to worry. Going forward, the House will return to normal, serving to protect magic as it should have been doing from the very beginning."

Decar lifted his glass and clinked it against his brother's before taking a sip, strangely enjoying the extra warmth it created in his body.

CHAPTER THIRTEEN

The smell of coffee didn't bring the same warmth it usually did as Liv raised the full mug to her lips. She held it away before taking a sip, the aroma making her stomach turn.

Usually, Liv didn't drink coffee, but circumstances required it. She'd returned home from the House of Seven and found it impossible to sleep. For hours she'd tossed and turned, seeing strange bright lights like fireworks when she closed her eyes. It wasn't until three in the morning that the shocking display had stopped jolting her awake.

When her alarm clock went off at six, she nearly threw it across her apartment. Exhausted and with a dull buzzing in her ears, Liv had pulled herself from the bed, showered, and put on a fresh set of clothes before going down to open the repair shop, remarkably on time.

No one ever showed up at seven in the morning to have their toasters or vacuum cleaners repaired, but John wouldn't listen to reason. He'd always insisted that the shop be opened early. Usually Liv didn't mind, because she could use the extra hour or two before customers arrived to work on the projects that always seemed to pile up in the back.

On that particular morning, though, Liv could hardly find the energy to keep her head up. She tried holding the mug of steaming hot coffee to her mouth again, but the smell instantly made her stomach rumble with unease.

"You need sleep," Plato observed from beside her on the workbench.

"You're right," she said flatly, setting down the cup of coffee. "You watch the shop. I'll take a nap in the back. If anyone needs anything, tell them that you're a talking cat and I'm a magician who was up all night trying to make sense of my new, strange life. Cool?"

Plato pretended he hadn't heard Liv and angled his head in the direction of her hand, which was tapping the mug still in front of her. "Maybe the ring will make more sense to you in the daylight. You could try studying it while the shop is quiet."

Liv looked down at the ring, which was the strange object Sophia had passed to her from Ian. Her mother's wedding ring, an heirloom that had been passed down in the Beaufont family for ages—but that didn't explain why Ian had told Sophia to give it to Liv if anything ever happened to him.

The ring was a monstrosity, but Liv had decided to wear it, not trusting leaving it hidden somewhere in her apartment. The center diamond was giant at approximately five carats, and round cut. Around the main gem were fourteen smaller diamonds of various colors, lights and darks of blue, green, red, yellow, orange, purple, and even black.

The band was platinum, and carved on the inside were the words, Together we are strong and balanced.

Liv searched the workbench for the magnifying glasses John often wore for small repairs. Finding them, she slipped them on and took a closer look at the ring. The craftsmanship was incredible—not that Liv had studied many gems, but she could tell immediately that the diamonds were of the highest quality. And the band didn't have a single scratch on it.

"This must be protected by magic," she muttered, turning the ring around and looking for anything that would explain why her brother wanted her to have it. Frustrated, she pulled off the glasses.

"I don't get it," she said to Plato. "Was Ian telling me not to waste my youth alone and that I should get married?"

Plato shook his head, squinting at the ring between Liv's fingertips. "I don't think so, but I strongly suspect he's left you a clue."

Liv dropped her hand and let out a soft growl of frustration. "But why? Why would I need a clue unless there's some mystery to be solved?"

The toaster next to her on the workstation shook. Thinking the big earthquake was finally coming, Liv shot up and grabbed Plato, bolting for the doorway that divided the storefront from the back.

She looked around tentatively, waiting for the major tremor. When nothing happened, she looked down at Plato in confusion.

"What exactly are you doing?" he asked dryly.

"I'm saving your ass from an earthquake," she explained, glancing at the toaster and the other objects on the work table that were still vibrating.

"What earthquake?" Plato asked.

Liv looked around, noting that the appliances lining the dusty shelves weren't vibrating like those on the workbench. Her brow furrowed in confusion. Plato wiggled his way out of her grasp and hopped to the floor, springing swiftly back up onto the worktable.

"Might I suggest that the trembling is less a result of tectonic plates shifting and more to do with a certain magician who needs to learn to control her magic?" he said boldly.

Liv blinked dully at the objects. "Me? *I'm* the one doing that?"

Plato nodded. "Just like last night when you changed your name on the Tree of Seven or made the flames flare in the torches."

"Are you sure that was me?" Liv asked.

Plato simply gave her a look that said, "Come on, get real."

"Well, how do I get it to stop?" Liv asked as the toaster rattled even harder and fell over on its side.

Plato laid down, putting his head on his paws. "Get trained. But for now, you better take care of *that* customer."

Liv's eyes widened in shock and her gaze flew to the entrance, where a figure stood on the other side. His back was to the door, and he pressed it open with his rear end since he was carrying a large printer in both hands.

Liv darted forward, sweeping the various tools off the

workbench and onto the floor where they continued to bounce around as if possessed.

Shane, a semi-regular, startled when the tools clattered to the floor, spinning around as he entered.

"What was that?" he asked, looking around for the cause of the noise.

Liv slammed both hands down on the toaster, which was jumping around wildly. "Oh, nothing. The dumb cat just knocked over my tools."

Plato cracked an eye open at her briefly and nestled more into a sleeping position.

Shane shook his head, his stringy black hair hitting him in the face. He wore his usual Metallica shirt and a silver loop in his right ear. A decade earlier he'd been a touring rockstar with various well-known bands, playing bass. Presently, he owned the pawn shop down the way.

"That's why you shouldn't have animals in the shop," Shane stated, giving the cat a disapproving look. "Besides, many people are allergic to animals."

"Yeah, but he's sort of my comfort animal, so I must have him here with me," Liv replied, pinning the toaster with her elbows. Like a possessed weasel, it was still trying to escape her clutches. On the ground, the tools continued to bounce around, clanging gently.

Shane chuckled. "I don't believe in all that comfort animal mumbo jumbo. I just take drugs, and I feel fine."

"Drugs. I'll remember that," Liv said tersely. "Thanks."

Shane peered over the side of the workbench to where the tools were dancing. "What's going on over there? You have another cat?"

"Rats," Liv stated. "Get off your ass, Plato, and take care of the vermin already."

Plato lifted his head and yawned before setting it back down again.

"Damn cats are worthless," Shane stated. "My Doberman would have eaten those mice for breakfast already."

Having had enough of this conversation, Plato stretched into a standing position, arching his back. He hopped off the workbench and disappeared behind a rack of tools.

"So, you have something for me to repair?" Liv asked, picking up the toaster, which was growing antsier with what felt like combustible energy by the minute.

"Yeah, some punk sold me this," Shane said, sliding the printer onto the table. "It worked for all of two minutes, but the moment the guy was gone, it stopped working. He's not coming back to get it, and I figured John or you might be able to fix it."

Liv held the toaster to her chest like it was a cuddly teddy bear. "Yeah, just leave it here, and I'll take a look at it."

Shane eyed her as she hugged the toaster and shook his head. "Actually, I wanted to show you something. I think the board is fried, but there's also a problem with the rollers. That was why it kept jamming on me when I first used it."

Liv looked over the table as Shane opened a panel.

"You see, in there." Shane pointed. "I think there's something lodged between the rollers."

"Yep, I see it," Liv said quickly. "I'll take care of it. No worries."

"You can't see it from over there," Shane stated. "Actually, if you hold open this panel, I can try to get my fingers in there."

The tools on the ground banged louder than before in a protest of sorts.

"Don't worry about it!" Liv yelled, her exasperation erupting, making several appliances fall off the shelves. Dust and small parts scattered from the impact.

Shane shielded his face from the minor explosion, jumping back.

Liv cringed, holding the toaster even tighter.

"What the hell was that?" Shane asked, looking at the appliances littering the ground.

"I think we're getting tremors," Liv insisted in a rush.

Shane's brow wrinkled. He withdrew his phone, pulling up an app. "I didn't get any notifications, and usually I do if they are in my area."

"They are small," Liv argued.

"That mixer flew off the shelf," Shane said, pointing. "And look at that wrench!" He pointed to the tools hopping around on the concrete floor.

"Yeah, I agree that you should probably get back to your shop to see if everything is okay," Liv stated, ushering Shane to the door.

He gave her a confused expression, as if he'd misheard her. "I didn't say anything about going back to my shop."

"Didn't you?" Liv asked. "I could have sworn that you said you were worried about how the earthquakes were affecting your place."

Shane looked at his phone, which reported there had been no earthquakes. Then his confused expression changed to a relaxed one, like he was suddenly in a trance. "Yeah, you're right. I should go back to my shop."

"Exactly," Liv agreed, pushing Shane out, the toaster still pressed to her chest. "I'll look at the printer and call you when I have a repair estimate."

"Printer?" Shane asked, looking over his shoulder. Seeing the electronic device he'd brought in, he nodded. "Right. Printer. That's weird, I forgot all about it."

The toaster finally broke free of Liv's arms, leaping over her head. She jumped, grabbing it and yanking it back against her chest.

"What in the he—"

"Earthquake," Liv said at once, cutting Shane off. "Get back to your shop. Nothing strange happening here."

Again his perplexed expression dropped and he nodded dully. "Yes, you're right."

As Shane left, another set of appliances jumped off the shelves, bursting on the ground.

Plato peeked his head out from the far corner of the room, only his face visible. "Well, that was the most entertaining thing I've seen in a long time."

Liv opened a vintage trunk full of moving blankets and stuck the toaster inside, slamming the lid before it could escape. She sat on the trunk, bouncing from the movement of the toaster. "What am I going to do? Plato, can you train me how to use my magic?"

"I'm afraid I can't," Plato answered, looking at the bits and pieces bobbing around on the ground. "But I *can* tell you that you need to relax. The more upset you get, the harder it will be for you to control your magic."

"How am I supposed to relax?" Liv asked. "The shop is a mess, and I think I just brainwashed a customer."

"Yes, that was quite impressive. Quick thinking."

"I didn't mean to do it!" Liv yelled. A jar of screws exploded, sending shards of glass in all directions. Plato ducked back under the shelf. Liv covered her face with her arms.

"Did I mention that you need to relax?" Plato asked. "Try meditating. If you don't get your emotions under control things will just get worse, since they are tied closely to your magic."

"Meditate?" That seemed like a very hard thing for Liv to do with so many panicked emotions running wild inside her.

"Either that or you can take a shot of whiskey," Plato suggested.

"Whiskey?" Liv asked. "It's early morning."

"Alcohol dulls magical abilities, as well as having a depressant effect on emotions," Plato explained.

Liv launched herself off the trunk, and the toaster nearly broke out. She didn't pay it any attention as she pulled out the top drawer of a filing cabinet beside the workbench. Yanking out a bottle half-full of whiskey, Liv tugged the cork out with her teeth.

"Remind me that I need to buy John a new bottle of whiskey," Liv stated, taking a drink while more appliances jumped from the shelves as if attempting suicide.

"Keep drinking, or it will be more than a bottle of

whiskey you owe the poor man," Plato suggested from his hiding place.

Liv pressed her eyes shut and continued to drink even though the whiskey burned her throat. She gulped, feeling the fire within her being smothered as the liquor hit her belly. Not until the bottle was empty did Liv stop drinking. She coughed, whiskey coming through her nose and burning her sinuses.

Looking around anxiously, Liv watched as the bits and bobs on the ground rolled around a couple of inches and then back the other direction, almost like a drunk staggering. Her head swam from the alcohol and she belched, entertained by the toaster knocking against the top of the trunk. All at once, the appliances went still.

Liv let out a giant sigh. "Finally," she muttered, looking around at the mess.

"Yeah, and not a moment too soon," Plato said, ducking back under the shelf and disappearing completely.

Liv looked up at the door as John entered the shop, shock covering his face.

CHAPTER FOURTEEN

"What in God's name happened here?" John asked, throwing his hand to his chest and stumbling back.

Liv's synapses apparently weren't firing at the moment. She couldn't believe what she'd done, or that she'd caused any stress to John. Shaking off the guilty emotions, Liv rushed forward. "It's totally fine. Some kids were in here this morning. I think they broke in through the back. They were in the shop when I entered and I ran them off."

John stared around in disbelief, looking at the various broken appliances. Then, as if his thoughts had caught up with him, he looked at Liv, worry making the wrinkles around his eyes deepen. "Are you okay? They didn't hurt you, did they?"

She shook her head, the well of guilt overflowing. "I'm fine. I was just trying to clean up before you got here."

John pointed to the empty bottle that was still in Liv's hand. "I'm guessing the shitheads drank all my good whiskey."

Liv found herself nodding as she covered her mouth so John couldn't smell the booze on her breath. "I'm afraid so. I was just about to chuck this in the trash."

"Did you file a police report?" John asked. "And the door in the back? Do I need to fix the lock?"

Liv was going to have to tell him the truth soon…once she understood it better. "No, you're fine. I fixed the lock already. You won't even be able to tell that anyone broke it. And no, I haven't had a chance to file a police report."

"Those hoodlums," John asked, pulling out his phone. "You get a good look at them?"

"Oh, yeah," Liv said, putting the whiskey bottle in the trash can and grabbing the broom and dustpan. Her dumb magic had broken more than a dozen appliances. She had to figure out how to fix this for John.

"What did they look like? How many were there?" John asked, dialing the police and pressing the phone to his ear.

"There were three of them," Liv began. "One had short black hair, like a bowl cut. Another had sort of poufy brown curly hair, and the last was bald."

John covered the phone with a hand. "Liv, did you just describe the Three Stooges?"

Sweeping the floor, Liv covered the blush on her face. "I was still half asleep when I came into the shop. Maybe I didn't get such a good look at them."

It took Liv longer than it should have to clean up the shop while John spoke with the police. It was hard for her to concentrate with the whiskey rolling around in her stomach. With each passing minute, she worried that the alcohol was going to wear off and her magic would be out of control once more. That was why her training was crucial. If she couldn't get things under control soon, she was going to have to ask the House for help. That was the last thing she wanted after her display of independence the night before.

"Okay, that's done," John said with a heavy sigh as he reentered the shop after talking to the police out front.

"What did they say?" Liv asked, dumping her dustpan into the trash.

"Apparently, there's been a string of similar incidents in the area," John reported. "Damn kids have nothing to do."

Liv's chest lightened.

John looked at the trash bin filled with appliances too broken to repair and grimaced. "I'll have to credit or pay most of those customers for their devices."

"You can take it out of my paycheck," Liv offered.

John gave her a confused look. "Why would I do that?"

"Well, because maybe I was running a few minutes behind this morning," Liv insisted in a rush. "If I'd been here on time, maybe the kids wouldn't have done all this."

John laughed good-naturally. "You haven't been late to work a day in your life. No, these things happen, Liv. We'll clean up and be fine. Don't you worry."

"Hey, John," Liv began, her tone careful. She wanted to tell him everything—about her magic and Plato and her family—but the longer she stalled, the more she thought she couldn't. What if he rejected her? Pushed her away? Kicked her out? No, she would tell him in time, once she could prove she wasn't a danger to anyone or anything.

"Have you taken your heart meds today?" she finally asked.

He looked at her absentmindedly and then nodded. Pulling the pill bottle from his jacket pocket, he opened it and took one of the small white pills. "Today I won't fight you on that, although I wish those heathens had left me some whiskey."

Liv turned her back to John, pretending to tidy one of the shelves. *Buy John more whiskey*, she reminded herself silently.

"Maybe Rory will bring me some stuff today," John mused. "I could use the work after this."

Liv spun around, an idea occurring to her. "How much does he sell those to you for?"

"Sell?" John asked. "He doesn't. Rory just gives them to me. He says it's stuff he finds in the junkyard."

"Really?" Liv asked.

"Yeah, and most of it doesn't even need much repair. You know that from working on the stuff in the past," John stated, waving at the display in the front of the shop where the repaired appliances were on sale. "So it's really all profit, whatever Rory brings me."

"Are you expecting to see him today?" Liv asked hopefully.

John scratched his head. "I never know when I'll see the fellow, actually. He just sort of shows up."

"Well, do you know where he lives?"

John looked up from the pile of appliances he'd started to sort through. "I'm not sure. Why do you want to know?"

"I'm just wondering where he gets his stuff," Liv lied. "I

was thinking I could do some scavenging for you. Help to make up for what happened here today."

John picked up an electrical heater, examining it. "Think we can salvage this one." He handed it to Liv. "Maybe you can try fixing it. And don't worry about doing anything to make up for today. It's not like it was your fault."

The guilt was almost too much for her. She gripped the heater and bit down hard on her lip.

The toaster banged strongly into the top of the vintage trunk, making the lid pop open slightly.

Liv's eyes bulged at the sight. *Damn it, what the hell was up with that damn toaster?*

John turned around at the sound, eyeing the trunk suspiciously. "Is Plato knocking around somewhere?"

"Yep," Liv said, hightailing it for the back. "That trouble-making cat is probably getting into stuff."

"Where are you going?" John asked.

"To the back to fix this heater," Liv said, disappearing before John could protest. They both knew the better tools were sitting on the workbench out front, but Liv couldn't chance being around John right then or she might make an even bigger mess.

She let out a giant exhale, pressing her eyes closed. The whiskey was wearing off faster than she would have expected, or maybe her magic was that difficult to subdue.

Liv counted down from ten, picturing herself riding an elevator down. It was a technique she often used to get to sleep. When she was almost to the first floor in her mind, she felt much more relaxed.

"You going to hide back here for the rest of the day?" Plato's voice called, making Liv's eyes open.

She nodded at the cat standing on the cluttered workbench in front of her. "I think that's the best plan for right now, unless you have a better idea."

"Blaming all your problems on me seems to be part of most of your plans," Plato said, offense in his voice.

"Yeah, sorry about that," Liv said, using a screwdriver to open the back of the heater.

"Why don't you use your magic to fix that like you did with the microwave?" Plato suggested, nodding at the heater.

"Because I don't know what I'm doing," Liv argued. "What if I blow it up or make a disaster of the back of the shop too?"

"What if you fix it?" Plato countered. "And now that you're relaxed, you appear to be in better control. You just can't let your emotions get away from you again."

Liv peered into the back of the heater. "It's fried—another appliance that can't be salvaged."

The objects on the table began to shake.

"Calm down," Plato warned.

Liv's eyes widened as the objects on the table began to bounce around more wildly. She closed her eyes and started to count back from ten again, trying to block out the gentle knocking sounds. When they died away, she opened her eyes again, a relieved smile on her face.

"Good," Plato said. "Now try focusing that power on fixing the heater."

Liv drilled the broken appliance with her gaze, seeing it as repaired as she'd done with the microwave. She felt the energy pour out of her like wisps of smoke, lacing around the heater's parts and changing them.

In her mind, she saw the heater working. Somehow, she could see deep into the appliance, observing as the parts were returned to working condition. It was like being in multiple places at once, her intention transporting her. It was brilliant and inspiring, and absolutely one of the most amazing feelings she'd ever experienced.

Sparks shot out of the heater, making Liv shield her face. Plato jumped from the table, once again taking cover. Smoke billowed from the heater, which had caught fire.

Liv ran for the back where the fire extinguisher was located, and she yanked it off the wall and returned as the fire grew, scorching the workbench. She sprayed the heater, sending white foam all over the place.

"What's going on back there?" John called from the front.

"Nothing!" Liv yelled, stopping the extinguisher and waving her hands to disperse the smoke.

"Do I smell smoke?" John asked.

"Damn it. Damn it. Damn it," Liv muttered under her breath, setting down the fire extinguisher and starting to clean up yet again. "No, you're just going senile, old man."

"Yeah, that seems about right," he replied with a chuckle.

Picking up the heater, Liv tossed it in the trashcan. "I'm useless today. I should just go home and stop making trouble for John."

"Or you could go to the House of Seven and accept their training," Plato offered, materializing on the table again and sniffing the white foam.

Liv grimaced at the notion. "I'm not sure I'm that desperate yet."

"Or," Plato said, drawing out the word, "you can try asking the giant for advice."

Liv sighed, looking at the spot where the heater had been. It was now permanently scorched. "I would, but I don't know how to find him."

"I know where to find him," Plato stated.

Liv looked up. "You do? Why didn't you say anything? Where is he?"

"In the front of the shop with John," Plato said, a hint of amusement on his face.

CHAPTER FIFTEEN

"Wait," Liv said, striding to the door and peering through.

Rory was, in fact, standing next to John, looking around the shop with a worried expression. He was so tall that John had to crane his head to look up at him. Beside him was a large box with various wires hanging over the side.

Liv looked back at Plato. "Why didn't you tell me he was here?"

"I thought you might be able to fix the heater," the cat answered.

Liv looked at the mess she'd made, and the objects on the table began to rattle again. "Next time have a little less faith in me," she said, poking her head through the swinging door dividing the back of the shop from the front.

"Hey there," she said casually, getting both men's attention. "Oh, Rory, you're here. I had no idea."

The giant eyed her suspiciously, not saying a word.

"Well, since you are here, would you mind grabbing

something off the top shelf back here for me?" Liv asked, pointing behind her. "It's way up on the top shelf and I can't get to it."

"Why don't you use the ladder?" John asked.

"It's broken," Liv lied.

John frowned. "That too? Damn this place is falling apart before my very eyes."

"I'll fix it," Liv stated. "Don't worry. But Rory, if I could have your help, that would be great."

The giant nodded, showing John a calm expression. "I'll be back in a moment. Pick through the box and let me know what you want. You can have it all."

John nodded, digging into the box in front of him.

Liv rushed back into the work area, starting to pace back and forth. What was she going to say to this giant? How could he help her? She wasn't sure, but of all the people she knew, he was the only one she was sure knew anything about magic. At least, she hoped her instinct was right about that. Otherwise, she was about to make a fool of herself.

Liv froze when Rory ducked through the doorway. His gaze fell on the scorch marks and foam on the worktable and the objects vibrating around it.

"I knew I sensed magic," he said, his voice a low whisper.

"You did?" Liv asked with relief. "When you showed up here?"

Rory shook his head. "I felt it from miles away. It was like a magical bomb went off. That was why I came down here."

Liv's face flushed. "Yeah, so apparently you know about magic. That's a good thing. One concern down."

Plato crawled up the ladder by the tall shelves and perched at the top, looking down at them.

Rory eyed the cat for a moment before looking at Liv. "So you don't need my help retrieving something from up high?"

Liv twisted her fingers together, trying to figure out the best approach. "No, I actually have a confession to make, and I need your help."

"Besides the fact that you're the one who destroyed the shop and that your cat talks to people?" Rory asked, not looking at all impressed.

Plato lifted his paw and licked it. "I only talk to Liv, not to people."

"Yes, besides that," Liv said sheepishly, looking at the objects that continued to vibrate on the table.

Rory crossed his large arms over his chest and frowned. "Go on, then."

Liv took a slow breath, and on the exhale, the tools settled down a bit, not making as much noise. "So, as it turns out, I'm a magician, and have just had my magic unlocked. I don't have the slightest clue how to use it, and I desperately need someone who can help me or I fear I might destroy this shop."

Rory looked at the scorch marks on the table. "I fear you'll do worse than that. Keep this up and you might destroy half of Los Angeles."

Liv forced out a laugh. "Now, let's not exaggerate."

The screws on the worktable all rolled off at once, bouncing on the floor like Mexican jumping beans.

Rory gave her a challenging look.

Liv combed her fingers nervously through her hair. "Yeah, well, maybe I'm a bit out of control. It's just that I'm not used to my magic, and apparently, my emotions are affecting it."

Rory nodded. "What do you want from me?"

"I was thinking that maybe since you're a magical creature—"

He coughed tersely.

"Magical person," she corrected, but the look on his face didn't soften. "Anyway, I'm not good with the terminology, but I thought you might be able to direct me to someone who can help me."

"Help you do what?" Rory asked.

"Train me on how to use my magic," Liv answered.

"Why are you asking me?" Rory questioned. "If you're a magician who has just had your magic unlocked, you have access to the House of Seven. They will surely train you."

Liv shook her head. "That's the thing. I don't want their biased help."

For the first time ever, the skeptical expression on the giant's face disappeared. A commonality seemed to connect the two. "So you're not with the House of Seven?" Rory asked.

Liv looked down at the floor. Giants weren't fans of the House of Seven. Liv wanted to tell Rory everything, but she didn't know him well enough to know if he'd reject her at once. She had to play this carefully. "It's complicated," she admitted.

"Why was your magic locked?" Rory asked.

"I didn't want it, and I gave it up so I didn't have to be

governed by the House," Liv stated. It wasn't a lie, but it wasn't the whole truth.

"And now?" Rory asked.

"Well, *you* have magic, right?"

He blinked impassively at her, not answering the question.

Liv coughed. "Right. Yes, of course, you do. And you know how much better your life is with it. I decided I'd embrace my magic."

"But you have zero idea what you're doing, obviously," Rory pointed out, waving at the front of the shop, his arm like the wing of an eagle.

"I know what I'm doing," Liv argued. "I just don't know how to control it."

Rory offered her a skeptical expression.

Liv softened. "Okay, fine. I don't know what I'm doing. That's why I need your help. Do you know someone who can train me? I don't have any money, but I can work in exchange for help."

"Those I know wouldn't want anything in exchange for helping," Rory replied. "Keeping a magician from abusing their powers would be enough for them."

"Wow, so you're going to send me to someone who knows about magic? Are they well-trained? Where can I find them?"

Rory considered her for a moment and then nodded. "Yes, they are the best I know for training, but know that if you're going to work with them, you have to take every-thing they say seriously." He looked at the objects clinking around on the table. "You're going to have to work on disciplining yourself, or I suspect they won't keep training you."

Liv nodded. "Yes, I can do that. I'll do whatever it takes. Just tell me where I can find this person."

Rory slipped his hand into his jeans pockets and withdrew a jagged piece of paper. He handed it to Liv. "Here's their address. You can find them there."

She unrolled it, confused. "Wait, there isn't anything on this. It's blank."

Rory nodded. "Go to find this person right after work today. Once you set off, the address will appear on the paper."

"Oh, like magic?" Liv asked with a laugh.

Rory didn't appear amused. "And in the meantime, stay away from electronics."

Liv gawked at him. "Um, how am I supposed to do that? I work in an electronic repair shop?"

Rory looked at the tools teetering toward the edge of the table, about to jump over the side. "I'll tell John that you're in the back office working on accounts today."

Liv brightened. "We *are* behind on filing and stuff."

"Yeah, paper is fine," Rory said. "Just don't go near anything electronic. It thrives on unharnessed magic."

Liv nodded, backing toward the office crammed with past-due invoices and accounts-payable receipts. When she was almost to the door, she paused. "Oh, and this person I'm meeting later… What's their name?"

Rory looked down at the floor uncertainly. "I'll tell them to expect you. They can make their own introduction."

CHAPTER SIXTEEN

For the rest of the day, Liv didn't leave the office. To her relief, no other strange mishaps occurred related to her magic. As a bonus, Liv found a rebate that John had forgotten to cash in, as well as three clients they hadn't billed. The found money more than covered the damage she'd done to the shop. It didn't make her feel completely better, but it softened the guilt slightly.

When Liv left the back office, she was relieved to find the area where the scorch marks had been from the heater was now pristine. Sitting on the table next to a row of neatly arranged tools was the heater, looking as good as new. Liv didn't dare get any closer to the workstation. Instead, she backed toward the exit.

"I'm heading out, John," Liv called to the front.

"See you tomorrow," he replied, poking his head through the swinging door. "Oh, and good news. They caught the hoodlums already."

"What?" Liv asked, pausing in the doorway.

John nodded proudly. "They deny breaking in here but admitted to a lot of other disturbances in the area. The police say our report put them on their trail, so good going today."

Liv nodded, plastering a fake smile on her face. "That's great. Well, we're off for the day. Take care, and don't stay here all night."

"Oh, I don't have to work late at all tonight," John stated, striding in Liv's direction "Rory cleaned up for me when I went to grab lunch. By the time I got back, the place was spotless. I actually don't want to do anything in the front, I'm so afraid that I'll mess it up."

Liv laughed. "Yeah, keep it clean as long as possible."

"And the appliances Rory brought me were all in pristine condition," John continued, "which made my job easy. I just put them on the retail shelf, and they all sold in no time."

Liv smiled for real this time. "Well, then it wasn't such a bad day after all."

"Best one I've had in a while, actually," John told her.

"That's wonderful." Liv beamed. "And the back office is clean, and I found some overdue accounts. The report is on your desk."

John peeked into his office, his face brightening, which made him look younger. "Oh, well, looky there. The top of my desk is light tan. I haven't seen it in so long that I'd forgotten. I can't believe you made so much progress today."

Liv looked down at Plato. "I had help."

John chuckled, picking up the report on the corner of

his desk. His eyes widened when he read the bottom line. "Is this right?"

Liv nodded. "Yes, and it was just money sitting around waiting to be claimed."

"Well, I'll be," John declared, laughing harder. "It's like my luck has changed. Maybe I'll renovate your apartment with some of this money."

Liv shook her head. "No, please don't. I like my apartment the way it is. But the shop could use a better sign."

John agreed with a nod. "A new sign it is."

Liv waved to John as she and Plato went out the back of the shop into the cluttered alley. Maybe that would be her job tomorrow: to clean up the old boxes and junk they threw back there. Anything to keep her away from electronics and from making another mess for John. However, so far, no real harm had come out of the incident that morning. Quite the opposite. And hopefully, whoever Rory was sending Liv to would help her so that she never lost control of her magic again.

Shoveling a spoonful of macaroni and cheese into her mouth, Liv stared at the piece of paper Rory had given her. It was still blank.

"When is it going to give me the address?" Liv asked, eating over the kitchen counter, which doubled as her desk and dining area. She didn't mind the small apartment, because she could clean the whole thing in under fifteen minutes. Also, she only had to walk ten feet from her bed to the sink to grab a drink of water in the middle of the night.

"He said that the address will appear when you set off for the place," Plato said, also eating at the kitchen counter, his bowl of food nearly gone.

"Yes, but how do I know which way to go?" Liv asked.

"I'd vote for going the more rural route to avoid setting off electronics by accident," Plato advised.

Liv looked down at the cabinet where she'd stuck most of her appliances upon entering her studio apartment. "That's probably a good plan."

She stuffed the last bite of macaroni into her mouth, feeling much hungrier than usual. To her surprise, after eating an entire box of macaroni and cheese, she was still starving.

Liv opened her refrigerator and scanned the pathetic options: three cheese sticks, a bag of carrots, and a jar of pickles.

"I seriously need to go shopping," she grumbled, slamming the refrigerator door closed and opening the pantry.

"And you're going to do that when? After you've had your magic lesson today, but before your first shift as a Warrior for the House of Seven?" Plato asked, finishing his bowl of food and looking quite satisfied.

Liv opened the pantry, a smile popping onto her face. She grabbed the bag of Doritos with delight. "Score! I thought I'd eaten these already."

Plato licked his chops, cleaning himself after his dinner. "Why does most of your diet consist of cheese?"

Liv opened the bag, inhaling the lovely scent of powdered dairy and spices. "I'm a cheesetarian."

"That's not a thing," Plato said dryly.

"*You're* not a thing," Liv fired back through a mouthful of crumbs.

"Back to talking about your schedule and lack of time to properly shop," Plato began.

Liv crammed three chips into her mouth at once, pinching the sides of her mouth in the process to make them all fit.

"I think you might need to reconsider your responsibilities."

"You're just afraid I won't have time to pick up kitty food," Liv teased.

Plato shook his head. "It might surprise you to know that I'm not dependent on you to feed me. It's just sort of a thing I let you do."

"It doesn't surprise me at all," Liv said, licking her fingers. "You magically appear on a regular basis and avoid telling me where you've been, and you know things that most magicians I grew up with don't even know. I'm certain you can feed yourself as well as do many other things you haven't shared with me."

"I trade stocks when you're sleeping," Plato admitted. "There, are you happy? I shared a secret about me."

Liv laughed. "I don't think for a second that you're lying about trading stocks, but I fear that only scratches the surface of your mysterious façade."

"So, back to your workload," Plato said. "Working cases as a Warrior will take up large chunks of your nights, and possibly the days."

Liv looked into the once-full bag of Doritos to find only

a few chips in the bottom. *Where had they all gone so fast?* She frowned, looking at the cat. "Yeah, so?"

"And you're going to need to train during the day as well," Plato reasoned.

Liv pinched up the crumbs at the bottom of the bag. "Again, so?"

"So, you might want to consider cutting your hours at the electronics shop or quitting altogether."

Liv gawked at the feline. "Well, it looks like I've accidentally poisoned your food and the result is that you've lost your damn mind."

Plato shook his head. "I think it's worth considering."

Liv wadded up the empty chip bag, still feeling strangely hungry. She grabbed a mug from the washboard and filled it under the tap. "I'm not quitting on John. Besides, I need that job."

"You don't, actually," Plato argued. "You might not have signed any formal HR agreement with the House, but Warriors make a comfortable living. You turned down the perk of living at the House of Seven, but you'll still make a handsome wage for the cases you work."

Liv rolled her eyes. "Living at the House of Seven isn't a perk. It's full of stuffy magicians who think they are better than everyone else." She looked around fondly at her tiny studio apartment, decorated with watercolor paintings and acrylics she'd bought from street vendors. Her sofa and coffee table were secondhand from the Native American man who used to live below her. The sofa was in great condition, covered in fabric with a pattern of pastel feathers.

The coffee table looked brand new, and on the surface

was a dream catcher. Under that were the words: "You are born free to be anything you dream to be."

The man had sold the furniture to Liv for a pint of cookies and cream ice cream and a bag of fruit rollups. It was all she had to pay him with, but he probably would have given it to her for free, wanting to unload the furniture before his unexpected move. However, Liv didn't take handouts, so she had insisted she pay him with *something*.

She sort of wished she still had that pint of ice cream now, but she definitely loved her sofa, which folded out into a lumpy bed.

"Besides, the House doesn't have the same charm and character as my place," Liv went on.

"There's a giant black chasm and a hall with a secret language," Plato argued. "I'd say it's got plenty of character."

"And no matter how much I make as a Warrior, I *do* still need the job working for John," Liv insisted. "It grounds me, and makes me feel like I have a place where I belong."

"You're a Warrior for the House of Seven now, the most prestigious organization of magicians in the world," Plato said. "I'd say you have a place to belong."

"They are a governing body, just like a bunch of politicians in some stuffy capitol building," Liv said, taking a sip of water.

"You're not quitting your job, then?" Plato asked, but there was something different in his eyes suddenly— possibly a spark of mischief.

"Absolutely not," Liv stated. "I'll just have to make it all work."

"I figured you'd say that," Plato said, jumping down from the countertop.

Liv's mouth popped open. "Then why did you ask?"

"Just to see if the magic was going to your head yet." Plato looked back at her from the front door. "Well, are we going or not? We shouldn't keep this mystery trainer waiting."

Liv shook her head at the cat and grabbed the blank piece of paper. "Yeah, I'm ready."

CHAPTER SEVENTEEN

"You've got to be kidding me?" Liv said, reading the address on the small bit of paper.

"Is it far?" Plato asked, looking up at her from the ground.

She shook her head and flashed him a look at the paper.

"I can't see it," Plato stated.

"Oh, well, it's—"

"Don't speak the address," he warned, cutting her off. "There's a charm on the paper that makes it so only the person it was given to can read it. If they share the address, they automatically forget it."

Liv's brow furrowed. "I've never heard of magic like that."

Plato nodded. "The giants and other magical creatures have a different way of using their magic. It's tied to enchanting objects."

"Well, I hope whoever Rory is sending me to knows about magician magic," Liv stated, striding down the sidewalk, following the map in her head. She'd spent the last five years exploring this city and falling in love with most of its oddities. She'd hadn't been from a specific place when living at the House of Seven, since it wasn't a part of anywhere, but rather its own location, like a self-sustaining city. Once she had gotten out of there, it had been nice to explore Los Angeles and find her identity in the many strange neighborhoods.

Liv turned a corner and paused. The street was dark and tall trees lined the sidewalk, casting most of the area in shadow. She looked up at the burned-out street lamps, wishing they were lit. Down the road, homeless people shuffled around, pushing carts or making camp for the night next to various buildings.

"You're not scared, are you?" Plato asked in a whisper.

Liv scoffed at him. "Speak for yourself, scaredy cat."

"Ha-ha."

From behind one of the trees, a figure staggered out—a man wearing entirely too many clothes and a stocking cap that obscured one of his eyes. In one hand, he held a bottle of liquor, and the other reached out for Liv. "Hey, darlin'. What brings you down here? Looking for some fun?"

Liv jumped back several feet.

The homeless man didn't take the hint, coming at her faster.

Liv halted, throwing her hand up to stop him. "Dude, if you come any closer, I'm going to roundhouse-kick you in the face."

She didn't really know how to pull off such an attack, but she knew how to talk shit. That was better than knowing how to fight, she reasoned.

"Awe, I'm just trying to be friendly with you, honey," the man said with a thick laugh.

"Take your friendly behavior somewhere else," Liv said, heat starting to build in her chest.

"Oh, fellas, we got a feisty one here," the man sang.

Behind him, more figures shifted before coming into view: two men, who looked similar to the first in their baggy, dirty clothes, wearing hungry expressions.

Damn it to hell, Liv thought, taking another step back. She looked around for Plato and was unsurprised to find he'd disappeared. *Must be nice.*

"Now, come over here, darlin' and tell me what a nice girl like you is doing down here?" the man suggested before taking a long sip from his bottle. He handed it to the man beside him and lurched in Liv's direction.

She ducked down, sliding to the side as the bum dove for her and he stumbled, falling to the pavement from the momentum. One of the other men reached for her, but she spun to the side faster than him and rammed her shoulder hard into his, knocking him into the third. When they collided, the bottle dropped from the man's hands, shattering on the ground.

The homeless man who had fallen to the pavement pushed up, his expression full of anger. He bent over and picked up a piece of the broken bottle, brandishing it at Liv.

"Now look what you've done," he said hotly. "You're going to have to pay for that."

The three men crowded around Liv, boxing her in with the trees and buildings behind her.

She held up her fists, ready to punch the first man in his

good eye if he took another step forward.

From the shadows came a loud growl, as if a giant lion was hiding in the dark.

The men all froze, looking at one another.

"What was that?" the middle man asked.

Again the growl sounded, this time louder than before. One man stumbled back. Another clapped his hands to his ears to try to block out the sound of danger. The ringleader jerked around and ran for the corner where the streetlamps still worked, the others right behind him.

Liv let out a breath of relief, grateful she didn't have to bruise her hands on those men's faces. She would have done it, and maybe she would have lost, but she wouldn't have backed down.

Turning to the shadow, Liv crossed her arms over her chest. "And here I thought you had abandoned me."

Strolling out of the dark with a smug look on his face was Plato. "I would never. I just thought I'd be more helpful to you if I wasn't seen."

"Thank you. And smart thinking," Liv said, glancing around. She pointed to a tiny house down the block. "I think that's the place."

"How charming," Plato said, looking the building over. It was nestled between an abandoned convenience store and a rusty warehouse.

The house had held onto its claim in this mostly industrial area while the rest of the neighborhood had been overrun with buildings that looked like they were close to falling over. Although the small cottage had probably been cute back in the day, right now it was in need of fresh paint, and half of the porch looked ready to collapse. The street outside the cottage was dark, but light shone from the house, each window illuminated.

Liv gazed at Plato tentatively. "Well, Hansel, ready to potentially become pie?"

"Sure, and don't worry, I won't let that happen," he replied calmly. "I've got your back." Plato's form flickered and he disappeared.

Liv sighed. "Thanks, but it would make me feel better if you had stuck around after making that statement."

Although Plato didn't answer, Liv knew he was there.

She paused, looking up at the strangely ordinary house in its bizarre location. *Okay, here goes nothing,* she thought, suddenly feeling exhausted after the long day. Liv shook that off and climbed up the porch carefully, afraid she might fall through.

Her hand was raised to knock on the door when it popped open a few inches and a green eye partially framed by curly brown hair looked down at her from up high.

Rory pulled the door back all the way to reveal his large form, which was hunkered down to avoid hitting his head on the low ceiling. He looked out past Liv and shook his head. "Wayne and his friends are harmless. You didn't have to frighten them off."

Liv looked over her shoulder before gawking at the giant. "He was harassing me. I was protecting myself."

"Protecting yourself is more about avoiding trouble than fighting your way out of it," the giant said, stepping back and holding a long arm out to welcome Liv into the house.

She stepped carefully over the threshold, expecting the house to open up into something grand like the House of

Seven did, although it appeared to be a rundown shop on the outside. However, the cottage looked absolutely normal when she stepped into it. Actually, it looked like it belonged to a grandmother with its old, cushy furniture covered in hand-knitted afghans.

On the walls hung oil paintings of horses grazing in green fields and kittens curled up in front of snow-flecked windows. The coffee and side tables were covered in ornate doilies, and on them stood dainty lamps with pastel shades.

Liv looked around as Rory trudged into the living room, where the ceiling was a bit taller than in the entry-way, allowing him to stand up properly. He took a seat in an armchair, making the springs groan.

"Well, do you want a tour first or can we get started?" Rory asked, eyeing her skeptically as she studied the living room's furnishings.

Liv blinked at him in surprise. "You? *You're* the one who is going to train me to use my magic?"

"What were you expecting, a magician?" Rory asked.

"Well, I just figured… I mean, I didn't know. And you didn't give me any information."

"And you no doubt wonder if a giant is good enough to teach you, a magician, how to use your magic," Rory grumbled, a hint of annoyance in his voice.

"I didn't say that," Liv protested. "I simply don't know how this works."

Rory looked at her sideways, an uncertain expression on his face. "What about your parents? You would have gotten your magic from them. Why aren't they offering to train you?"

Liv gulped. "They are dead."

Rory nodded almost like he'd expected this answer. "And your other family? Grandparents, aunts, uncles?"

Liv shook her head. "I don't keep in contact with any of them."

Rory pursed his wide lips. "Something isn't lining up about all this. You recently had your magic unlocked, but why? Usually, a magician doesn't do that by choice. Did you get in trouble with the House of Seven or something?"

Liv looked behind her at the door, wondering if she should just leave. The hostile undertones she was sensing from Rory didn't really make her feel welcome.

"What's that on your hand?" Rory asked, standing suddenly, which made the floor creak loudly.

Liv pulled her hand to her chest, covering the ring with her other hand. "It's nothing. Just a ring I found."

Rory narrowed his eyes at her, holding out his giant hand in a demanding fashion. "Let's see this 'nothing' ring you found."

Liv again considered bolting out of the small cottage, but that left her with only one option for training. Instead, she lifted her chin and proudly held out her hand. This was only going to work if she owned up to who she was, and instinctively she knew that.

Rory's gaze dropped, and he growled upon seeing the large ring. When he looked up at her, the expression of disapproval was heavy on his face. "You're one of the Seven."

Liv shook her head but then corrected herself. "I am, but only as of last night. My siblings were recently killed, moving me into the position of Warrior. I decided to take the role, and they unlocked my magic so I can protect my family's place within the House."

Again Rory growled, thundered back to the chair and taking a seat. "Why would you, a potential Royal, be living in a studio apartment and working for John? Why was your magic locked in the first place? Did you do something wrong?"

Liv sighed. "Yes. I challenged the House, showing strong disapproval of how they handled my parents' deaths. When I got fed up with the Institution, I abdicated my place within the House and because my family are Founders, they decided my magic should be locked if I was to go out on my own."

Rory nodded. "This is starting to make sense. The House would not want a powerful magician who shows tendencies toward rebellion to have magic."

"Well, it was *my* choice," Liv argued. "I didn't want anything to do with magic. I wanted to be as far from it as possible."

"Until now," Rory stated.

Liv let out a heavy breath. "I can't run from who I am forever. Even with my magic locked, it still found ways of coming through."

Rory arched an eyebrow at Liv. "Are you certain of that? The House's lock on a magician's powers is strong."

Liv nodded. "Yeah, I figured I was just losing my mind, but Plato can attest that I've used it several times."

"I believe you," Rory admitted. "I knew I sensed something magical about you before today."

"So, can you help me?" Liv asked. "I can't have a repeat of today. I feel the energy of the magic flowing within me, and it's taking everything I've got to keep it bottled up this evening. I feel like it might explode if I'm not careful."

The giant regarded Liv for a long moment and shook his head. "I don't know. Helping a rogue magician get their magic under control is one thing. Helping a Warrior from the House of Seven is another entirely."

"I get that the House abuses their powers and set up a system that mostly serves magicians," Liv began. "My parents fought against many of those practices for years. I saw from an early age that the House created laws but didn't serve justice. It's not the same thing, and I guarantee I'm not like the rest of them."

"But you're working for them now," Rory replied coldly.

"Yeah, well, I figured that if I didn't like how they operated, I could be a part of the change," Liv countered. She'd mostly been trying to save her family's place in the House, but deep down she *did* want to take on her parent's crusade. They'd tried to make a difference by changing how the House worked, and maybe they would have succeeded if they had lived.

"And you don't have any objections to being trained by a giant?" Rory asked after careful deliberation.

Liv shrugged. "As long as you know what you're doing and can help me, I don't care who you are. The last thing I want to do is have to go to the House and accept their training."

Rory regarded her with a skeptical expression that made the lines on his forehead deepen. "Most magicians prefer socializing and training with other magicians. You live and work around mortals. You rejected a role most magicians would have killed for. And now you're asking me, a giant, to train you. Why are you so different, Liv?"

"I abdicated because I was tired of watching magic mess up everything in my life," Liv began. "I didn't trust it. And I do trust mortals because with them, what you see is what you get. I don't care if you're an elf or a centaur or whatever. If you can help me, then that's what matters."

"You are one strange magician." Rory rose from his chair and lumbered through an open doorway to a bright kitchen.

"Ummm, what does that mean? You'll train me?" Liv called.

"I'm going to attempt to train you," Rory said from the kitchen, making a lot of noise. "But before we begin, there's something you need."

A moment later Rory returned carrying a plate of meat and cheese.

Liv eyed it with hesitation when he set it on the coffee table.

"Go on and eat up," the giant said.

"Wait, what I need is meat and cheese?" Liv questioned.

Rory nodded. "Doing magic when you're hungry and tired is a recipe for disaster, and using magic will deplete your reserves fast, so keep something to eat on you at all times. It's also important that you always get as much rest as possible."

Liv picked up a piece of meat, cutely rolled up and pinned with a toothpick. She took a bite, enjoying the savory flavor as she looked around at the strange living room. "Thanks. Has anyone ever told you that you remind them of their grandmother?"

CHAPTER EIGHTEEN

Liv's mouth dropped open when she followed Rory into his backyard. The lights from the house and the flames from a firepit made the yard visible. The oversized lawn was bordered by lush shrubs and towering trees that blocked out the view of the warehouses and the dirty alley. Row after row of flowers burst with color in the overflowing beds. Fruits and vegetables filled the boxes in the middle of the yard, and on the patio was a yellow swing, the firepit, and a hammock.

"I was wondering where you'd magicked your house," Liv said, looking around the pristine yard.

Rory regarded her incredulously. "This isn't magic. I built every inch of this garden. Although I use magic to enhance parts of it, this was mostly done with hard work."

Liv looked at various sections of the yard again, not believing that it was all real. "Wow. You did all this?"

"Magicians prefer to use magic to create their homes, enhancing every aspect so that it deceptively looks like something else. They aren't happy with dwellings that are in fact small. Instead, they fit a mansion into a bungalow or change something perfectly normal and fine into something outrageous, just because they can't accept the way things are. They are never happy with mediocre or simple."

"Well, by definition, mediocracy isn't something most strive for," Liv argued, although she didn't disagree with everything Rory had said. Still, she needed to play the devil's advocate. Always.

"Enjoying things the way they really are is an art form," Rory countered. "Magicians get in trouble for over-enchanting their houses or revving up their cars until they are dangerous, or using too many youth potions on their faces. It's rare for a magical creature to get in trouble for one of these crimes."

"So this garden…" Liv asked, reaching out and touching a soft hibiscus flower.

"I created it on my own, digging up the beds, putting in the plants, and tending them every single day," Rory stated.

"With little or no magic?" Liv questioned.

He shrugged. "I'm all for making my life easier with magic, but what you see is real. Also, I do most of the chores myself. There's something honest about doing things without magic. Being overly reliant on it is dangerous."

"Why gardens?" Liv asked, noticing a pair of reflective eyes she recognized somewhere in a shrub.

"Giants and many other magical creatures feel most at home in a garden or forest," Rory explained. "Many of my ancestors fought the movement that we should have proper homes instead of living in the woods. However, the

House of Seven pushed back for many years, and now most people I know live in a house and pretend to be mortals instead of embracing our ways."

This wasn't a part of the history that Liv had been taught. Her history books said that the House had saved many magical creatures from famine and disease by educating them on the ways of sophisticated living. How many times had she heard that it was magicians gifting giants with the technology of plumbing and electricity that had helped save their race?

"So how will this magic training work?" Liv asked.

"Magic is the same as any of your senses," Rory began. "It can be passive, like when you stroll through the garden and smell a rose. Or it can be active, like when you're on the hunt for a ladybug and must use your eyes to find it. However, unlike your other senses, magic is tied to your emotions, and if you don't have a handle on those, it will overwhelm everything."

"Okay, handle on emotions," Liv stated. "I can do that. What's next?"

Rory shook his head. "No, first we practice that, *then* we move onto honing your magic skills. Right now you probably don't know how to use your magic to make a cup of tea, but if you first conquer your emotions, doing the hardest spells will come naturally."

"Well, should I stretch out on this hammock so we can have a therapy session?" Liv asked.

Rory pointed to an empty flower bed. Beside it, a shovel materialized, then a pair of gloves. "I want you to dig a hole."

Liv held up her finger, trying to remember the spell for

digging. It was stuck far back in her memory; too far back for her to recall with the giant scowling at her.

Rory wrapped his large hand around Liv's, covering her fingers, wrist, and part of her arm.

She looked up at him in confusion. "Am I not supposed to use a spell to dig the hole? I guess there are other magical ways to do it."

"There are, but I want you to use a nonmagical one."

"What?" Liv asked. "You want me to dig a hole by hand?"

Rory nodded and swung into the hammock, which was oversized. He looked like a large man-baby in a swing. "Get to it. We don't have all night."

Liv pulled her phone out of her back pocket and eyed the time. "I actually only have an hour or so before I'm due at the House."

Rory pointed to the pile of dirt. "Then get digging."

Liv grumbled as she pulled on the gloves and picked up the shovel. The tool hardly made much progress as Liv dug it into the soft dirt. She looked back at Rory with a questioning look. "Where do you want me to put the dirt?"

He shrugged. "It doesn't really matter."

Liv nodded and tossed the dirt in his direction.

He crouched, fanning away the dirt the wind carried over to hit him in the face. "That's not what I meant."

"Well, next time you might want to be specific, magic instructor," she said, pitching the shovel into the dirt and then emptying it a few feet from the hole.

"Are you certain you're not just trying to get free labor out of me?" Liv asked after a few minutes.

The giant eyed her and then the hole. "Believe me, if I wanted free labor, I'd pick someone with a bit more muscle than you. As it is, I'll be here all night waiting for that hole to be dug."

"How deep do you want it?" Liv asked.

"Deep enough."

She rolled her eyes. "Again, I fail to see how this is supposed to help me with my magic."

"It's about control, little Grasshopper."

She brought the shovel around and tossed its contents in Rory's direction again. With a flick of his wrist, the dirt flew back at Liv, hitting her in the face.

Rory laughed at this, making a booming sound as his face transformed.

"Hey, you don't look like such an ogre when you laugh," Liv observed.

"And you look like a bride fit for a troll with that dirt on your face," Rory said, still laughing.

Twenty minutes later, when the hole was several feet deep and wide, Liv spun around to face Rory, who was snoring. "Hey, is this deep enough yet?"

He cracked open one eye and sat up more. "Yeah, that will do."

"Okay, now what?" she asked.

Rory flicked his finger at the hole, and all the dirt rose into the air and refilled it.

"Wait! Why did you do that?" Liv yelled, her face flushing with heat. The fire in the pit next to the swing flared, her vision was momentarily covered in red, and the sounds in the garden were amplified.

"Dig the hole again," Rory insisted.

"What? That's insane!"

"Dig the hole again," he repeated

"But—"

"That's an order," Rory said. "If you don't like it, leave."

Liv cursed under her breath, pulling the gloves on tighter. Her hands were already sore from digging, and her back ached. Digging the hole was probably one of the hardest things she'd ever done physically, which was proven by the sweat pouring into her eyes.

"I'm not complaining, I just don't understand how digging a hole teaches me how to use my magic," Liv stated between ragged breaths.

"I'm not teaching you how to use your magic," Rory said through a loud yawn. "I'm teaching you how to control it."

"What's the difference?" Liv asked.

"You already know how to use your magic," Rory answered. "It's part of your instincts, like using your senses. What you *don't* know how to do is to isolate it from everything else. It's blurred together with your other senses, which was why you nearly destroyed John's shop."

"Everything worked out, though," Liv said defensively.

After another twenty minutes, the hole was identical to the last one. Liv turned around and rested her arm on the shovel. "Okay, I dug you another hole. Now what?"

Rory pointed at the dirt, and it swept back into the hole. "Dig it again."

Liv's eyes widened with frustration, and suddenly her vision was tinted dark-red. Her hand tightened around the shovel handle, and the wood splintered in her fingers. The ground started to shake under her feet. The windmill in the corner of the yard spiraled out of control as a sudden wind rushed across the yard.

Rory sat up, looking victorious. "Only two times to dig the hole. As I figured, you're a hot head."

"I'm not either!" Liv yelled and the shovel broke in two, falling to the ground in pieces.

Rory eyed the broken bits with amusement. "Now, isolate your emotions from your magic."

"How do I do that?" Liv asked, her insides vibrating with anger.

"Visualize putting them in a compartment, where they won't have the ability to affect your senses," Rory instructed.

Liv clenched her eyes shut, feeling even more frustrated than before. The ground continued to rumble under her, nearly throwing her off balance.

"Take the anger you feel at yourself and me and lock it away," Rory continued. "Then feel what's left."

When Liv was little and afraid, her mother brought out a "fear" box made of wood and supposedly protected by a special enchantment. Liv would then pretend to stick each thing she was afraid of in the box. Her mother said that when the box shut, the fears could no longer affect her. It always worked...well, until it didn't, when her parents died and the fears were too big for the box.

Liv pictured a similar box in her mind. This time it was labeled "emotions." She visualized sticking all her frustrations and insecurities and anger in the box, then she closed and locked it.

As if she were standing on a desert plain, Liv looked out

at the expanse of her mind, the "emotions" box sitting right beside her.

The constant shaking under her feet gently faded until the ground was still once more. The loud rustling of the trees subsided to a gentle melody. The red light tinting her vision disappeared. She suddenly felt each of her senses acutely: The taste of the autumn air, the smell of grass, the feel of the air gently catching in her hair. In her body, she became aware of a force, one that ticked like a clock while also flowing like a river. It was in all parts of her, connected to everything and bound by nothing.

For the first time in her entire life, Liv felt her magic in its purest form. It was all-encompassing, unstoppable, and completely mesmerizing. She saw it in her mind's eye, flowing like strands of ribbon, gliding across the plains of her consciousness. It moved like a dragon, flying free, unrestricted in this form. She looked down at the emotions box and understood how she now held the reins on her magic. This was completely different than before, when her feelings had been driving the wild beast, allowing it to charge in any direction it wanted.

Opening her eyes, Liv found herself smiling.

"Well, good thing you got that under control before you pushed up all my bulbs," Rory stated, looking around the now-calm garden.

"So, you made me mad in order to teach me how to control my emotions?" she asked, sort of peeved and also impressed.

"Hard labor is the best way to learn how to restrain your feelings because it's a humbling act."

Liv looked at the place where the hole she'd dug twice had been. "It was definitely humbling."

"Well, and I also knew that the physical exertion would keep your magic from getting out of control," Rory admitted.

A glass of ice water appeared on the table next to the swing and Rory pointed at it. "That's for you."

"Thank you." Liv strode over, picking up the drink and enjoying the cold condensation on the glass against her aching fingers.

"So, you see how to untie your emotions from your magic," Rory began. "Now you have to keep them that way."

"But how? What I feel colors everything from my mood to my tone of voice."

Rory nodded. "It used to, but now you need to be more careful. People often say that something makes them feel a certain way, but honestly, emotions are always choices. You chose to get angry about me making you re-dig the hole, and then you allowed your emotions to take over. It's like when someone drives a car. If they become upset, they might start driving erratically, but someone who has mastered their emotions knows better. They deal with the frustration and keep it separate from how they drive. You'll have to practice doing this with your magic. *You* have to drive it, not allow your emotions to."

"Hmmmm...that actually makes sense." Liv wiped her hand on her jeans, before pulling her phone from her pocket. It was ten minutes to nine. "Oh, shit! I'm late. I've got to go to the House of Seven!"

She froze, realizing there was no way she could get to Santa Monica in such a short time.

"You appear lost," Rory observed.

"I need to get across town in only a few minutes."

He yawned, unconcerned by her problem. "Make a portal, then."

"I don't know how to make one," she admitted.

"You know where you're going, right?"

She nodded.

"Then you know how to make a portal," Rory stated. "Magic is about intention and energy. Combine the two, and you can do many amazing things."

"But isn't there a spell or something specific I need to create a portal? I always thought portals were incredibly difficult to produce."

Rory pushed himself out of the hammock and stretched. "Most magicians overcomplicate magic. Yes, there are spells and potions and many other things we can get into, but the most complicated magic is the simplest to perform. It might tax you greatly, but all you must do is focus."

Liv nodded and pressed her eyes shut, visualizing the portal location for the House of Seven. Her eyes popped open at a sudden thought. "What if I can't do it? Can you open a portal for me?"

Rory shook his head. "Confidence is key. The most successful magicians have an ego the size of a giant's mansion. Believe you can do something and you will. Couple that with humbling activities, and maybe you won't turn out like most of the magicians I know."

Liv sighed. *Confidence.* She had always pretended to

have that, but magic couldn't be fooled. She truly had to believe in herself, not just fake it until she made it, which had been her motto for the last five years.

In her mind, she pictured the location of the Santa Monica entrance of the House of Seven. She also felt the reins of her magic firmly in her control. They could take her anywhere, based simply on her will, so with all her soul, she tried to make herself believe she could go anywhere. She'd seen Clark open a portal last night. She'd seen her parents do it throughout her childhood. There was no reason that she, a powerful magician, shouldn't be able to do the same.

A light so bright it nearly blinded her with her eyes closed shone in front of her. She thought for a moment that Rory had shined a floodlight on her, but when she opened her eyes, she saw a shimmering archway full of blues and greens.

"That was me?" Liv asked in disbelief. In the same instant, the lights began to fade.

"Remember, confidence is key," Rory prompted.

Liv nodded, bolstering herself. "Hell *yeah*, that was me. I created a portal."

She took a step, about to enter the portal, when Rory chuckled. "Let's just hope you made it right or it might distort your ugly little human face."

Liv halted. "Wait, what? Distort my face? And hey, what's up with the insults?"

He strode over, standing next to her and looking at the portal. "Humans are funny-looking with their tiny features."

She shook her head at him. "You're funny-looking, and take up entirely too much space."

"And you're stalling, afraid that your first portal will sever you in half."

"Well, can you blame me?" Liv asked the giant.

"Nope, and that's why you need tough love." Rory clapped a hand on her back, thrusting her forward and straight through the portal.

CHAPTER NINETEEN

Liv held her breath as she fell through the portal, a flash of anger at Rory surging through her. She clamped down hard on that emotion though, putting it in the box before it caused her to shake the Earth upon landing.

Her feet hit the ground with a thud, and Liv's fingertips touched the concrete softly as she realized she was in a crouch. The portal shielded her appearance momentarily when she landed, giving her a chance to right herself before it blended her into her surroundings. Or that was supposed to be how a portal transitioned a person. She'd never made one, and usually had a ton of trouble coming through them.

Liv looked around upon landing, highly curious to see if she'd made the portal right and also wanting to orient herself. Passing out from portal travel would be no good, with no one to help her. The salty ocean air hit her right away, and the sounds mimicked the ones from last night.

Liv looked at her right and was relieved to find the Pacific Ocean there, as well as shops and bars on her left.

"So you did it," Plato said, standing next to Liv and looking around.

"Where have you been? And where did you come from?" she asked.

"Watching you be a gardener, mostly." He looked at the portal. "Might want to close that thing unless you want to create all sorts of problems."

"How do I do that?" Liv asked.

"It's like closing a door," Plato explained. "You just do it."

"Oh man, why am I seeking advice about this magic stuff when it's so easy to use?" Liv said, sarcasm oozing in her tone.

Plato walked a few paces away before turning back. "It's not easy to implement, but the process is mostly straightforward. You'd be amazed how hard it is for people to focus. The keys to a successful life are simple and riches and fame can be achieved through habitual practices, yet few ever get there."

"If you're so smart about all this stuff, why aren't you rolling in dough?" Liv asked, closing the portal and striding after the cat.

"How do you know I'm not?"

She rolled her eyes. "I forgot that you trade stocks. Never mind."

The pair stopped in front of the Palm Reading shop.

Liv looked at her phone. "Hey, I made it with two minutes to spare."

She had held her hand up to the door and was

preparing to enter when Plato said, "Yeah, too bad you don't have another extra few minutes."

"Wait, what?" Liv asked, looking down at him. "Why?"

He shook his head. "No time for that now. You don't want to be late."

"What are you wearing?" Clark asked when he caught sight of Liv as she strode down the hallway.

She looked down. Her jeans and t-shirt were caked with dirt, and she realized that it was probably also streaked across her face in places.

"Oh," she said. She looked around for Plato but realized he'd disappeared again. That was what the feline had meant. "I had a long day, and just came from another thing."

"Another *thing*?" Clark asked, eyeing her with disgust. He, conversely, was wearing a dark-blue pinstriped suit and white tie. "You look like you just dug a ditch."

Liv laughed. "I sort of did. Twice."

Clark sighed. "You're supposed to be taking this seriously. Did you even look into getting training or just play in a community garden all day?"

Liv sighed. "I wasn't off playing. As hard as it is to believe, I was getting trained. I even opened the portal to get here."

Clark shook his head. "Look, I don't have time for your games. We need to get into the Chamber of the Tree."

Liv gawked at him. "I'm not lying to you. I opened a portal. It's not that hard. Just focus, and bam."

Clark gave her an annoyed look. "Yeah, 'focus and bam.' Very funny. Do I need to pay for your taxi?"

Liv shook her head and charged past her brother. "No, I'm good. I paid for it with the produce I sold at the farmer's market. Don't worry, Bro."

She only heard half the grunt Clark made before it was muffled by the Wall of Reflection. Again, she felt blind. Saw indistinct figures. Heard the chanting. When she could take no more, it spat her out into the Chamber of the Tree, where the Warriors and Councilors stared at her in disgust. In comparison to the regal appearance of the other Warriors, Liv looked like a homeless person. The Councilors all put their snotty noses in the air once they caught sight of her, as if fearful they might catch whatever degenerate gene she possessed.

Liv ignored the stares and marched over to her blue light, taking her position as Clark came through the Wall of Reflection.

"As soon as Mr. Beaufont is in place, we'll get started," Adler said, disapproval heavy in his tone.

"Yes, I'm sorry, sir." Clark climbed the stairs to where the Councilors sat.

Once he'd taken his seat, Adler began. "Now, everyone here knows how the day-to-day meetings are carried out except for Ms. Beaufont, so I'll take a minute to explain the process quickly for her."

Bianca smiled and nodded in Adler's direction, apparently appreciating his consideration of Liv's newbie status.

"The Councilors meet prior to this to review the various cases that have come in," Adler continued. "During that meeting, we decide the best way to intervene, and also assign cases to the Warriors at our disposal. We have the benefit of knowing which Warrior's profile best matches up with the level of difficulty each case is coded with."

"Has my magic level normalized?" Liv interrupted.

Adler lifted a white eyebrow, giving her an impatient stare. "Olivia, I really haven't had a chance to review your stats." He looked down the table at the Councilors. "Has anyone else?"

Raina Ludwig cleared her throat. "It appears that your magic is still surging, and might need another day to even out."

"Is that normal?" Liv asked.

"Really, Olivia, we don't have time to discuss the specifics of your magic levels," Adler stated. "If you need to discuss that, you'll have to schedule a private meeting with the Councilors."

"I don't think my inquiry into my abnormal magic levels is out of line," Liv countered boldly. "This is my first day on the job, after all."

The white tiger strode out from the side of the bench, his green eyes on her.

Adler glanced at the white tiger, then redirected his attention to Liv. "Your magic level is the concern of the Councilors, and we've taken it under advisement when making assignments today."

"I thought you said you were unaware of what my magic level currently was," Liv challenged.

Adler sighed heavily. "I really can't be expected to remember everything about every new Warrior. Now, if you have nothing else to interject, we will be making assignments."

Liv stretched her arm out dramatically, offering the floor to the Councilors.

Adler cleared his throat, lifting a pad to read. "Firstly, Trudy and Stefan, we've located a group of unregistered magicians somewhere in Bali, Indonesia. The readings have been haphazard, but we believe that there are at least half a dozen. You will go there and bring in the offenders. You have authority to use lethal force on those who resist."

Liv bit her tongue, although she had a ton of questions and complaints. Lethal force was something that should be applied to those who committed heinous crimes. Someone not registering their magic seemed like a minor infringement.

The two figures beside Liv, a man and a woman, nodded before striding for the door.

"Maria," Adler said, looking at the Warrior on the far side who had two long black braids framing her face. "A shop in Manhattan has been selling enchanted merchandise to mortals. There have been a series of explosions and some near fatalities. You are to round up the merchandise after bringing in those responsible. You can use any method you deem necessary to apprehend them."

The woman nodded and marched for the exit without a word.

Adler's attention shifted to his brother, who was in front of him. "Decar, you're to continue to work on your current case. The Councilors have reviewed your reports, and we think you're on the right track."

The tall Warrior beside Liv strode off at once, earning a glance from the white tiger as he left.

"Emilio and Akio, there are several cases involving

gnomes and elves operating outside our agreement," Adler stated. "You should divide the cases and deal with them accordingly."

Neither Warrior said anything, only spun and charged for the exit.

"Olivia," Adler began.

Liv pointed up at the tree where her name was etched. "It's Liv, actually."

Clark partially covered his face with his hand, hiding his embarrassment.

"Right. As I was saying," Adler said, his voice tight, "there is a troll loose in Las Vegas on the Strip. You are to track down this creature and dispose of him quickly."

"'Dispose of him?' Are you insinuating that I should kill the thing?" Liv asked.

Adler nodded. "Naturally. It has violated the treaty."

Liv scratched her head. "Right. And it's strolling down the Strip doing what, exactly?"

"It doesn't matter," Adler answered, his attention on something in front of him. "A public sighting of a troll is unacceptable."

"It's not like anyone on the Strip is going to notice," Liv argued. "The drunk tourists probably think it's just a guy in a suit."

Adler's eyes cut to Liv. "It doesn't matter what the mortals think. The troll must be punished for his violation."

"How do you suggest I find this troll?" Liv pointed over her shoulder. "Actually, how are any of the Warriors finding those they are assigned to 'handle?'"

Adler turned to the woman on the far end. "Do you have Ms. Beaufont's digital codex?"

Hester nodded, flicking her hand and sending a small device over the edge of the bench. It floated down, landing in Liv's hand.

"You will find the details of your cases in there from now on," Adler explained. "It will give you some information, but tracking the troll will be up to you."

"How do I—"

A sharp glare from Clark cut Liv off.

Adler gave Clark a sideways look. "Are you wondering how to track the troll, Ms. Beaufont? Because if you had taken our offer to train, you wouldn't need to ask."

"Oh, the House's training covers troll-tracking on the first day, does it?" Liv asked sarcastically.

Adler peered over the edge of the bench, exaggerating the effort of looking down at her. "What did your training today teach you? How to farm?"

Bianca covered her mouth as a tight laugh fell from it.

"I learned how to control my emotions," Liv said reflexively, feeling her temper flare. The irony of her statement and the emotional blaze wasn't lost on her. She pressed all her frustration at the Councilors into the box, kicking it into a corner in her mind.

Adler looked down the row at the Councilors to the left. "Our new Warrior spent the entire day learning how to control her emotions. Isn't that something?"

"It sounds like a complete waste of time to me," Lorenzo Rosario said, looking bored as he combed his thin fingers through his goatee.

"I didn't spend the entire day learning that," Liv spat. "I worked most of the day."

Most of Clark's face was covered by his hand as Bianca laughed even louder.

"Worked at that electronics shop, you mean?" Adler asked, sounding too amused for Liv's liking. "Do you plan to continue to work in this mortal job?"

"I don't believe what I do in my own time is the concern of the Councilors," Liv fired back.

The entertained expression on Adler's face evaporated as he leaned forward. "Although you might be right, you will find your role as a Warrior much easier if you don't fight us on everything. The Councilors are here to help you, Ms. Beaufont."

Catching the humiliated look on Clark's face, Liv decided to back down. "I'm grateful for the help. I simply choose to live my life outside of this place in my own way."

"Well, if you decide to change your mind on training, then—"

"She created a portal," Hester cut Adler off, looking down at her pad and scrolling through the report on Liv's magic.

A small laugh escaped his mouth. "That's impossible. Portal magic is complex and requires a lot of focus."

"Not for magicians who learn how to control their emotions," Liv fired back, earning a questioning look from the white tiger. He stood and strode over to her gracefully. When he was in front of her, he sat, looking at her in an evaluating manner.

Liv tried to pretend that he wasn't dangerously close and giving her a look that made her feel like dinner.

All the Councilors were busy reviewing their own pads. After a moment, Adler looked up, wiping his arm roughly across his forehead. "Well, a likely explanation is the current surge in your power. It will normalize soon, though, so you shouldn't get used to it. Portal magic is something second-year magicians begin but don't master. I guarantee it takes more than controlling one's emotions to pull off."

Liv looked at the tiger, trying to decipher the strange message in its eyes. "If I'm supposedly not ready to attempt portal magic, how did you expect me to get to Las Vegas?"

Adler sighed as if bored by this conversation. "All of the notes for your case are in the codex, Ms. Beaufont. I urge you to study it carefully and return to us with questions or concerns tomorrow."

"So when do you expect me to complete the case?"

Adler looked down the bench both ways, although he didn't seem to register the various faces before he spoke again. "That's entirely up to you, but please understand that your first case is always challenging, so don't be deterred."

"Right," Liv said, drawing out the word.

A moment later, Adler glanced at her with an edgy glint in his eyes. "Ms. Beaufont, just so you know, after your case has been assigned, you're dismissed for the day."

Liv found herself nodding, just as the other Warriors had done. She backed toward the exit, and only turned and sped away when the white tiger rose from his position, once again giving her the look she recognized but couldn't read.

CHAPTER TWENTY

Outside of the Chamber of the Tree, Liv slipped into one of the shadowy edges of the hallway. She waited for a breath, until Plato materialized on cue.

"Did I handle that all wrong?" she asked the feline.

He gave her an impassive look. "Depends on what you were going for."

"I think a little disdain mixed with dumbstruck awe."

"I think you achieved that," Plato answered.

Liv backed up as several Councilors exited through the Door of Reflection, none of them talking, but rather hurrying for the large door across from the chamber. A cold so startling it nearly made her scream crept over her back and arms. Liv caught the yell before it escaped her and spun to find she'd nearly fallen into the strange abyss down the hallway. She took a step away, careful to remain hidden if anyone else exited the Chamber of the Tree.

"What do you suppose that's all about?" Liv asked, pointing at the black chasm.

"I have some speculations about what it could be."

"Let me guess… You're not going to tell me, are you?" Liv asked, listening as the Councilors retreated.

"So, this case you've been assigned?" Plato nodded at the device in her hand.

"Right," Liv said, raising the codex. "How do I turn it on—"

The codex lit up, brightening the space around her.

"Well, that was strange timing," Liv stated.

"I don't believe it was," Plato said. "Try thinking about what you need from the device."

Liv did this, reflecting on the troll case. The screen flickered, bringing up a report.

"So it works off my thoughts?" Liv asked.

"Intentions, really," Plato corrected. "Remember what Rory said about magic being related to intentions?"

Liv nodded, squinting at the screen. Her mouth fell open. "They expected me to drive or fly to Las Vegas for this case?"

Plato didn't look as offended as she felt. "How else were you supposed to get there?"

"Portal magic."

"You're not supposed to be able to do that."

"And yet I can," Liv replied. "And they have me going to round up a troll. If I didn't know any better, I'd say they were giving me shit cases."

Liv scrolled through the report. It offered her multiple modes of transportation, none of them using magic. She also had an expense account and a credit card that would cover her airfare or a car rental.

"This says I'm supposed to use a tracking spell to find

the troll," Liv stated, reading the report. "Do you know how to do that?"

"No, but I've got an idea," Plato answered.

Liv smiled down at the cat, holding out her hand and preparing to create a portal. "Okay, get your party clothes on. We're headed to Vegas, baby."

Liv tried to open her mouth to yell at the eight-foot-tall troll who even by Las Vegas' standards wasn't wearing enough clothes. However, every time she opened her mouth, she felt like she was drowning in a puddle of water.

"Hello," the troll said, his diction perfect a chain dangling between the piercing in his earlobe and the one in his nostril. "Are you okay?"

Liv gawked up at the troll, careful to keep her eyes averted from whatever was not completely shielded by his loincloth. People strolled around them on the Strip, their eyes fixed on the lurking beast who smelled strangely like sour milk and cherry gelatin.

"Liv, wake up, would you?" the troll said, again his voice reminding her of someone.

She peered up at the creature, mesmerized by its docile demeanor.

Something shook her. She turned, but there was no one nearby. Still, the shaking continued.

"Hey, wake up!"

Liv jolted upright, her eyes squinting from the brightness of the shop's lights. Liquid dripped off her chin. She brought her arm across her mouth, sopping up entirely too much drool from her face.

"There you are, Sleepyhead," Shane said, gazing at her quizzically.

Liv looked around, trying to orient herself. The past twelve hours fast-forwarded through her brain until she remembered how she came to be sleeping on the workbench in John's shop.

"Hey, Shane," she said, her voice croaky. "What can I do for you?"

He pointed to the printer sitting next to her. "Did you have a chance to check that out?"

She blinked at the device. "Um, I haven't, actually. Things got crazy here yesterday."

Shane whistled through his teeth. "I'll say. I heard about the kids who roughed up the shop. On top of the earthquakes and vermin, John's got his hands full." He looked around. "However, the shop looks better than I've seen it in a while."

Liv agreed with a nod. Rory had done a good job. She'd tried to continue to help that morning by fixing various devices, including the printer, but it hadn't worked. Every time she pointed at something, a weak spark shot out of her like her magic was broken.

"I'll take a look at the printer this morning," Liv promised. "If you stop by tomorrow, I'll have an estimate."

"Oh, give yourself a break if you need it," Shane stated. "Looks like you tuckered yourself out cleaning up this place."

"It wasn't... Yeah, thanks," Liv stammered, waving at

Shane as he backed for the door. There was no point in getting herself in deeper trouble.

When the door to the shop closed with a rattle, Liv pulled the printer closer to her. She might not have magic to fix the equipment at the moment, but she had her brain, which was almost better. Then something Rory had said rang clear in her head: "There's something honest about doing things without magic. Being overly reliant on it is dangerous."

Liv smiled, the words resonated with something deep within her—a core belief that had made her different from most in the House of Seven. From an early age, she hadn't trusted magic. Not because she feared the role it had played in her parent's death, but because she thought it spoiled otherwise good people. It made things too easy. It created appearances and deceived. Magic at its core was deception, or at least, that was what she used to believe. She wasn't so sure anymore.

"You have a gummy bear stuck to your cheek," Plato said after he jumped up on the workbench.

Liv swiped at her face and pulled a cherry gummy bear away from her cheek. She eyed it tentatively before popping it in her mouth.

Plato gave her a look of disgust.

"Hey, I'm hungry," she protested.

"I understand why. You haven't had that much to eat." He nodded at the package of powdered donuts, empty bag of roasted almonds, and the half-finished gummy bears.

Liv ignored him and grabbed the bag of gummy bears, pulling a handful free. She sprinkled the little bears into her mouth, imagining she could hear them scream as she chomped, just like the troll could have done with her last night if he pleased.

The sugar didn't wake her up as she would have liked, but it did take the edge off her constant hunger.

Again, she pointed her finger and her intention at the printer, willing a repair. When nothing happened, she sighed.

Shaking off the nearly incapacitating exhaustion, Liv set to work. She had a lot of appliances to fix, and apparently magic would not be coming to her rescue.

CHAPTER TWENTY-ONE

The door was wide open when Liv arrived at Rory's cottage that afternoon after work. She'd grabbed a protein bar from a store and demolished it on the way over. Although she'd tried to open a portal to his house, it hadn't worked, meaning she had to walk the mile and half there, which would have been fine on any other day except that one. Each step felt like a million. Each minute, a year. Every sound was an orchestra of noise, and the lights were blinding.

"You look like shit," Rory observed when she sidled into his place and leaned against the doorway.

Liv glanced down at Plato. "Are you going to let him talk to you like that?"

Ignoring her, Plato jumped onto the nearby armchair and stretched before fluffing the cushion several times with his claws and lying down.

"I was referring to you, magician," Rory said.

Liv brushed a blonde strand off her cheek casually. "Oh, well, I forgot to brush my hair."

SARAH NOFFKE & MICHAEL ANDERLE

"Or sleep," Rory added.

Liv nodded. "Yeah, I only managed to get like two hours or so, but I'll be all right."

"The hell you will." Rory picked up a small leather pouch beside his chair and jiggled the contents absent-mindedly.

Liv waved him off. "It's fine. I can go days without getting a full night's rest. I just have to make up for it at some point."

"That may have been true before your magic was unlocked, but things are different now," Rory explained. "If you're not rested, magic will leech from your life. I hope you haven't tried to use any spells today."

Liv's eyes darted to the side. "Not successfully."

Rory nodded. "Good thing you came here before you killed yourself, you dumb magician. No more using magic until you've had a proper rest."

"But what about our lesson?" Liv asked.

Rory tossed the pouch back and forth in his large hands. "It's canceled. And if you ever show up here this tired again, the lessons are off for good. Watching an idiotic magician kill herself isn't on my bucket list."

"But insulting her is?" Liv pretended to ask.

"Go home and get a full night's rest," Rory ordered. "If you do that, we can resume lessons tomorrow."

Liv shook her head as a rogue yawn escaped her mouth. "I can't. I have to go to the House of Seven tonight."

Rory's eyes fluttered with annoyance. "You're not any good to them like this."

"Doesn't matter," Liv stated. "They already treat me like

I'm a loser. If I don't show up, I'll give them one more thing to ridicule me about."

"Wow," Rory said with zero emotion. "Sounds like the kind of upstanding individuals *I'd* want to surround myself with."

Liv couldn't argue with that. "The Seven are a bunch of jerks, but I'm not doing this for them. I'm doing it for my brother and sister. For my family."

Rory regarded her for a moment, the brooding expression he wore most of the time fading slightly. "Then I guess you'll be quitting the repair shop."

Liv shook her head. "No, I work there for me. A girl has to have something."

Rory considered the pouch in his hand for a moment. When he looked up again, he had an expression of indifference. "Then you're going to have to figure out how to manage this all on your own, because you seem to have made up your mind."

Plato lifted his head. "I told her that too."

Rory looked directly at the cat. "I thought you said you only talked to Liv?"

Plato's head dropped back down as he closed his eyes.

"Damn lynxes always think they are so clever," Rory complained.

"That's the second time someone has called Plato a 'lynx,'" Liv stated. "What does that mean?"

Rory lifted one of his bushy eyebrows at her. "He's your cat, and you don't even know what he's all about?"

"He's not my cat," Liv argued. "Plato belongs to himself, just as I belong to myself."

Rory nodded. "Yes, very true. And he's technically not a cat. Well, not by traditional standards."

He stood, brushing off his pants, although they weren't dirty. From a nearby shelf, he retrieved a book and handed it to Liv.

"I'd tell you to read that in your free time, but that's sort of a joke at this point."

She read the cover aloud. "*Mysterious Creatures* by Bermuda Laurens."

Rory pointed at the volume. "Not everything in that book is accurate. A lot of it is conjecture because the subject matter is a bit hard to pin down."

Liv laughed. "Yes, this Bermuda lady probably made a lot of this stuff up…like her name for instance."

Rory shot her a disgusted look. "Bermuda was my mother."

Liv covered her mouth. "I'm sorry. I just meant that it was a strange name for a book on mysterious creatures."

"Why?" Rory questioned.

"Well, because Bermuda is a place cloaked in mystery."

Rory shook his head at her. "It's a place where mortals have seen a lot of things they shouldn't have or things they can't explain. The actual area is quite normal by our standards."

"'Our standards,'" Liv repeated dryly.

"Well, read the book when you can. Maybe you'll learn something about your little friend."

Liv held up the book, laying her head on it. "I'll read it through osmosis when I'm sleeping."

"No reading while you're sleeping until you've rested. You need to dream to rest properly."

Liv shot him look of surprise. "I was only joking. Reading while sleeping is a thing?"

"Reading while sleeping, or exploring, or doing just about anything," Rory explained. "How do you think that the Great Pyramids got built so fast?"

"Aliens?" Liv answered tentatively.

Rory sighed. "For a Seven, you're sure dumb. I'd expect your education to be more...well, doctrine-oriented."

Liv shrugged. "I forgot a lot of it, and my parents did a lot of my teaching, which was sort of organic. It was only the formative years when I was subjected to the strict teachings, which my mother always called 'subtle brain-washing.'"

Rory pressed out his large lips, his eyes narrowed. "It sounds like your mother and I would have gotten along."

Liv wanted to agree, but the idea that Rory would have enjoyed a conversation with her mother made her throat ache. It almost made her jealous to think that someone else would have had her mother's attention when she wanted all of it. Pining for someone's love you couldn't have was Liv's curse.

A knock on Rory's door startled Liv and she jumped nearly a foot in the air, her reflexes unpredictable due to her exhaustion.

Standing on the porch was a squatty old woman who had her head covered with a shawl. She had a large wrinkled nose, and hardly any teeth when she smiled. "Sorry to have scared you. I was looking for Rory."

The giant came around Liv, nearly pushing her out of the way. "Birdie. I told you I'd come to you."

"I know, I know," the woman said, waving a withered hand at him. "But it's good for me to get out."

Rory handed the woman the leather pouch with a smile. "I understand that. Here you go."

"I promise that next month—"

"Let's not speak of it," Rory said, cutting her off and ushering her away.

Liv watched as he helped the woman down the porch, whispering something in her ear. The giant had to bend in half to reach her.

"Bye, bye, Rory," the old woman called when she was to the walkway, waving behind her as she trudged forward.

"What was that all about?" Liv asked, her arms across her chest.

Rory shook his head. "It was nothing, and definitely none of your business."

"That's fine. I'll just catalog it with the rest of your suspicious behavior."

Rory halted after ducking into his house. "You shouldn't waste any of your time doing that. Don't you have more important things to worry about?"

Liv yawned. "Yes, namely sleeping. If I get home right now, I can get a few hours of sleep before I go to the House tonight."

Rory stared at her for a long moment and then said, "Why are you still standing there? Shouldn't you have left already?"

"Yeah, about that. I'm sort of beat. Would you open a portal for me to get home?" Liv asked.

He shook his head. "Portal magic isn't a giant's specialty."

"How do y'all get anywhere then?" Liv inquired.

Rory shot her a defiant look. "We use a different kind of magic, little grasshopper."

"Well, can you teleport me or slingshot me or whatever you do to travel long distances?"

"I can call you a cab," Rory stated.

"Oh, so you're not going to tell me what kind of magic you giants use for traveling?"

Rory crossed his arms, matching her stance. "There are some things that magicians don't need to know."

CHAPTER TWENTY-TWO

When Liv entered the Chamber of the Tree, there were only three Warriors standing in their places. She thought for a moment that she was strangely early, but then Adler said, "Now that Ms. Beaufont has joined us, we can get started."

She took her spot, earning a curious look from the guy next to her. Stefan Ludwig's jet-black hair contrasted with his porcelain skin. He wore a traveling cloak that was splattered with blood in several places.

Liv returned his look of curiosity before directing her attention to the Councilors.

Clark eyed her, probably relieved that she wasn't covered in mud, although she hadn't had time to change her jeans and knit top, which were wrinkled from her long nap.

"Trudy and Stefan, you've returned," Adler said. "Did you successfully contain the unregistered magicians?"

Stefan's chin raised slightly. "Three have registered with

the House and state that it was only a mistake. The other three tried to flee."

"And?" Adler asked, drawing out the word.

"We were unable to apprehend them alive," he answered.

The black crow Liv had noticed on her first visit to the room flew down from an unseen perch, landing in the center of the half-circle on the ground and looking up at the Warrior.

"Very well," Adler stated.

He turned his attention to Liv, his cold eyes scrutinizing her. "And Ms. Beaufont. You've returned. That should mean that you properly disposed of the troll in Las Vegas."

"I did," Liv answered at once, her arms clasped behind her back and her ears burning.

"May I inquire how you took care of the troll?" Haro Takahashi asked, his hands steepled in front of him.

Liv eyed him, appreciating the intricate patterns on his red, silk robes.

"Yes, I'm especially curious to know how you defeated it, and so quickly," Bianca said. "We didn't expect you back this soon."

"Well, apparently the fluke with my magic continues, because I can still create portals," Liv replied.

"I do expect that to fade soon," Adler stated. "But the troll…what did you do with it?"

Liv opened her mouth to tell the story, but nothing came out. It was probably the pleading look on Clark's face that kept her from divulging the truth. She tried to come up with a passable lie.

"I show here that you didn't attempt a tracking spell?" Hester said, studying her tablet, which detailed the various magics Liv had used recently.

She shook her head. "No, I decided to use a straightforward approach. I simply asked around on the Strip."

"You *asked*?" Bianca exclaimed with a sudden laugh.

"Yes, like a detective. I took the Sherlock Holmes approach," Liv answered.

Bianca looked at Haro and then Adler. "That would have taken all night."

"It took about twenty minutes," Liv corrected. "You'd be surprised by how many people recognized a large, disgusting troll carrying a club and grunting loudly."

Bianca grimaced. "What disgusting beasts."

"That was a conservative approach," Raina said, earning a quick look from her brother beside Liv.

"I could have used a tracking spell, but I decided not to," Liv lied.

"And quite right you were," Raina said, her tone more sympathetic this time. "I think it was a smart move. Tracking spells cost a lot of energy and can take quite some time to use. It sounds like you found the troll faster than if you had employed magic."

"I don't know about that," Bianca interjected.

Raina's kind expression dropped as she glanced down the table at Bianca, the two exchanging heated stares.

"How did you deal with the troll?"

Liv was surprised that it was her brother who asked the question. He looked so different as he peered down at her, not like the boy she remembered.

"I-I-I…" Liv stuttered, unable to look at him. "I took him to a remote part of the desert."

"And then?" Adler asked, leaning forward.

Liv chewed her lip. This wasn't going to be so bad. She just had to have confidence. "I left him there."

A great commotion erupted from the Councilors. Stefan and Trudy shot her cautious looks. Even the Warrior on the far side of the room, Maria Rosario, was regarding Liv with shock.

"Why would you do that?" Lorenzo asked. "Were you unable to subdue him?"

"She doesn't know any combat spells," Bianca said. "I warned you all this would be a problem for her."

"That's not it," Liv insisted, taking a step forward and making the crow hop back a foot. "The troll wasn't hurting anyone. He was just a dumb troll."

Adler rubbed his temple, his eyes narrowed. "Ms. Beaufont, you were supposed to dispose of the troll, not take him through a portal to some place in the desert where he'll continue to be a problem."

"But that's just it," Liv said, her voice growing louder. "He wasn't a problem. He was lost and confused."

Bianca laughed. "He's a troll. They are born that way, and they die that way."

Liv ground her teeth, shoving all her hostile emotions into the "box" before they got the best of her. She felt her power come back to her when her emotions were in check.

"The troll may not have spoken English, but he understood me when I told him I was there to help," Liv stated. "He likes the desert, and now he's away from mortals and not bothering anyone. I don't see what the issue is."

"The issue," Adler said, seeming to try to quell his own anger, "is that you were told to dispose of the troll. That was an order, not something up for negotiation."

"Why kill him? Because he's a troll who got lost and stumbled into mortal territory?" Liv asked.

Every single one of the Councilors nodded at her.

"No!" she yelled, making the crow jump again. "He wasn't doing anything wrong. I watched him. He didn't harm a single person, and they all thought he was a part of some show. Even when the tourists taunted him, he didn't act out. He just looked around to try to figure out where he was."

"It's about enforcing the law, which is what your role as a Warrior is supposed to be," Adler argued.

Liv crossed her arms over her chest and regarded the Councilors with a pointed stare.

"So I'm just supposed to follow the law, even if it's dumb and makes no sense?" Liv looked at the other Warriors. "Is that what you all do? Do you just dispose of people blindly without questioning whether they are guilty of a crime or not?"

Trudy shook her head at once, but Stefan and Maria seemed unwilling to engage, keeping their eyes focused forward.

"Is enforcing the law going to continue to be a problem for you, Ms. Beaufont?" Haro asked, his tone not punishing, but rather curious.

"It depends," Liv began, earning a frustrated look from Clark. "Are the laws going to operate without concern for actual justice? What's the point in upholding the law if we throw out our concerns for how empathetic justice works?

It sounds like you all have blind laws that state that if a creature violates a rule, they are punished without regard to circumstance. Not everything in life is black and white. Sometimes people break laws for perfectly good reasons, or by mistake. Like, how do you know that those magicians in Bali were entirely at fault? Maybe they didn't know any better, and were scared and reacted out of self-preservation? What if—"

"Enough!" Adler yelled, cutting Liv off.

The Chamber fell silent, except for the sound of the crow pecking at the ground as if it were trying to loosen one of the tiles.

"Ms. Beaufont," Adler began slowly, "it is the council's prerogative to assign cases as we see fit. We determine the law, and your job is to enforce it."

"But sometimes when you're in the field—"

Adler held up his hand, halting her. "The law is the law, regardless of the situation. It is our responsibility to bring objectivity, which is why we review and assign cases. Your judgment is too clouded when you're in the field. If every Warrior got to handle each case as they felt they should, where would the line be?"

"The line is drawn around justice," Liv argued. "It doesn't have to be difficult if one can think for themselves."

This caused an uproar from the Councilors, but the Warriors stayed completely still.

"That's quite enough!" Adler yelled, making his contemporaries quiet down. He stared coldly at Liv. "You are to return to where you left the troll and dispose of him as you were ordered. The creature violated our agreement, and the punishment is clear and non-negotiable. Besides, we can't leave him out there where he can commit the offense a second time. There's being understanding, and then there's being careless." Adler looked down the bench both directions. "Do all Councilors agree?"

There was a collective yes from the group, although a few of them, including Clark, didn't appear as adamant as others.

"Very well," Adler stated victoriously. "You will dispose of the troll and give us a full report tomorrow. Is that clear?"

Liv realized then that she needed to get a whole lot better at lying.

CHAPTER TWENTY-THREE

When John showed up to the shop the next day, Liv was already working on her second breakfast. She didn't have any graceful way of eating the giant cinnamon roll, so she just took a large bite, getting frosting all over her cheeks and nose.

John regarded her for a moment before looking down at the printer. "You said the rollers were jammed. What else?"

"Da cigicts ere fried," she said through the large mouthful of moist dough.

John shook his head at her. "Liv, can I ask you a question?"

She wiped her mouth with a napkin and took a gulp of orange juice. "No," she said simply when she'd swallowed.

He gave her a long-annoyed stare.

"I sort of hate it when people ask that question," she replied. "Like we all know that you're going to ask your question. Why do this preface business?"

"It's polite," he replied.

"Oh, and when did you start with the niceties?"

"The doctor said it would be good for my heart if I wasn't so moody with everyone," he shared.

"Sounds like you need a new doctor who understands you." Liv licked her fingers, eyeing the cinnamon roll and trying to determine where to take her next bite. "Did you get your meds fixed?"

He nodded. "Yes, but my question is about you. Are you…well, I don't know how to ask this."

Liv set the roll down, trying to keep her expression normal. Did John know? Had he seen her that morning when she'd been using her magic? Had he heard Plato talking? It was only a matter of time. "John, I can explain."

He shook his head at her. "It's fine. But you had to know that I'd figure it out eventually."

"I guess you're right."

"I've known something was up for a while. You've been sleeping all the time." He held up one finger. "And eating nonstop." John ticked off another finger. "You're more moody than usual, and you disappear all night. I know I shouldn't notice, but I do. I'm protective of you. But this change you're going through… Well, it doesn't have to be alone."

Liv looked down at the cinnamon roll, suddenly not as hungry. "John, I actually *do* have to do this alone. My new life and old one can't really mix. I mean, not entirely."

"But the baby," John began. "What are you going to do about that?"

Liv's mouth popped open and stayed that way, her eyes following suit. "Wait, you think I'm pregnant?"

John chuckled uncomfortably. "Well, it's obvious, now isn't it?"

Liv joined in laughing with him. She doubled over as it sank in. John stopped laughing, apparently not thinking it was as funny as she did.

When she came up for air, her face was red. "John, I'm not pregnant. I'm... I just took a side job. That's why I'm hungry and tired." Again, she had the urge to tell him everything. Maybe he'd love that she was a magician and that she could make their lives easier with magic. Maybe he'd rejoice in the fact that she was staying loyal to him and the shop, even though she was now a coveted Warrior. *Or maybe he'd freak out and think she was crazy.* She shook off the impulse, shoving it down. No, she couldn't risk telling him the truth. Not yet.

"You're not... Wait, you took another job? Where?"

"In Santa Monica," Liv said, not wanting to lie to John. The Councilors were different, but John deserved her honesty and trust. Well, as much as she could give him.

"Oh, well, if you need a raise, I'd be happ—"

"No," Liv cut him off, not able to bear the caring look in his eyes. "It's not like that. I'm doing it to help a friend."

"Friend?" John asked, now giving her a skeptical expression.

She rolled her eyes as Plato jumped up on the work-bench and sniffed her cinnamon roll. She shooed him away. "Believe it or not, I have friends."

"I'm not sure I *do* believe it," John teased. "But if you say you don't need a pay raise, then I believe you. I just don't want you overdoing it. Maybe you're taking on too much."

Join the club of people who don't think I can do all this, Liv thought.

"So the printer works fine," Liv stated, redirecting the conversation.

John pointed to the row of appliances on the shelf. "And you say that you fixed all of these too?"

"I did." Liv took a bite of her roll, enjoying the creamy sweetness.

John looked around and sighed. "When did you have the time to repair half a dozen electronics this morning?"

She shrugged, her mouth full.

"Well, that doesn't leave me a lot to do, then," John said, momentarily lost.

Liv swallowed, offering him a smile. "Why don't you take a day off?"

He waved her off. "We both know that would be a form of torture for me."

Liv's phone buzzed on the workstation. She looked at it, surprised by who had sent her a message; she didn't know Rory had her number. Then she remembered that whole bit about magic and tech. Her phone was officially "smart."

The message read, **I'm busy tonight. See you tomorrow**.

John wore an inquisitive expression when she looked up.

She grabbed the phone and stuck it in the pocket of her hoodie. "It's my friend. Looks like I have the night off."

"Oh, well, then do you want to help me with the truck?" he asked, a glint of enthusiasm in his eyes.

The 1940s Willys hadn't run in years. John worked on it

on the weekends, but there were too many repairs and never enough money or time to get it up to standards. Still, Liv had enjoyed the chances he'd given her to work on its electric motor conversion with him. Usually it was "his" project, so his invitation was a welcome gesture.

"Sure thing!" Liv exclaimed, but then remembered her shift at the House of Seven. She added, "I can't stay too long, though. I have a thing I have to do."

"I thought you said you didn't have to work tonight?" John asked.

"I don't, but I have to give Plato his worm medicine."

John and the feline looked at her and then at each other in unison.

"Oh, poor fella," John said kindly. "He has worms?"

"Yep," Liv lied. "Vet says it's from eating out of garbage cans and licking his butt."

John nodded like this made perfect sense. "Good thing he has you to take care of him."

"That was the best lie you could come up with? I have worms?" Plato asked when they stepped through the portal into Santa Monica a few hours later.

"You're a cat," Liv said. "No one cares."

He held his head high. "*I* care."

"I didn't know what else to say." Liv halted in front of the House of Seven. She was actually quite early for once since she hadn't met with Rory and John had dismissed her when it had gotten too dark to see. Still, they'd changed out the battery and Liv had repaired the radio, which John had thought was toast. Without magic, it probably would have been. She still didn't know exactly how her magic worked, but with her focus honed, she'd been able to repair quite a few things in the shop that day.

Once they were through the long hallway, Liv went through the large door. She'd promised Sophia that she'd visit, and she wasn't about to start letting the little girl down. However, once she was on the other side of the large door, Liv didn't know where to go next. She hadn't learned which door led to the Beaufonts' quarters. She could have tried a locator spell, except she didn't know how to use them. Fixing stuff with magic was easy, Plato had reasoned, because she already knew how to fix things. But doing things with magic that one didn't know how to do was different, he'd explained.

At the landing to the long staircase , Liv froze. Looking at the stairs that climbed up seven flights filled her with emotions she hadn't allowed herself to feel in a long time.

"Are you lost?" a voice called at her back.

Liv jolted and turned to find Stefan Ludwig standing only a few feet away. She hadn't heard him approach. Stepping back a foot, she found the wall.

"I was looking for the Beaufonts' quarters."

His black eyebrows knitted in confusion. "I'm sorry for being obtuse, but shouldn't you know where they are already?"

Liv let out a hot breath through her nostrils. "I don't live here."

"Oh, well that explains why I've never seen you around." He held out his hand. "I'm Stefan, one of the Warriors you pretty much convicted of following the law blindly yesterday."

She didn't take his hand. "I regret nothing."

He laughed easily. "I never would have expected Liv Beaufont to apologize, so don't worry." He eyed her. "You have quite the reputation already, you know?"

She nodded, looking at his cloak, which was clean. "Have you killed any magicians today?"

Again he laughed, this time louder. "I haven't, but the day is still early."

Liv narrowed her eyes at him, shaking her head.

"What have *you* murdered?" he said, pointing at her.

She looked down and sighed. Her jeans and t-shirt were covered in grease from the truck. Liv zipped up her hoodie, but that didn't cover all the stains. "It's from a truck, which by the way, I didn't murder. I'm working on saving it since it didn't do anything wrong, but you wouldn't know anything about that."

Stefan's expression shifted to mild contempt. "You know, we're not all bad."

"You know, when you're not all bad, you don't have to tell people that. They simply realize it."

Stefan took a step forward, invading her personal space. "Sheep's blood."

Liv narrowed her eyes. "What?"

"That was the blood on my cloak last night."

She stepped around him, trying to get some distance. "That's awful. You went and slaughtered sheep after murdering magicians? You're sick."

He laughed so abruptly that it made Liv freeze.

"I didn't kill the sheep or the magicians."

Liv was momentarily speechless. That didn't make any sense, but the steady look in his eyes told her he wasn't lying—or so she wanted to believe.

"Stef?" a voice called from behind her.

He looked over Liv's shoulder and smiled.

Liv spun to find Raina Ludwig standing in the doorway.

The woman's expression shifted to one of welcome at the sight of Liv. Raina was wearing a long gown of muted reds and blues. On her hip and shoulder, the material was gathered into elegant flowers. Her flowing black curls cascaded over her shoulders. "Oh, you've come for dinner. That's marvelous. I'll tell them to set an extra place for you."

Liv shook her head quickly. "No, I haven't actually. I already ate, but thank you. I'm here to see my sister."

Raina smiled wider. "Oh, Sophia is my favorite. She's the brightest child I've ever met." She strode over and offered Liv her hand. "I'm Raina. We should meet formally, I think."

Liv wrung her hand, offering a lame smile. "Nice to meet you."

Raina leaned closer, which didn't cause Liv the same trepidation that her brother had. "I liked the way you handled the troll. It made sense to me. I'm only sorry you had to go back and dispose of him."

Liv's face nearly gave her away. She tightened her hand in Raina's, shaking it harder. "Yep, too bad I had to slay that beast, but my freezer is stocked with troll meat to last me for eons."

Raina winked at her, pulling her hand free. "Your sister

is taking her dinner in her quarters, as usual. It's the door marked with your family crest. May I show you up?"

Liv suddenly felt dumb for not remembering about the family crest. Of course, that was how the quarters were marked. "No, I'm good. I don't want to keep you from your dinner."

Raina nodded good-naturedly. "Nice to meet you, Liv. I look forward to seeing you more."

Liv didn't know how to respond to this seemingly genuine comment, so she simply waved at Raina and her brother and headed up the stairs.

Sophia nearly launched herself at Liv when she opened the door. Then, seeing the thick grease marks on her clothing, she paused. "What are you covered in?" the little girl asked.

She was wearing a pink and silver sweater dress with a belt and leggings that made her look older than she was. Liv remembered pulling at the tight-collared dresses her mother made her wear and complaining about how the patent leather Mary Janes hurt her feet. She looked down at her Converse shoes and smiled with delight at how comfy she felt.

"It's grease," Liv answered.

"What sort of spell calls for grease?"

"Mechanics."

Sophia gave Liv a curious look. "I haven't heard of this branch of magic."

"And you probably won't," Liv said, peering around Sophia. "Hey, is Clark here?"

Sophia shook her head. "No, he likes to hobnob with the old wrinklies."

The confused expression on Liv's face told Sophia that she'd misunderstood.

"Oh, I mean Adler and his brother and Bianca and Emilio, who aren't old but act like they are," Sophia explained. "And Haro and Akio are there some of the time."

"They eat in the dining room downstairs?" Liv asked.

"No, they meet in Adler's private quarters." Sophia rolled her beautiful blue eyes. "They are too good for the rest of us."

"And you eat up here alone?" Liv asked.

Sophia looked both ways down the hall and sneakily waved Liv inside. "I'm not alone."

When she passed through the door, Liv froze. There, sitting in a circle on the rug were a dozen stuffed animals. In front of them were plates and teacups. "You're having dinner with your stuffies?"

Sophia clapped her hands. "It's all right, guys. She's cool."

The animals all sprang to life, picking up their teacups and chatting with one another or toddling around the room.

"Ummm, you enchanted your stuffed animals to have parties with you?"

"I simply activated the side of them that was dormant. But I'm not supposed to do such things, and no one but Clark, and now you, know I have magic strong enough to do this kind of thing. I shouldn't be able to until I'm twelve, when my magic is registered."

"So the Councilors have no record of your magic, do they?"

Sophia nodded.

Liv looked down at her stained clothes. "Well, can you help me, so I don't look like a mechanic? Clark will shoot me judgmental looks all night."

"Sure," Sophia said. "You don't know how to do that yet?"

Liv shook her head. "No, I haven't really been taught much. When I was your age, I didn't dabble with my magic."

"Why?" Sophia asked.

Liv watched as a toy giraffe stuck its face into a teacup, nearly getting it stuck on his nose. "I didn't trust it. I had seen magic do a lot of bad things. I'd heard the stuff Mom and Dad talked about..." Liv stiffened, afraid she'd said something wrong.

"You don't have to worry about it," Sophia said, suddenly looking way too mature. "Thinking about them doesn't make me sad. Not as sad as it would make you."

Liv didn't know what to say, so she watched as a teddy bear spilled tea down its front and then dabbed it with a napkin. Something on the far wall caught her eyes. A set of words she hadn't seen in a long time. Etched onto the wall, were the words her parents had said often: Familia Est Sempiternum

Family is Forever.

Liv coughed to loosen the tension in her throat.

"I bet your education was different than mine," Sophia went on, sensing the sudden emotion building in her older sister. "Clark says that Mom and Dad didn't push things on you. He said that you would pick them up on your own, and it would be better that way."

Liv nodded. "Yes, that's true."

"I've had to go to the House's school most of my life, and it's sort of strict," Sophia explained.

"But you're good with your magic," Liv pointed out, looking around the living room full of animated stuffed creatures. Then something occurred to her. "But why don't you join the others for dinner?"

"I sometimes do," Sophia explained. "But I'm with people all day, so it's sort of nice to just be with my friends."

Liv wanted to hug the little girl. Instead, she pointed at Plato, who had materialized at some point. "That's sort of how I feel about him, but don't tell him I said that or I'll never hear the end of it."

Sophia cupped her hand to her mouth and whispered, "I think he can hear you."

Liv copied her. "He can always hear me. It's why I say half the stuff I do."

Plato sauntered over to the stuffed animals, his eyes dancing from one to the other as they paraded around.

"So, do you think you can clean up my outfit?" Liv asked her sister, looking down at her grease-streaked clothes.

"I can do one better." Sophia pointed at her sister, and a moment later Liv felt constriction all over her body. She looked down, certain she was being strangled around the waist.

"What have you done to me?" Liv asked, gawking at the flowing gown she was wearing. The bodice was tight and lined with ribbons, and there were buttons down the back. The corset made it hard to breathe, and she didn't have to move to know that the weighty train behind her would make walking difficult.

"It looks beautiful on you," Sophia gushed.

"I'm a Warrior, and I need to look like one."

Sophia thought for a moment and then nodded. A moment later Liv found herself wearing a black suit, like something a ninja would wear.

"Ummm...no?"

"Fine," Sophia said, thinking again. "How about this?"

Liv felt something wrap around her, but not as tight as before. When the transformation had finished, she was wearing black leather pants and top, and a jacket with various zippers and compartments and a hood.

"I don't hate this," Liv said, admiring how stealthy the suit made her appear.

"It makes you look tough," Sophia replied.

Liv winked at her. "I *am* tough. But really, I was only asking you to clean up my old clothes."

Sophia nodded and returned the wink. A second later Liv's clothes materialized in Sophia's hand, folded and clean. She passed them to Liv. "There, now you have them for later when you go back to doing that mechanic thing."

Liv laughed. She was definitely going to make time to spend with this little girl. There were few things that renewed her spirit, but Sophia Beaufont was one of them.

CHAPTER TWENTY-FOUR

L iv expected to receive curious looks when she walked into the Chamber of the Tree. What she hadn't expected was to find a small dragon flying through the room. It was red, with iridescent scales that caught the overhead lights indicating the registered magicians.

The crow watched from the floor as the dragon soared back and forth, shrieking. Liv grimaced at the awful sound but tried to ignore it as she took her spot next to Stefan. Decar was still gone, as well as Emilio and Akio. Liv guessed that some cases took longer than others, which kept the Warriors away.

Stefan shot her a look of surprise when she sidled up next to him. He had probably expected her to still be covered in grease.

When Liv caught Clark's eyes, he too appeared flabbergasted, but pleasantly so. He gave her the smallest of thumbs-ups. If he had known that Sophia was responsible for her wardrobe, he might not have looked so pleased.

That made Liv wonder where Sophia got the clothes. They had to have come from somewhere.

The small dragon dove, heading straight for Adler's head. Liv hoped it would collide with his face, but it leveled out and landed beside the magician. Adler lifted his hand, and the dragon rubbed his head against it like a cat wanting attention. The dragon then curled up next to him, its narrowed eyes on the Warriors.

Didn't realize it was Bring Your Pet to Work Day or I would have... Never mind, Liv thought.

"Trudy and Stefan," Lorenzo began, reading from his tablet. "You've had moderate success at rounding up unregistered magicians, adding a total of twelve in the last day. But there have been quite a few casualties."

Stefan cleared his throat. "It was unavoidable, sir."

Lorenzo waved him off. "The unregistered do tend to be the most unsophisticated amongst us."

"Sir," Trudy began. Liv hadn't heard her speak before, and her voice was higher-pitched than she would have expected since she had broad shoulders and masculine features. She had the same short spiky hair as her sister Hester, although hers was still blonde, whereas Hester had gone completely gray. Still, Hester had a femininity to her that made her appear soft, and Trudy seemed rough.

"Yes?" Lorenzo asked, looking down his long nose at the woman.

"Are we to continue to round up these unregistered magicians?"

Lorenzo appeared distracted for a moment, tapping on his device.

"The Councilors think that's the best use of your and

Stefan's skills for the time being," Adler interjected. "You two have the best track record, and appear to work well together."

"I understand that, sir," Trudy began. "I was only wondering if we could be assigned to something different for a little while."

Adler blew out a breath, making the dragon stir. "We haven't cleaned up unregistereds in a while. This is necessary."

Trudy nodded. "Very well, sir. Thank you. I'm happy to continue."

"And if these rebels give you too much trouble, feel free to stop offering them the chance to register and just dispose of them," Adler added.

"Wait, we're not even giving magicians the chance to surrender?" Liv asked out of turn, as usual. "We're shooting first and asking questions later?"

Adler didn't try to hide his eye roll. "We are magicians, Ms. Beaufont. We don't shoot people or anything of the sort. And all magicians are warned of repercussion if they don't register their magic upon coming of age. Ignorance isn't an excuse for delinquency."

"A warning still seems like the first course of action," Liv argued. She was about to say more, but she knew it was useless. Clark's face had blossomed into an embarrassing shade of pink.

"Do you want to tell us how you dealt with the troll?" Adler asked.

"I killed it," Liv said flatly, making Clark close his eyes for a half-beat from mortification.

Adler sighed. "How did you do that?"

"Well," Liv said, drawing out the word, "first I used a binding spell to tie up its arms and feet. Once the sucker was on his back, I used a suffocation enchantment, but he was pissed by that point, rolling around and knocking rocks down from the cave ceiling."

Liv knew that the Councilors would have a record of her using these spells since Rory and she had practiced them the night before. They just didn't know she hadn't performed them on a troll.

"You were in a cave?" Hester asked intently.

"Oh, yeah," Liv answered. "The brute had made quite the home for himself. And he was relentless, breaking free of his restraints—"

"See, I told you she wasn't ready for combat spells," Bianca whispered loudly in Haro's direction on her left.

Liv counted back from ten before continuing her rehearsed speech. "Rocks were raining from the ceiling, but I wasn't out of options—"

"How did you kill the troll?" Adler interrupted.

He wasn't a patient man, Liv observed.

"I shot him with a paralysis curse, followed by a trauma shot," Liv said.

"You know how to do a trauma shot?" Haro asked.

"That's right," Liv stated.

Haro looked down the bench, nodding. "That's the right way to take out a troll."

"How did you dispose of him?" Adler asked.

Liv blinked. "I just told you."

"No, Warrior, I mean what did you do with his body? You didn't leave it behind for mortals to find, did you?"

Liv scoffed. "Of course not. I burned it."

So when the Councilors said "dispose of," they really meant to erase all evidence of a magical creature or person, Liv realized.

"Very good," Adler said without inflection. "We have another case for you that we believe is right for your new skills."

Liv caught the shift in Clark's demeanor. He lowered his head, his ears turning red.

Lorenzo began reading. "Recently, we've become aware of some sort of creatures that are apparently leeching power in the Los Angeles underground."

"Wait, LA has an underground?" Liv asked.

Lorenzo nodded. "Yes, apparently, most of the tunnels were thought to be shut down and the open ones used to travel between government buildings. However, we've learned that there's extensive networks which are operating. More investigation needs to happen, but once you locate the creatures responsible for leeching power, they need to be—"

"Disposed of," Liv said, finishing his sentence.

"Exactly," Lorenzo stated. "There have been numerous reports of leeching, so we're not sure exactly what is going on. It's probably a case of enchanted termites or something left over from when trolls lived in those tunnels."

"So it's a pest control assignment?" Liv asked.

Lorenzo looked sideways at the other Councilors.

"It's a Warrior's assignment," Adler corrected. "Do you have any issues?"

Liv ignored the look on Clark's face and simply shook her head. "Nope. Sounds like a fun challenge. I'll be off."

She pivoted and trotted away, not needing to be formally excused like before. She felt the eyes of the Councilors on her back as she headed for the Wall of Reflection. When she was almost through the door, she heard the flapping of the strange dragon. Only then did she wonder where the white tiger was that day.

CHAPTER TWENTY-FIVE

For over three hours, Liv tried to locate an entrance to the LA underground. Instead, she found mostly sleek, clean tunnels that led between government buildings. Although they were creepy and dark in their own way, there was absolutely no sign of any strange creatures trying to leech energy. These tunnels weren't like the ones she'd heard of in Portland, Oregon that had been known for harboring smugglers back in the day. These had been used during Prohibition, but still, they looked harmless.

When she'd given a security guard the slip for the tenth time, Liv decided it was time to give up for the night. She had work the next day, and if she showed up at Rory's place exhausted again, he'd quit training her.

In the morning, she was surprised to discover that Plato had left early. She eyed the black outfit Sophia had put her in with fondness as she changed into a clean pair of jeans and her favorite sweater.

She stopped off at the Village Bakery, which should have been cited for filling the air with the smell of inviting, fresh-baked bread. Because of that intoxicating scent, she spent the last of her paycheck on a ham and cheese croissant with extra cheese and a protein shake. Liv had never gone through a paycheck this fast, but keeping up with her hunger was proving expensive. If she was living at the House of Seven, it wouldn't have been such a big deal since her meals would be provided, but then she'd have to stomach annoying magicians.

As she took a bite of the still-warm croissant, she smiled inwardly. Freedom and independence were worth more to her than anything else. She might not be rolling in cash, but she had a life she had built. That was more important to her.

Once she had settled into her usual spot at the shop, Liv looked around aimlessly. There wasn't anything to do for once. She'd used her magic to repair everything last night before she left, when John had gone early to get the parts ready to repair the truck. Since no new appliances had come in, Liv had her first moment of respite in a while. She leaned back in her chair, enjoying the peace and quiet for once when something poked her in the back.

Leaning forward, she determined it was her bag. She reached into to find the source of her discomfort and pulled out the book Rory had loaned her, *Mysterious Creatures*. Laying her head against the volume, she pretended to sleep.

"Reading while sleeping," she said, shaking her head. "Yeah, right. Until then, I'll have to just do it the old-fashioned way."

Liv opened the dusty book, impressed by the artwork that filled the first few pages. There was a map of a world that the author, Bermuda Laurens, had titled the "Original Planet." The continents looked like Earth's except that they were shaped slightly different. There were also extra masses of land that Liv didn't remember seeing on the regular globe.

Liv continued to turn the pages and found something that struck her as odd, which was the dedication page. It read, "Dedicated to the Seven, for it is your mystery I cannot unlock, no matter how hard I try."

Liv looked down at the ring on her finger. The largest diamond caught the light overhead.

"That makes two of us, Bermuda," Liv said aloud.

Liv hadn't had much time to think about the clue of sorts that Ian had left behind. She'd tried to tell herself that he was only passing along a family heirloom, but if that was the case, he wouldn't have had Sophia give it to her in secret. She didn't know what kind of person Ian had become, but she remembered that he didn't do anything without good reason. That was why she'd been careful to hide the ring in her pocket at the House of Seven. She desperately wanted to ask Clark about it, thinking he might know something, but she wasn't sure he wouldn't tell Adler or someone else.

No, if Ian had asked Sophia to keep it a secret, he didn't want anyone else to know about it.

"What were you trying to tell me?" Liv asked aloud.

Liv flipped through the thick book, which was full of beautiful drawings of different creatures. Everything from horvendi, a small and loyal breed of fairy, to sacros, a species of dwarf that was rarely ever seen.

Liv had grown up around many different magical creatures, but nothing like these. Honestly, the ones she'd known were more like pets. She'd only met elves or fey on a number of occasions and it had never seemed like pleasant interactions between them and the magicians. After one such situation, everything had gone haywire in the House of Seven, and all the children were forbidden to interact with any advanced magical creatures from that point forward. It had been a silent war, Liv had realized later.

She turned the page and found the introduction to the next chapter surprising. *We are all creatures. However, there is a species among us that sees themselves as civilized and regards the rest of us as magical animals.*

It wasn't hard to figure out who Bermuda was referring to. Actually, much of the book seemed to be a commentary on the magicians and how they held themselves separate from the rest. Liv didn't have to wonder if Bermuda was held in high esteem among the House of Seven. They'd been trying to regulate the giants' magic for a long time.

Several pages farther in, Liv stopped at an image she recognized. Under it the caption read, *This is how the magical lynx appears to most, although this is not its true form.* The picture showed a common house cat, but the tip of its tail was white, as were the tops of its ears, just like Plato's.

Liv continued to read.

Lynxes have been known for centuries to be the great secret-keepers. Whose secrets they keep, we may never know. They can take the form of a lion, a tiger, a bobcat, or a mountain lion, but they are most often seen in their most deceptive form: the domes-ticated house cat. They are masters at hiding and can disappear at will. Most believe them to possess more knowledge than they

let on, and they tend to be very choosy who they share informa-
tion with. Because of this, they are often seen as untrustworthy.
Also, lynxes might have the ability to see through objects, which
is why they are often associated with veiled truths. However,
those who make friends with a lynx should be warned: they are
not prone to friendly behavior. Therefore, if one makes your
acquaintance and doesn't leave, as lynxes are prone to do since
they are natural nomads, you are a part of a secret they are
trying to hide.

Liv looked up suddenly, feeling as though she was being watched. "Plato, are you there?"

Silence followed her question. Feeling self-conscious, Liv looked around. Was she a part of a secret Plato was hiding? And if so, what did she not know? He had arrived, seemingly out of nowhere, the day she had left the House of Seven. She had never asked about his presence and he hadn't left her side since then, but now it felt necessary to question his purpose in her life. And yet, she worried that the more she did, the more likely she was to lose him. That thought was followed by a sinking feeling in her gut.

Shutting the book, Liv gazed around the organized shop. There might be a lot she didn't know about Plato, but at this point, she wasn't sure it was necessary to find out anything new.

Liv started to worry when her shift was over at John's Repair Shop and she still hadn't seen Plato. Was it possible that he was hurt? Maybe he knew that she'd read about his race in the book, and that had broken some sort of silent agreement between them. She couldn't figure it out, and there was no way to track him down. She instinctively knew that if Plato wanted to be found, he would be. Otherwise, it was a hopeless cause.

Dispirited but bent on making the most of the day, Liv showed up at Rory's cottage right on time. Her stomach grumbled as she climbed the rickety porch. She hadn't even gone home to eat, because, in truth, there was nothing in her pantry or refrigerator. She didn't get paid for two more days, and although she *could* ask John for an advance, that was not going to happen. He'd worry about her and try to give her a pay increase she didn't deserve. No, Liv would just have to make do. She'd eat dinner at the House of Seven if she had to, or maybe Rory would teach her how to manifest her own food, although she doubted it. She knew from her childhood that creating food was a complex spell because food was one of the Three Requirements of Life.

"Food/water, air, and sleep are the most complicated spells to cast," her father had once told her. "To manifest food or take away air or put someone to sleep is extremely difficult. Magicians are strong and live for centuries, but we are susceptible to death if our basic needs aren't met."

The door was open when Liv got to Rory's house, and a thick, savory aroma wafted from the kitchen as she entered, as if it were there to tempt her.

"Hey?" Liv called.

"I'm back here," Rory responded, peeking around the corner with something frilly hanging around his neck.

Curiously, Liv trotted to the kitchen, her nose leading the way. "What are you making?"

"Pies," Rory answered, grunting as a pan banged against the oven.

Liv came around the corner to find a sight she hadn't expected. Rows upon rows of pies sat on cooling racks stacked all the way to the ceiling. Steam rose from the tops of the pies, sending various smells spiraling through the air.

Rory stood in front of the oven, pulling out a large pie using floral oven mitts. He spun, his brow beading with sweat as he smelled the crust. Hanging around his neck and tied around his waist was a frilly apron decorated with birds and nests.

He set the large pie on the bottom rack as Liv glanced at the dozens of others spread around the room.

"Ummm, let's start with the obvious question," Liv began. "What are you doing?"

Rory counted the pies. "I'm making pies."

"Why?" Liv asked.

"To eat," Rory stated simply, continuing to count.

"Is this, like, your dinner tonight?"

Rory shook his head. "I couldn't eat all of these in one sitting."

Liv patted her stomach. She felt she was up for *that* challenge.

Rory turned to face her. "Besides, I'm gluten-intolerant. It gives me an awful rash, and irritates my stomach for days if I have it."

"So who are all these pies for, then?"

"Friends," Rory replied, untying the apron and hanging it on a hook on the wall.

"And again, has anyone ever told you that you remind

them of their grandmother, with your floral prints and vintage kitchen?"

Rory looked around at the room, which was decorated in mint greens and soft pinks. He shrugged. "I kept some of my grandmother's effects, but I think this place has a nice balance of masculinity and femininity."

Liv didn't really care to argue that point. "So these friends… Am I considered one of them?"

"Is that your way of asking for a slice of pie?" Rory asked.

Liv nodded, salivating from the intoxicating smell.

"What would you like?" Rory pointed to the first row of pies. "We have chicken pot pie, meat pie, apple cinnamon, blueberry crumble, peach vanilla, cherry marmalade, and strawberry rhubarb."

Liv was stunned by the options. Her mouth hung open as her anticipation sought to burst out of her.

"No time for pie," Plato said from the entrance to the kitchen. "We've got work to do."

CHAPTER TWENTY-SIX

"Plato, where have you been?" Liv asked, looking the cat over.

"I found the network of tunnels," he answered.

"You've been off looking for those all this time?" Liv questioned.

Rory looked at Liv and Plato, confusion growing on his face.

"It didn't make any sense that the tunnels were giving off readings of a leeching magical creature but that we couldn't find evidence of it," Plato stated. "So I investigated until I found what we were missing. Or rather, *where*."

"Are you going to tell me or make me guess?" Liv asked.

Plato nodded in the direction of the front door. "I'll show you."

Rory cut into the biggest of the pies and pulled out a steaming slice, sliding it onto a decorative plate. He handed it to Liv but looked directly at Plato.

"She needs to eat, or she'll be no good to either of us," he said. "First chicken pot pie, then whatever else."

Plato sighed impatiently and disappeared into the living room.

"Want to tell me what's going on?" Rory asked Liv as she shoveled the still-steaming pie into her mouth, burning her tongue.

Liv explained about the case she'd been assigned and handed Rory her digital codex with the notes.

"So you went to this location in the underground and didn't find anything?" Rory asked, reading the device.

"Nothing out of the ordinary, but it sounds as though Plato has found a new lead."

Rory gave her a skeptical glance. "Firstly, it's not like a lynx to be so helpful."

"Plato is different," Liv said, polishing off the last of her pie and taking the glass of cold water Rory offered her right on cue.

"And secondly, he's talking an awful lot lately," Rory continued.

"Plato is different," Liv repeated.

"That's the thing," Rory said in a whisper. "Lynxes are never different. You read about him in the book I gave you? They are deceptive and self-serving. If he's helping you, well…"

"Do you think I'm part of a secret he's hiding?"

Rory regarded her uncertainly for a moment and then nodded. "That makes the most sense, but it's never so straightforward. I'll just caution you not to trust the creature."

Liv finished the glass of water, finally full after the wholesome meal. "There's no one else alive I *do* trust."

Rory shook his head. "Oh, you're one dumb human, but

I'll let it pass." Rory swiped his hand at the row of pies, and they were instantly packaged in white cardboard boxes tied with ribbons.

"Who are these friends you're giving these to?" Liv asked.

Rory ignored her. "What I don't understand is, if the House of Seven got reports of leeching, why do they not have a better reading on where it was happening or who is doing it?"

"Isn't that my job to detect?"

"Still, the report had to come from somewhere. Something about this doesn't sound right to me," Rory said, scratching his wide chin.

"Well, why don't you come with me and see what you think if you have such suspicions," Liv offered.

Rory gave her a quizzical glance. "You, a Warrior for the House of Seven, want to bring me along on one of your illustrious cases?"

"I've been assigned what sounds like a bogus case in the sewage-filled underground of LA," Liv stated. "I don't know how illustrious this one will be."

Rory hesitated for a moment, considering Liv.

"Hey, you *do* owe me a lesson." She picked up a large leather jacket hanging on a dining room chair and nearly doubled over from the weight of the oversized garment. "I need you to teach me some more combat spells." She tried to throw the jacket in Rory's direction, but it fell short, landing at his feet.

He directed his hand at the jacket, making it hover above the floor before it flew up to his outstretched hand.

"If you want to learn how to do a trauma shot, you better get a whole lot stronger."

"Oh man, you're not going to make me dig another hole, are you?"

"Nope," Rory said, striding toward the door. "I don't have all day to sit around."

Liv followed Plato as he led the way through the tunnels she had spent hours investigating the day before. She didn't have to read minds to know that he was less than thrilled about the giant accompanying them. Yes, Rory was suspicious of Plato, but he was also a source of information on other magical creatures, and Liv could use all the help she could get solving this case.

Plato stopped abruptly and Liv ran into him, then Rory rammed into her back. Looking up at Rory with pure disdain, Plato said, "Watch where you're going."

The giant only shook his head, not looking offended.

"This is what I found earlier," Plato explained, indicating a solid wall.

"Wow, a concrete wall that we walked past a bazillion times last night," Liv exclaimed with mock amazement in her voice.

"It has a glamour on it," Rory said, walking straight up to the wall and putting his hand even with the surface.

"Yes, I figured you could see through it, giant," Plato stated dryly.

Liv looked at the cat and Rory. "Does someone want to tell me what's going on?"

"Giants can't be fooled by glamour or any magic used to deceive," Plato explained.

"Oh, so that's why you don't do anything to your house to make it look less run down," Liv stated.

Rory gave her an annoyed look. "And also because it's wrong. Remember, it's better for us to try to enjoy things as they are."

"Yes, I remember, but it doesn't work for you anyway, so the point is a little less poetic than the first time you tried to make it." Liv pointed to the wall. "But you can see through this? What's on the other side?"

"More tunnels," Rory observed, ducking to peer at the wall.

Liv shot Plato a look. "You think this is where the leechings are happening?"

He nodded. "I know they are, but the giant is right that something is amiss. The House gave you this case, but the details aren't specific enough. It seems like they are almost sending you on a wild goose hunt."

"Why would they do that?" Liv asked. "I'm a Warrior, meant to help and protect."

Rory put his head through the solid wall, and a moment later, he pulled it back through. "You're a pain in the ass that they probably want to keep out of their hair until you're better trained."

"What did you see? Anything?" Liv asked.

Rory shook his head. "I'm not sure what I saw. It's going to take more investigating."

Liv gestured. "Giants before beauty."

Rory looked at the wall and back at Liv and laughed. "I can't fit through that opening."

"How big is it?" Liv asked. "Big enough for Plato?"

"Yes, and you, if you bunch up real tight, human," Rory answered.

"But where's the opening? All I see is a wall," Liv said.

Plato sighed and jumped up, disappearing behind the glamoured wall.

"See? Just follow the cat," Rory explained.

Liv rolled her eyes. "Oh, right. Follow the cat." She felt around on the wall until her hand went through. "So I just go through this hole?"

The wind was knocked out of Liv when her torso fell through the hole, but her legs remained stuck on the other side. She fell head-first, her face smashing into the other side of the wall. Pushing herself up, she looked directly at Plato, who was sitting on the ground in front of her.

"Someone could have told me the dimensions of the opening and that it was suspended two feet off the ground," Liv complained.

Rory laughed on the other side of the wall. "It was more entertaining this way."

Plato laughed with him.

"Oh, now you two are getting along?" Liv asked.

"No, but watching you fall through the hole was pretty entertaining," Plato said.

Liv kicked her feet, trying to get them through. "Can I get a little help here?"

Rory grabbed her feet and pushed them, making her do a somersault. "Thanks."

"Not a problem," he said, still laughing.

"So, what,…are you just going to wait over there for us?" Liv called.

"I'm going to keep an eye out," Rory answered. "Something doesn't feel right about this, but mark where this spot is in case you lose the lynx. You'll need a way to find the exit."

Liv looked down at Plato. "I won't lose you, will I?"

He gave her a noncommittal expression. "Honestly, I don't know exactly what's down here, but something tells me that having a backup option in case you lose me is a good idea."

Liv agreed with a nod and pointed, making an "X" appear on the wall.

She then turned, and her breath hitched in her throat. Before her was something she'd only read about or seen in movies.

CHAPTER TWENTY-SEVEN

A shimmering transparent figure floated by, gliding across the cold concrete. Liv blinked at the figure, trying to make out the details. It was a man with short hair, carrying a baseball bat and looking confused.

"Is that a…" Liv asked Plato in a whisper.

"A baseball player?" he answered sarcastically.

"Ha-ha. You know what I mean."

"Oh, yes, it's one of those."

"One of what?" Rory asked from the other side of the wall.

Liv leaned closer, careful not to fall through the other side. "It's a ghost."

"Mmmm…that's interesting."

"Yes, that's what I was thinking," Liv said as the ghost disappeared through a solid wall. "And why is it interesting?"

Rory chuckled slightly. "Well, because of the notes on the case. Leeches and ghosts go hand in hand."

"Exactly what I hypothesized," Liv stated with confidence. "And why do leeches and ghosts go hand in hand?"

Rory sighed. "Just go see what else you can find and let me think about this. Something isn't right."

"Well, they don't send Warriors on cases where everything is hunky-dory."

"Liv? You should see this," Plato called. She turned to find what he was talking about.

A stream of green dust spiraled through the air in the distance. The tunnel disappeared into darkness ahead, but the green bobbed on, lighting the walls as it moved.

"What's that?"

Plato shook his head. "I don't know. I'm all for following strange green lights, although if it's a will-o-the-wisp, we're screwed."

"What's that?"

"It's how all great travelers have gotten lost," Plato explained.

"Well, I guess it's a chance we have to take," Liv stated. "Let's go down the dark tunnel after the unknown and ghosts."

"We only saw the one, and it's probably unrelated." Plato led the way, his tail high in the air.

When they'd traveled several yards, the light from the other tunnels evaporated, leaving them in near-darkness.

Liv held up her hand, trying to remember the spell for light. The harder she tried to recall it, the more it felt like it slipped away, like a dream upon waking. Then she thought about when she fixed appliances and didn't mutter an incantation, but rather just thought of the repair. She tried to think about light. Something that illuminated her path. Her mouth opened, and in a deep voice she sang, "*Raaaam.*"

The vibration of the word felt strange in her throat, but a moment later a ball of light materialized in front of her, lighting the path ahead.

She looked down at Plato victoriously. He was wearing a curious expression. "Hey, *you* might be able to see in the dark, but I can't."

"That's not it," Plato said. "You just spoke the ancient language of the Founders."

"What? No, I didn't. I said the incantation for light."

"In the ancient language," Plato argued.

"How do you know? I thought only the Seven could read or speak it?"

"I recognized it," Plato replied. "How did you come up with that incantation?"

"I just thought about light, and that word came out." Liv hesitated, then asked Plato, "Is there a secret you want to tell me?"

He thought for a moment. "That's a very general question, and no. I think we'd better follow that green thing before it gets away." He indicated the green light bouncing ahead.

Liv conceded with a nod. "Yeah, good idea."

They sped up, trying to close the distance between them and the floating light. The tunnel went on and on, its stone walls and concrete floors giving them no way to know how far they'd gone. After several minutes, the tunnel split. The green light bobbed briefly and then sped to the right.

Liv gave Plato a tentative glance before hurrying after

the green light, then halted at the sight before her. A few dozen balls of green light flew around a large cave-like room. Liv thought she'd gone unnoticed when they all halted, hovering in the air. Then, one by one, the green figures turned around. With the lights illuminating the creatures, Liv recognized what they were—the ugliest fairylike creatures she'd ever seen.

The little beasts had pale freckled wings that resembled a butterfly's, and a short tail that flared at the end hung between their stubby, clawed feet. On their abnormally round, bald heads were large black eyes, and their mouths contained several rows of razor-sharp teeth. The green light radiated from a substance they were carrying in their hands, which they were also pressing into the cracks in the walls in this room.

"Oh, hell," Liv breathed, backing away from the hovering creatures who stared at her uncertainly.

"What are they?" Liv asked.

"Ugly," Plato answered, staying in place.

The creatures gave a collective shout of fury before dropping the bundles of glowing green material and flying in their direction.

"No!" Liv yelled, raising her hands to cover her face.

She was certain she was about to get mauled by those razor-sharp teeth, but instead, she heard knocking sounds. Liv lowered her hands to find the creatures colliding with an invisible wall between them and the ugly fairies.

"Nice barrier," Plato said proudly.

"Barrier?" Liv asked, blinking at the wall as the creatures rammed it again and again.

"Specifically, a defensive barrier," Plato said. "Usually a

magician throws one up intuitively when they feel threatened."

"Yeah, well, the idea of being eaten alive by ugly fairies sort of made me feel threatened."

"Well, now that you've got them contained and we're safe, want to attempt some diplomacy?" Plato asked.

Liv looked around the room, the orb of light hovering beside her illuminating the places she wanted to see using her inclination to direct it. The bits of green glowing material was crammed into the corners between the wall and the ceiling and the floor, making the room look like it was radioactive. Liv didn't understand what kind of magic this was, but she knew it was her job now to control and stop anything that put others in danger.

She took a step forward and cleared her throat. "I'm here to stop you all from leeching magical powers."

"Oh, good, you're going with the direct approach," Plato said dryly.

"What am I supposed to do, shoot first and ask questions later, as the Councilors would suggest?"

"No, I'm just curious how this will pan out."

"Leech? Leech? Leech?" the fairies said in unison, their voices high-pitched and squealy.

"Yes. You can't keep taking magic power," Liv continued. "I'm going to give you one warning, and then I'll have to stop you."

"Stop. Stop. Stop," they repeated. As if they'd coordinated this dance, they formed a solid figure of a man and made him walk over to the wall where the glowing green was stuck. "Stop. Stop. Stop."

Liv shook her head. "Yes, I'll have to stop you if you won't quit leeching energy. We know it's you."

"Ghosts. Ghosts. Ghosts," the creatures said, breaking out of the figure of the man and flying around haphazardly, some of them knocking into the invisible wall again.

"Wait, why are they talking about the ghosts?" Liv asked.

"I think the more important question is what they are doing to your wall," Plato said.

She figured out what he meant; they were ramming into her barrier or taking bites out of it with their teeth, making sawing noises. Liv couldn't tell what was happening to the barrier, but she could put two and two together well enough to figure it out. Following her instincts, she scooped up Plato and spun in the opposite direction just as a loud buzzing sound like that of a swarm of bees started after her. The ugly fairies were angry about the interruption and threats, and no barrier stood between her and them anymore.

CHAPTER TWENTY-EIGHT

The orb of light sped ahead of Liv, just close enough that she didn't trip on her feet in the dark. Clutching Plato to her chest, Liv felt the rush of air at their backs as the little creatures came on faster, closing the distance.

"Do you have any bright ideas about how to not get eaten?" Liv asked between ragged breaths.

"Run faster," Plato offered.

"I could try throwing up another barrier," Liv said.

Plato looked over Liv's shoulder. "You don't have enough distance to do it successfully."

Liv pushed on, willing her feet to move faster. She concentrated on making them seem as light as possible as they touched the ground and left it again. Running had never been her thing, but with a number of bloodthirsty, ugly fairies chasing her while making squeaky, chirping noises, she felt like an Olympic sprinter.

The light from the connecting tunnels was visible ahead, which didn't make Liv feel any better since she knew that the entrance to the other side was a hole she couldn't see. She might run straight into the concrete wall before she found the door. And what was to prevent the ugly fairies from following her through?

Sweat dripped into her eyes as she continued to run. Willing the orb to disappear, Liv pictured transferring that energy to her legs to help her move faster. The tunnel blurred as she picked up speed, now moving so fast she thought she'd roll forward out of control.

"You're gaining some distance," Plato said, still looking over her shoulder.

Liv caught sight of something ahead. She thought it was the X she'd drawn, but blinked and made out Rory's curly hair. He had stuck his head through the hole, making it look like he was mounted on the wall like a hunter's trophy.

His eyes widened when he caught sight of Liv. She was about to tell him to move when the loud buzzing of fairies stopped suddenly. Liv thought she'd finally put enough distance between them using her super speed and she spun, her hand in the air, ready to cast another barrier spell. However, the ugly fairies were all hovering a safe distance away. Their beady eyes watched Liv hungrily, but none of them dared move any closer.

Keeping her hand up, Liv backed away. "I think they got the message."

Plato, wiggled free of her grasp, jumping to the ground and looking the other way. "Yes, I think so, but I don't think that message came from you."

Liv quickly glanced over her shoulder and then back at the fairies, still hovering several yards away. She gave a double-take once the image behind her sunk it. Rory's head was still hovering on the wall, but his usually green eyes were red, brutal hostility on his face.

"Rory?" Liv asked looking between him and the fairies. It seemed to be a standoff, the creatures' round faces turning scarlet as they hovered angrily.

"Get through," Rory commanded.

Plato didn't hesitate, crawling through the hole around Rory's face.

"Ummm, I don't know how," Liv said, not knowing where the hole began and ended and not wanting to bump into his face.

A large hand reached through the seemingly solid concrete. Liv flinched from its sudden closeness, but didn't react before Rory's fingers grabbed her around the collar and hauled her off her feet. She gulped, holding her breath as he yanked her through the hole like she was a rag doll. Liv's arms covered her head to protect her from a collision with the wall, but to her relief, Rory pulled her through cleanly and plopped her on the ground.

Liv was ready to take off running again, but she hesitated when she saw Rory's slumped figure. He was leaning against the wall with his head hanging between his knees.

"Ummm, are we okay?" Liv asked. "Are those ugly fairies coming after us?"

Rory shook his head. "Zonks. And they can't see the opening."

"'Zonks?' That's what those things are called?" Liv asked.

Rory looked up, the red of his eyes fading back to green. "Yes, and they're sensitive, so if you called them ugly to their faces, no wonder they're mad."

"Well, I also told them that I was there to stop them from leeching power," Liv replied. "They probably didn't like getting shut down."

Rory shook his head. "They aren't the ones who are leeching."

"I saw them," Liv argued, glancing at Plato for backup. "*We* did. They had this green substance they were putting into the cracks in the walls."

Rory wiped the sweat off his forehead and started forward, crouching to avoid hitting his head. "Come on. I need a drink after dealing with you. I'll explain in a bit."

"Hey, what do you mean, 'after dealing with me?'" Liv asked. "I'm not the problem here. Those Zonks tried to eat us for dinner."

"After you called them names," Rory said. "And convicted them of something you don't know if they did. You're a lot more like the House of Seven than you realize, throwing accusations out and asking questions after the fact."

Liv muttered to the ground as they marched toward the entrance to the tunnel. She didn't want to admit that Rory might be right. Actually, it burned her up inside that she had offended a race of magical creatures and also judged them without evidence, as the House of Seven would.

CHAPTER TWENTY-NINE

L iv had to take three steps to each one of Rory's to try to keep up with him as he exited the underground tunnels. When they reached the surface, she was surprised to find it already dark. Liv hadn't thought they'd been gone for that long and at first worried she was late to the House of Seven, but then she remembered that she didn't have to attend until she made progress with this case.

"There's a pub down this away." Rory pointed to a dingy alleyway that was mostly cloaked in darkness.

"Please tell me that there's glamour over this place and I'm just not seeing the clean bar you're pointing to?" Liv asked.

Rory grabbed the back of Liv's shirt and half-led, half-dragged her until they arrived at a Chinese restaurant.

"When you said pub, I was thinking beer and brats, not tea and dumplings," Liv admitted.

"Speakeasy," Rory clarified.

"Speak for yourself," Liv replied.

He groaned, not appreciating her humor, and opened the

door. The smell of tempura and fish hit them immediately. Rory breezed by the hostess, who merely nodded as if seeing a giant who had to duck to enter the place was a daily affair.

Liv followed Rory as he led her down the hall to the bathrooms. She was about to protest when he opened the last door and the soft sound of a fiddle filled the air.

The next room was starkly different than the bright Asian restaurant with pastel furnishing and dusty statues. The pub they entered was full of dark wood and smelled of sweat and licorice. Around the ornately carved bar were three of the largest men Liv had ever seen, including Rory. Playing cards at a rickety old table were a few gnomes with fat noses and shifty eyes, and in the corner was a three-piece band that included a flute, a tambourine, and a fiddle. Playing the instruments were two men and one woman. Liv didn't have to stare at them long to recognize their elvish features, which were more subtle than the characteristics that distinguished gnomes and giants. Even though they had long hair and hats, it was impossible to fully disguise their pointy noses, chins, and ears.

"Ummm, I'm not sure it's a good idea for me to be in here," Liv said in a whisper.

"Know a better place to learn about Zonks and how to measure leeched magical energy?" Rory challenged.

Liv looked down for Plato but immediately realized that he was gone or hiding.

Rory took a seat in a chair that didn't look like it could withstand the challenge of supporting his weight. He waved to the bartender, a woman, who in comparison to everyone in the pub looked to be almost normal. Her strawberry-blonde hair framed her face with curls, and she wore a long skirt, which she used to dry her hands as she strolled over to the table.

"Mr. Laurens, what brings you here?" the bartender said, batting her eyelashes at Rory. "I told you that we were good after the slump, and—"

"It's nothing like that," Rory interrupted. "Can my friend and I get a mug of whatever you have on special right now?"

The woman nodded, acknowledging Liv reluctantly. "Sure thing."

"That's okay," Liv said after the woman had trotted away. "Honestly, I'll just take water. They have water here, right?"

Rory dismissed her with a shake of his head as he studied the people around them. "I've got the beers."

"Thanks, but it's not necessary."

Rory kept his eyes trained on one of the other giants at the bar. "I don't drink alone, so either you drink with me, or we leave, and you're that much farther from solving your case."

Liv grudgingly agreed. "Fine. So these Zonks…tell me about them. And what was that thing you were doing with your eyes?"

"That was simply a repercussion of using my elemental magic," Rory explained. "And Zonks don't leech energy. They are actually fix-it fairies by nature."

"Who live in the underground and carry around radioactive particles?"

"Those must have been a material they repurposed for

SARAH NOFFKE & MICHAEL ANDERLE

making a repair," Rory stated. "You said they were putting it in the wall? Like in a crack?"

Liv nodded. "What were you saying before about ghosts?"

Rory gave her a look that said, "cease and desist" as the bartender approached.

"Yeah, anyway, so did I tell you about the troll?" Liv asked, hurrying to cover the conversation as the bartender set down two mugs that easily held a gallon of beer each. She slid them onto the table with a shaky smile.

"Anything else for you two?" the woman asked. "Share some fries or something?"

Rory snorted with laughter. "No, it's nothing like that, Cindy. We're good."

Relief flooded the woman's face. "Oh, good. We were wondering." She indicated over her shoulder where the other three giants stood.

"What were they wondering?" Liv asked when Cindy had left them with their beers, which Liv didn't know how she was going to tilt to drink from.

"They thought you were my date," Rory said. "It's common to share food on a first date in giant culture. The idea is to show restraint and give the woman most of the food as a sign of humility and selflessness."

Liv burst into laughter, making everyone in the bar look at them. She couldn't stop herself even when the elves played more quietly, interrupted by her constant chuckling. "They thought you and I..." Liv wiped her hands under her eyes, pushing away the tears flooding them.

Rory easily lifted his beer and took a long drink, swal-

226

lowing a third of it. "So this troll? That was your first case?"

"Yeah, and they wanted me to...you know..."

"No. What did they want you to do with it?" Rory asked, although the look on his face told Liv he was messing with her.

She pulled her finger across her throat and let her tongue fall out of her mouth. "You know."

He nodded. "And what did you do?"

"I took him to a place in the Amazon and made sure he was as far from civilization as possible," Liv explained. "I told the big fella that he was never to go near people again."

"And he understood you?"

"I'm not sure. He grunted and nodded a lot."

"What did you tell...well, you know?"

"I lied," Liv confessed. "It might come back to bite me on the ass, but I wasn't going to dispose of a troll who was doing nothing wrong."

Rory looked mildly impressed. "Which is why you can't exterminate the Zonks."

Liv agreed with a nod. "You mentioned the ghosts, and that it was related to leeches?"

"Yeah. Ghosts, in essence, are bundles of magical energy, like vaults of it," Rory explained as Liv lapped beer from the top of her mug. She half-stood to give her the right angle to drink like a dog. "You want to try a straw, half-pint?"

She shook her head. "Nah. I almost got this."

"Sure you do." Rory scoffed. "When you or I use magic, we draw on power sources, like elements, for instance. However, a ghost's energy is trapped within it."

"So they are like batteries, in a way?"

"Exactly," Rory said. "It makes a lot more sense to me that whoever is leeching magical energy is using the ghosts somehow."

"Like drawing them in?"

Rory lifted his mug and drank another third. "Maybe. We need more information."

"Which is why we're here." Liv picked up her mug with both hands and tilted it to her mouth, but it slipped in her fingers, spilling beer down her chin and front.

Rory howled with laughter when she dropped the mug. It looked like she'd taken a bath in the lager.

Liv brought her arm across her mouth, then shook like a dog and sent beer all over Rory.

"So why did you bring me here, except for your entertainment?" Liv asked, attempting to lift the beer again. Having lost half its contents, it was easier to pick up. Liv took a long drink and set it down with a thud.

"Who's your friend, Rory?" one of the gnomes asked, pulling up a barstool to their table. He was only about three feet tall and wore an expression like the mustache under his nose was washed in sour milk.

Rory scrutinized him and nodded in Liv's direction. "This is Helga Dobo."

Liv couldn't cover her grimace. *Helga?* What kind of horrid name was that?

"Helga, you keep drinking like that and our friend Rory will have to carry you out of here," the gnome advised her.

"Where're the glasses you use?" Liv asked him. "That might work better for me."

The other gnomes around the table looked up like she'd

just said fighting words. They all pushed away from the table in unison, slipping off their chairs.

Liv looked at Rory. "What? What did I say?"

Rory leaned closer as the other three gnomes waddled over. "They don't like to be reminded that they aren't as big as giants."

Liv looked at the four three-foot-tall gnomes and then Rory and laughed. "Isn't that about like walking around in a bikini during a snowstorm? You can pretend all you want, but the truth is evident."

"Liv…" Rory cautioned.

"Liv?" the gnome questioned. "I thought you said her name was Helga, a good strong gnome's name. Who is this 'Liv?' That's a magician's name."

Liv looked at Rory and then the gnomes. "Wait, you thought I was a gnome?" She stood up, looking down at the gnome and his friends. "I'm obviously not a gnome. I'm, like, almost five feet tall."

"Liv…" Rory said again.

"As a female gnome that makes you slightly above average, but by magicians' standards, you're a runt," one of the gnomes said.

Liv picked up her beer mug and took a long drink, finishing its contents. Well, nearly finishing it, since some dripped down her chin and dribbled down her front again. She let the mug thud on the table, earning the attention of everyone in the bar.

Rory leaned back in his seat, looking at the ceiling. "And I thought that bringing you in here would be a mistake."

Liv waved him off, swaying slightly. "I got this, Mr.

Laurens." She looked down at the gnomes. "If I said something to offend you, I'm deeply sorry."

"We don't take kindly to people looking down on us," one of the four said.

"How are people *supposed* to look at you?" Liv asked with a hiccup.

Rory tossed his head back, sighing loudly. "Here we go."

Liv was about to ask if she could help him polish off his beer when a sharp smack knocked her across the shin. She hopped straight up, grabbing her leg, and looked down to see the closest gnome pulling his tiny foot back.

"You kicked me, you little shit!" Liv yelled.

"And there's a whole lot more of where that came from, magician," the gnome warned. "We will be outside, waiting to teach you a lesson."

The gnomes clapped twice in unison and disappeared.

Liv blinked dully and looked at Rory. "Wait, where'd they go? I thought they were about to break into a cute little song and dance?"

"They know better than to throw down in Cindy's pub. They went outside to wait for you," Rory answered dryly. "They plan on kicking your ass."

CHAPTER THIRTY

L iv laughed. "You've got to be kidding me? Those little guys want to scrap with me?"

Rory crossed his thick arms over his chest. "I wouldn't underestimate them. Gnome magic is strong, and you're not trained in combat."

Liv scoffed at him. "I know how to fight."

"You know how to start fights," he countered.

Liv grabbed Rory's beer, not asking permission, and drank. He didn't appear the least bit upset as he watched her gulp the rest of its contents. When it was empty. she put it back on the table and burped. "Let's go kick some gnome butt."

Rory looked at the giants at the bar and sighed. "You're on your own, magician."

"Fine," Liv said, taking a step forward and swaying as she headed for the exit.

When they reached the alley, Liv was grateful for the night air, which brought much-needed coolness to her cheeks.

Stretching between the buildings on either side of the alley were the four gnomes, standing shoulder to shoulder and blocking the path.

"They think they are so tough with their hostile looks and fat heads," Liv said, looking at the little men twenty yards away.

"They don't fight fair," Rory warned.

"Hence the fact that there are four of them and one of me."

"Yes, but you're a woman. In gnome culture that's considered fair, since the females are usually bigger and stronger."

"I don't resemble a gnome," Liv argued, putting her fists on her hips.

"Not an attractive one, that's for sure."

"Hey, I don't have a bulbous nose or hair growing out of my ears, so I think I'm far more attractive than gnomes."

Rory shook his head. "Your features are too dainty, and your shoulders too narrow. An attractive female has a nose that fills her face and is built like a linebacker, like Cindy."

"The bartender in there is a gnome?"

"Yes, and you're stalling," Rory said.

Liv looked at the gnomes, who hadn't budged. "I am not. I'm just giving them time to figure out their strategy." She puffed out her chest, holding out her arms wide. "You're going to need it, gnomes!"

"Talking smack will only delay the inevitable," Rory warned her, grabbing the back of Liv's shirt and hauling her off the ground.

Her feet kicked and she tried to bat him away, with zero success. "Hey, what are you doing?"

"I'm helping you," he told her.

"Helping me would have been teaching me combat magic before now."

Rory pulled back his arm. "It's never too late for a lesson." He threw Liv across the space, and she landed at the gnomes' feet.

She looked up at the little men and growled, "You boys want a fight? I'll give you one, but get ready to run home crying to Momma."

"Stop talking so much and start fighting!" Rory yelled.

Liv pushed up onto her hands and knees and looked back at him. "It's courteous to let them know what they've gotten themselves into."

"Gnomes aren't close to their mothers."

Liv nodded, looking up at the closest gnome. "Get ready to run home to your ugly wife."

The gnome to the side stepped forward, his boot stomping on Liv's fingers.

She howled in pain, yanking her hand to her chest as she rolled over on her back and popped to her feet. "Seriously, you little shits kick shins and stomp on fingers? That's so stereotypical. What are you going to do next, bite me?"

Two of the gnomes sprinted for her, their grubby hands above their heads as they yelled in rage.

Liv made a feint to the right, causing one gnome to run past her, and she pulled a trash can away from the wall and placed it directly in front of the other gnome. He ran straight into it, falling on his ass from the collision.

Liv laughed, reaching down and grabbing the lid for the trash can and holding it like a shield.

One of the two gnomes still standing raised a hand and a ball of red light poured from it.

"Hey, Roar? What's that?"

"What does it look like?" he yelled from his place on the sidelines.

"A fireball."

The gnome wound his arm up like he was about to throw a baseball.

"Bingo," Rory said. "Try not to get burned."

"Thanks, buddy." Liv held up the lid as the fireball soared at her face. She deflected it, bouncing it in the direction of the gnomes on the ground, who were trying to get up.

Both standing gnomes now produced fireballs and prepared to throw them at Liv. Beside her the other gnomes were baring their teeth, looking like they were about to charge.

"Ummm, any bright ideas, giant?"

"Stay vigilant," Rory answered, sounding amused.

Liv darted to the side as one of the gnomes charged, and a fireball whirled by her, nearly singing her pants. "Thanks, but I was thinking of a more tactical approach."

"Use magic," Rory suggested.

Liv ducked as a fireball soared over her head, landing with a blast on the brick building behind her and sending sparks everywhere. "Thanks, but again I need something more specific."

"What's the best way to fight fire?" Rory asked.

All four gnomes were now throwing fireballs, not giving Liv a chance to regroup after nearly being burned.

She used a trashcan to block her bottom half while using the lid to deflect anything higher.

"Fight fire with fire, right?" Liv asked.

"Nope, dumb human," Rory corrected. "Fight fire with ice."

"I don't think you know your clichés." As Liv jumped out from behind her trashcan three fireballs barreled into it, blasting it out of the way.

"Think 'ice' and try to pull the energy from your surroundings, since you're drunk and can't rely on your internal source," Rory advised.

Liv gawked at him, taking her focus from the fight for a split second. That nearly cost her all the hair on her head. A fireball whirled by, the flames singing her eyebrows. "I'm not drunk. Would a drunk be able to do this?"

Liv rolled over on her side as the gnomes lobbed consecutive fireballs at her. She bounced to her feet and darted around the gnomes, throwing off their formation.

"I'm not sure why one would want to," Rory answered.

A fireball ricocheted off the wall behind Liv and hit the back of her makeshift shield, making her drop it. She went to grab for it, but one of the gnomes charged at her, leaping into the air with his hands clawing forward.

Liv held up her palm and thought about ice, and a frozen sensation gathered around her. Pushing the energy out, she felt the confidence she'd come to associate with magic.

The gnome froze in midair for a moment before crashing to the ground like a statue made of ice. He rolled to the side, frost covering the end of his nose and his head.

"Hey, now!" Liv said, striking a fighting stance and

SARAH NOFFKE & MICHAEL ANDERLE

facing off with the other three gnomes. They paused, regarding her hesitantly.

"Don't use the same spell twice when fighting," Rory called.

"Because it will drain me of too much energy?" Liv asked, exhaustion suddenly sweeping over her.

"Because it's dumb and your opponent will know what to expect."

The gnomes held their hands close together, and something began to form between their palms. Snowballs.

"Seriously, what's y'all's fascination with balls?" Liv asked, looking around for her shield.

"See, now they've pulled on ice magic, which will make your freezing spell ineffective," Rory pointed out.

"So I use fire?" Liv asked.

Rory rolled his eyes. "Not now that you've told them what you're going to do."

Liv ducked and dodged, trying to avoid the snowballs coming at her with lightning speed.

"Damn, you boys should think about going into the minor leagues," Liv said, spinning to avoid another attack. "Well, maybe Little League. Not sure you're tall enough to play with the big boys."

The snowballs came faster. Liv felt like she was doing a horrible dance, trying to avoid getting hit by an ice attack. The balls that slammed into the trashcans left dents, which didn't make her feel any better about the snow versus the fire.

"Stop stalling and attack!" Rory yelled.

"I. Am. Trying," Liv shouted, jumping back and forth. She held up her hand and thought of how much she needed to disable the gnomes so she could plan an attack. Suddenly the closest one began to rise into the air. Liv squinted, trying to figure out what was happening to him. The one behind him also rose, and around him was a soapy film.

"I put them in bubbles!" Liv exclaimed and ducked as a snowball whooshed over her head.

She held up her hand at the only free gnome. "Hey! You ready for bath time too, little fella?"

The gnome froze, looking up at his mates, who were rising higher, the wind now pushing them sideways. Once they hit the side of the building, they would be falling straight back down again.

The snowball the gnome was about to throw dissolved as he took several steps back, then spun and raced in the other direction. His friends collided with each other as they crashed to the pavement. Both looked disoriented when they hit the ground, rolling over and giving Liv one last vengeful look before fleeing down the alley, leaving their frozen pal behind.

"Yeah, you *better* run!" Liv yelled, pumping her fist in the air.

She turned to Rory, looking victorious. "See, I did it!"

"You sure did," he said plainly.

"Now we can talk to whoever can help me track down the leeched magic."

Rory nodded in the direction the gnomes had fled. "Yeah, well, you better get running, because you just frightened them off."

CHAPTER THIRTY-ONE

"It was the gnomes who could help me?" Liv asked, her hands on her hips. "Why didn't you tell me?"

"I didn't have a chance. You'd already started a brawl with them, and then it was too late."

"Well, we'll have to find someone else," Liv stated.

Rory shook his head. "Gnomes are the only ones I'm aware of who have an energy meter for tracking stored magic."

Liv gave him a pointed stare. "Again, something I think you should have told me before I went and offended them."

"Looks like you're going to have to settle for option two," Rory said.

"What's that?"

"Go to the House of Seven and ask them if they have something similar that would work?"

Liv cringed looking down at her jeans, which were burned in places, and at her dirty t-shirt. "Right, well, I need to change first." She pointed at herself, but nothing happened.

"What are you trying to do?" Rory asked.

"I'm trying to change my clothes."

He shielded his eyes. "Don't do that in front of me. What if something goes wrong?"

"Well, then, I guess you'll see a boob."

"And lose my lunch," he said with a look of distaste. "Also, where are you pulling these clothes from? Your apartment?"

"Or wherever. I haven't done laundry, so probably not from my place," Liv replied. "My sister put me in clothes, but I have no idea where they came from."

"Magicians have a service they use to manifest things," Rory explained. "It consumes less energy than creating an object from nothing."

"A service?" Liv asked.

"Yes, the service has a storage warehouse of most of the common things magicians manifest."

"Like a black combat suit?" Liv asked, thinking of the outfit Sophia had put her into.

"Yes, as well as other things," Rory explained. "However, unless you have a subscription to this magician warehouse of supplies, you're going to have to summon from your apartment or create from nothing, which you look too drunk to successfully pull off."

"Again, I'm not drunk," Liv said, staggering a few feet to the side and then turning back around to face Rory. "Okay, well, maybe I'm buzzed. That seems like the way to show up to the House of Seven: buzzed and dirty."

The Chamber of the Tree was empty when Liv fell through the Door of Reflection. She was seriously tired of having the experience of going blind while indistinct figures huddled around her.

The white tiger stepped out of the shadows when she looked around the room, taking in details she hadn't noticed when standing before the Councilors.

He gave her a pointed stare that seemed to see all the way to her soul.

"So what's your deal?" Liv asked the white tiger, feeling hiccups coming on.

He blinked at her impassively.

"And the crow? What's that about?"

The white tiger strode over to her, halting when he was dangerously close. His gaze was on her pocket for a long moment before he looked up at her.

Taking the hint, Liv reached into her pocket, finding her mother's ring in there, where she'd put it that afternoon. She also found something she hadn't remembered being in her pocket: a one-hundred-dollar bill. Liv's brow scrunched in confusion. She'd just washed these jeans, which meant the money had recently been put into her pocket. But how? She shoved it back down and held up the ring. "Are you going to tell them I have this?"

The tiger didn't answer out loud, but his gaze seemed to communicate a whole host of information. She held the ring up to the light radiating from the tree. "I don't understand what I'm supposed to do with it."

Symbols like in the long hallway between the entrance and the Chamber radiated behind the ring. Liv pulled the ring down, startled. The symbols disappeared. Again she lifted the ring so it was even with the tree and the many names of the families. The symbols appeared behind the ring again, floating in the air.

"Wait, what's that about?"

"What's what about?" a voice called behind Liv.

She tensed, shoving the ring back in her pocket as she spun to face Decar Sinclair. The other Warrior wore a silver robe that accented his white hair, making him appear almost monochromatic. He studied Liv as she worked the ring into her pocket.

"Oh, nothing," Liv answered. "I was referring to the broken finger I got tonight." She held up her middle finger, showing him the bruised appendage while flipping him off.

He grimaced. "However did you do that?"

"Bar fight," she said simply. "Have you seen my brother?"

Decar nodded. "Yes, he's in Adler's study. I'll lead you that way."

Liv wanted to decline the offer, but she didn't know where Adler's study was. She was feeling a bit too sassy and sort of afraid she'd say something else to offend him.

Following Decar through the Wall of Reflection and the large door to the living quarters, Liv kept an eye out for Plato. Hopefully, he was somewhere close by and could aid her if she couldn't keep her mouth shut.

"You realize that Warriors aren't supposed to get into bar fights and act in a disorderly manner," Decar said, his tone overflowing with condescension.

"What? I totally thought that was in the job description. Well, shucks! I might have to rethink this whole protect magic thingy."

Decar looked back at her as he climbed the stairs. "For now, no one knows who you are, because you're new. However, in time, magicians and creatures will know you, and your behavior will reflect on the House of Seven."

"Which is why I wore my good jeans today."

Decar looked at her burned pants and shook his head disapprovingly. He pointed to a door marked with the Sinclairs' family crest. Liv remembered her father saying that he argued with Adler Sinclair more than any of the other Councilors. "It's healthy to have a devil's advocate," her father had said once, but Liv had sensed that there were more than common disagreements between the two.

Liv charged past him and knocked three times on the door, and a moment later it slid back.

Stepping through, Liv's nose was accosted by the strong incense in the air. She covered it and looked around the large room.

"Hello, Ms. Beaufont," Adler called from the far side of the room, where he sat across from Clark. "What can we do for you? Aren't you supposed to be on a case?"

Liv nodded. "Yes, but I have a question for my brother."

Clark stood and strode over to Liv, taking in her rough appearance. "Are you all right?"

"I'm great," Liv lied, her head swimming from the beer she'd drunk too fast. It was finally hitting her, or maybe it was the incense in the air that was making her woozy.

"You smell like you've been playing with gnomes." Adler sneered.

"Yes, there's a herd of them on my kickball team," Liv said, looking over Clark's shoulder.

"Was that how you broke your finger?" Adler asked, eying her over his spectacles, a wine goblet in his hands.

"She said she got into a bar fight," Decar offered.

"Are you drunk?" Adler asked.

"Are you ugly?" Liv questioned. Clark's hand shot to his forehead.

"Olivia, you must not—"

"Yes, it would appear that your sister has had a bit too much to drink, Mr. Beaufont," Adler stated. "Why don't you take her away until she's sobered up?"

"Won't help. You'll still be ugly," Liv said as Clark grabbed her arm and pulled her through the open door. He dragged her up another set of stairs and didn't release her until he'd opened the door marked with the Beaufonts' family crest.

The lights were dimmed in the living room and Sophia was asleep on the sofa, a teddy bear pressed to her chest.

"What were you thinking?" Clark asked, looking Liv over. "You offended Adler."

"I also flipped off Decar," Liv told him proudly.

Clark's eyes sank shut for a beat. "You need to learn to behave yourself. We operate with a certain level of decorum here."

"'Boring stuffiness' is what I'm calling it."

Clark pinched his nose. "You do smell awful. Were you really hanging out with gnomes tonight?"

"Kicking their asses, but sort of," Liv answered.

"Why would you go near them?"

Liv looked at Sophia for a moment before reconnecting with Clark. "Were you always such a snob, or did hanging out with Adler and Decar make it rub off on you?"

"Liv, gnomes are—"

"Just like us," Liv said, cutting him off. "That was what Mom and Dad used to say, remember? When the Seven threw the book at gnomes or other creatures, Mom and Dad fought for their rights, saying that magicians shouldn't be treated differently."

Clark shook his head. "I remember. Of course, I do! It's just that they aren't here, and the current administration—"

"Is the same as it used to be, except without Dad as a Councilor, there's no one to oppose Adler's cruel and unjust rule."

"You don't get it," Clark said dismissively. "You haven't been here long enough."

"Or maybe because of that, I get it a whole lot better than you do," Liv countered. "Anyway, I need your help. I found some Zonks in the underground tunnels where we think the leeching is happening."

"We?" Clark questioned.

She shook her head. "Plato and me."

Clark's expression didn't look like he was convinced. "So Zonks are behind the leeching?"

"No, they are fix-it fairies," Liv stated. "I think they were leading me to the cause."

"Zonks need magic to fix things," Clark said, starting to pace in front of Liv. "It makes perfect sense that it would be them doing the leeching."

"No, it doesn't," Liv argued. "They were sealing something. Maybe trying to prevent the leeching. I need to investigate more. I'm looking for a way to measure magical energy. Do you have something like that?"

Clark considered her for a moment. "No. If you've found Zonks at the place, then they are responsible. Protocol dictates that you apprehend and stop them."

"No, Clark. You're missing the point. They aren't the cause, I just know it, but I need to investigate more. Will you help me?"

Clark stopped pacing. "By giving you something to measure magical energy?"

"Yes. That way I can follow the trail and find out who is behind this."

"Zonks are behind this. That's obvious to me. Take care of them and close the case. The sooner you do, the better you'll look."

"The better *you'll* look," Liv countered.

"Hey, you're already getting enough heat for your behavior," Clark said. "The best thing would be to complete the case and prove to the Councilors that you're trying your best, especially after tonight."

"Hey," Liv said, using the same inflection as Clark had. "This is *my* case, assigned to me by you and your jerk cronies. I'll be solving it how I see fit, and you're just going to have to deal with it. This isn't an open-and-shut case. I know it. I can feel it."

Clark chewed his lip. "What did you do with the troll?"

"I killed it," Liv answered.

He shook his head and charged for his bedroom. "Damn it. This isn't going to work if you're going to lie and break rules."

"How else was this ever going to work?" Liv asked. "That's who I've always been, and I'm not changing now."

Clark slammed the door to his room, making Sophia stir on the couch.

The little blonde haired girl sat up, looking disoriented. "Liv?" she asked, rubbing her eyes. "What are you doing here?"

Liv came over to her sister and knelt beside her. "Just stopped in for a moment. Can I carry you to bed and tuck you in?"

The blue eyes that looked up at Liv made her knees weak. How had she missed the girl so much and never realized it until that moment? "Yes, please," Sophia requested, holding out a small hand for her.

Liv pulled her up and then scooped Sophia into her arms, carrying her to bed where she should have been all along.

CHAPTER THIRTY-TWO

Dropping wires and bolts and other parts behind her, Liv carried a mound of broken appliances to the front workstation. She dumped them on the table, allowing them to roll before coming to rest.

"You think you can do this?" Plato asked, jumping onto the counter and inspecting a broken compass.

"Why are gnomes the only ones who can make magic meters or whatever we're going to call it?"

"Because they have a natural tendency toward being able to gauge things. They don't even have thermometers and such."

Liv licked her finger and put it in the air. "I do too. It's a crisp sixty-eight degrees in here."

"You know I have complete faith in you, but what's your backup plan if this doesn't work?" Plato asked.

Liv began disassembling the compass. "That's not how 'complete faith' works."

"I just think having other options is important."

Liv tapped the compass, sending magic into the device

and making it spin wildly. "I'm going to make friends with the ugly fairies, I guess."

"They did say something about ghosts and formed that image of a man, so they obviously know something," Plato agreed, looking up as Shane entered the shop carrying the printer Liv had fixed.

"Hey, there," she greeted him, pulling the face off a clock. "Is the printer working okay?"

Shane slid it onto the countertop. "Thing is that it's working too well."

"Too well?" Liv questioned. "I think that's a first."

Shane pulled a sheet of paper from the tray of the printer and handed it to Liv. It was a color picture of a red sports car. All the details were crisp, and in the background, the trees were bright and perfectly framing the vehicle.

Liv looked the picture over and handed it back. "Color laser printers have come a long way recently."

"That's the thing," Shane said, looking at the image. "This isn't a color printer."

"Oh, I upgraded it for you," Liv answered, thinking fast.

Shane's brow furrowed. "But something else weird happens. It's got the copy option, right?"

"Yes," Liv said, looking between Plato and the printer, not excited about what else weird the printer might be doing.

Shane lifted the top of the printer and put the picture of the car flat on the scanner. He then pressed the green button, and the copier began scanning. A moment later it churned out an exact replica of the original.

Liv took it. "I'm not sure I see the issue here."

Shane held up the plug. "It's not plugged in."

"Oh," Liv said, her eyes widening. "That's weird."

"Really weird," Shane agreed. "I noticed it this morning after making a dozen copies and then realizing that my assistant had unplugged the printer last night. I can't even begin to understand how it's working. It's like magic or something."

Liv laughed abruptly and loudly. "Magic? That's ridiculous. I'm sure there's an explanation. I bet it has a built-in battery."

Shane scratched his head, staring at the printer. "I don't know…"

Liv waved off his skepticism. "Now I remember. This model does come with a backup battery that will last for a little while until you plug it in. That will recharge it for the next time you need to use the printer off the grid."

"'Battery?'" Shane questioned. "'Off the grid?' Is that really a thing printers have now?"

Liv laughed. "Oh, where have you been? Of course, they do."

Shane let out a giant breath. "Well, that's a relief. I really didn't know what to make of this. I thought I was losing my mind."

"Not quite yet," Liv answered, turning her attention back to her current project and silently dismissing Shane.

He nodded, picking the printer back up with a grunt. "Well, thanks. And I appreciate you upgrading it to color. That's a nice feature."

"You're welcome." Liv kept her eyes down as Shane exited, working to keep her expression neutral.

When the front door was shut, Liv let out a breath. "Well, that was close."

"How many of the other appliances you fixed are doing strange things, do you think?" Plato asked.

"If I know my luck, all of them."

"What are you going to do?" Plato questioned.

"Move away," Liv answered. "But seriously, how do I fix things with magic without getting unintended consequence?"

Plato thought for a moment. "Maybe try fixing exactly what's wrong."

Liv nodded. "Yeah. Most of the stuff I fixed, I just zapped it until it worked."

"Which meant that the magic would fix anything that was wrong, or even lacking."

"But if I know what's wrong and target that…"

"Then you won't have hand mixers that can make a cake without help," Plato said, finishing her sentence.

Liv's hand shot to her mouth. "Mrs. Holly. I hope the blender and hand mixer haven't taken over her house."

"I bet the old loon doesn't think a thing about it," Plato said. "And if she does tell anyone, they'll just think it's another of her far-fetched tales."

Liv nodded. No one was going to believe Mrs. Holly, but there were other clients who could cause a stir if their devices were working without electricity or trying to launch rocket ships.

"You made this?" Rory asked, turning the hand-held device over in his fingers.

"Well, I more or less put it together," Liv answered.

Rory switched on the device and watched as the needle toggled back and forth before pointing directly at Liv.

She furrowed her brow. "Why isn't it pointing at you?"

He shrugged. "I don't know how you have this calibrated."

"It's supposed to point to the largest store of magic," Liv explained. "I figured that would lead us to the leeched energy."

Rory lifted an eyebrow. "Then between you and me, the meter is stating you're more powerful."

Liv waved him off. "The House mentioned that my magic would even out. It's surging because I just had it unlocked."

Rory gave her an unconvinced look. "I've never heard of that before, but I also don't know many who have had their magic locked. Just those magicians who don't cooperate with the House."

"Anyway, do you think it will work?" Liv asked, taking the device back.

"There's only one way to find out," Rory replied. "But remember that I can't get into those tunnels, so you're on your own."

Liv pulled her phone out of her pocket. "Yeah, but it will be just like you're there the entire time."

CHAPTER THIRTY-THREE

"So where is the hole?" Liv asked, looking around for the hidden tunnel.

Rory pointed. "It's straight ahead."

Like a blind person, Liv reached forward, feeling across the concrete wall.

"The entrance is over here," Plato said from several feet away, looking up at the wall.

Liv glanced at Rory. "How long were you going to let me grope the wall before you told me?"

A smile cracked his face. "You'd have found it eventually."

"Giants are awful people," Liv said to Plato.

"I could have told you that," the cat said before jumping through the wall and disappearing.

Liv found the edge of the hole and began climbing through, careful to not fall on the other side. When she was safely on the ground, she raised her phone. Thankfully, she still had reception due to the magical enhancements the

House had made to the device. She video-called Rory, hearing his phone ring only a few feet away.

After three rings she said, "Would you pick up already?"

"I don't want to seem too antsy," Rory answered.

"Oh, for the love of all that is holy!"

Rory picked up after the next ring. "Hello, this is Rory."

Liv blinked at him on the phone. "Yeah, I sort of knew that, dumbass."

He shook his head. "Who is this? I can't make out your face in the dark."

Then, "Oh, it's Liv," Rory said, recognition dawning in his voice. "I can see your face now."

"Ha-ha." Liv held her hand up, recreating the ball of light without having to mutter the incantation this time.

She pulled out the magic meter she'd constructed from the bag strapped to her side and turned it on. At first, the needle toggled back and forth, halting on her for a moment before spinning in the opposite direction.

"Apparently you're not the most powerful source of magic down here," Plato said, looking at the device.

Ahead she spied the green light she'd seen before and slid up next to the wall. "The Zonks are here," she said in a whisper.

"Just avoid offending them and they should ignore you," Rory's voice came through the phone on her butt. "You can do that right? Not be offensive for once?"

Liv thought for a moment. "I'm not sure I can. It might pain me."

"Well, then suffer," Rory answered.

Liv continued down the tunnel. "How do you know

they will ignore me and not try to take a bite out of my body like before?"

"Zonks are used to ignoring humans while working," Rory explained. "They usually go unnoticed above ground, blending into their surroundings, but in this location, they aren't disguising their appearance. That probably means they are using most of their magic to fix whatever the problem is."

"I'd be disguising myself too if I looked like them," Liv said. "However, I don't think there's enough Botox and plastic surgery to fully fix their ugly faces."

"Remember what I said about not being offensive," Rory stated.

"Right," Liv chirped. "But that just means I have to insult you extra."

"Whatever it takes," Rory agreed.

When the tunnel split, Liv followed the meter, which pointed to the right, the opposite direction from where the fairies' green light was radiating.

Ahead she spied a shimmering figure. "I've located another ghost. Do you think that's the source of the magic?"

"Doubtful," Plato answered. "One ghost wouldn't hold more power than you."

Another transparent figure walked through a wall, falling into line behind the first.

"How about two?" Liv asked.

"There are two ghosts?" Rory questioned.

"Three, actually," Plato answered when another ghost slipped down from the ceiling, joining the others, which were marching forward like zombies.

"Three still wouldn't be enough," Rory stated. "In order to have more magic than you, I'm thinking it would have to be more like ten or twelve ghosts."

"Damn," Liv breathed, surprised.

She continued following them, keeping a safe distance from the ghosts, who were approaching a lit room ahead on the left.

A set of voices echoed from the area. Plato halted first, sidling up against the wall. His ears tilted as he listened.

"There are two men talking," he said when Liv looked down at him curiously.

"Be careful, Liv," Rory warned. "Whoever is up there has this major source of magic."

"How do we know they aren't the actual source?" Liv asked in a whisper.

"We don't," Rory answered. "Get a closer look but don't get caught."

"Copy that." Liv slid up against the wall as a ghost disappeared around the corner. She sensed something behind her and turned to find yet another ghost approaching.

"As long as the conductor is on, they'll continue to come," a man said up ahead. "However, we are going to have to shut it down soon to recharge."

"If those damn fairies would stop blocking our efforts, we would be done already," another man said.

"Yeah, whatever they are doing is hindering the ghosts from coming through any entrance but this one," the first man said. "But look, we are still getting a few through here."

The other man laughed, a cold, hollow sound. "Only a few hundred more and we'll have enough."

"But like I said, we need to shut this down in a few minutes."

"Well, I need to grab something to eat anyway," the other man said.

Liv looked down at Plato, her eyes widening. They didn't have much time. She needed to get closer and see what they were dealing with. She sped up soundlessly. When she reached the entrance to the room, Liv froze, pulling her phone out of her pocket.

She slipped it around the side of the door so that Rory could see what was in the room before she did. Once she was sure he had gotten a good look, she held the phone up and looked at him straight on. His face had gone completely slack.

He mouthed the words, "Get out now."

CHAPTER THIRTY-FOUR

L iv's heart was racing as she slid through the hole in the wall. Before her feet even hit the ground, Rory grabbed her by the wrist and pulled her forward.

"Look, just because you're bigger and stronger, you can't pull me around like a ragdoll," she scolded as he half-dragged her down the tunnel.

"Can't I, though?" he asked, his voice gruff.

"What did you see?" Liv asked when he'd slowed a bit.

"A magic battery powered by ghosts," Plato answered.

Rory nodded. "They have something that attracts ghosts, and then they walk into a large conduit. It looked like they were trapped in there."

"That's the leeched source of magic?" Liv asked.

"Yes, and I recognized one of the men," Rory added. "His name is Valentino, and he's not the kind of magician you want to mess with. He's been creating trouble for giants and elves for a long time."

"And now it sounds like he's trapping ghosts," Liv stated.

Rory stopped when they surfaced from the underground tunnels. "It makes perfect sense. He traps the ghosts, and they power the magical source."

"The question is, what is he going to do with all that energy?" Liv posed.

A troubled look crossed Rory's face. "It's not good. We're going to have to shut him down."

"'We?'" Liv questioned. "You can't even get down there. I need a plan. Maybe the House can help me? If there is that much energy, I shouldn't risk going in there on my own."

Rory nodded. "Yeah, I think this case just got a little out of your league."

Adler's eyelids fluttered with annoyance when Liv finished telling the Councilors what she'd found. She was the only Warrior in the Chamber of the Tree.

"Do you have any evidence of this thing you've seen?" he asked.

"No, but—"

"And you didn't see it with your own eyes, is that right?" Bianca questioned.

"Well, no, but my cat did," Liv said, wishing that Plato was standing beside her instead of hiding somewhere in the room.

"A lynx, you mean," Adler corrected. "They are notorious for being untrustworthy."

"Not Plato," Liv said defiantly. She couldn't tell them that Rory had also seen the source of the magic because mentioning a giant would immediately discredit the story, not to mention that they'd find out that she was working with Rory and Clark would probably die from mortification.

Adler sighed. "I'm sorry, but I'm not sure what you expect us to do here."

"There's a man named Valentino, and he's trapping ghosts," Liv explained for the third time. "We need to go after him."

"*We* aren't Warriors," Adler stated. "You are, and it sounds like the problem is with the Zonks. You saw them with your own eyes putting a strange substance into the walls."

"Ugly fairies aren't the problem," Liv insisted, catching the frustrated expression on Clark's face. His face had grown more annoyed as she'd told the Councilors what she'd seen.

Adler tapped his fingers impatiently on the bench. "Do you know that Zonks are notorious for creating disturbances all over the world? They hide behind this persona of being helpful, but they are actually a huge nuisance."

Bianca nodded. "It makes sense that they would be behind this."

"It was Valentino," Liv argued, nearly stomping.

Adler shook his head, his white hair swaying with the movement. "Valentino is a huge supporter of the House. He would never do anything to abuse magic. If he's working on something, you are to stay as far from it as possible." Adler looked down the bench quickly. "Do you all agree that Ms. Beaufont should go after the Zonks and dispel them? They appear to be the problem, agreed?"

There was a collective muttering of "yes" from the group.

Liv sighed. "We don't have any evidence of that."

Adler held out his hand and a ball of wax materialized above his palm. It floated through the air and hovered in front of Liv. "You are to take that and use it to get rid of the Zonks."

Liv reached out and took the ball. "How?"

Adler sighed. "If you had accepted the House's training, you'd know how to use a ShimVen."

Liv put the ball of wax in her pocket. "I still don't think the Zonks are the problem."

Adler slammed his hand down. "It's not a Warrior's responsibility to think. That's what we Councilors do. You are to take our advice and proceed. Is that clear?"

Liv looked to the other Councilors for back up. Clark had his face partially covered. Raina offered a sympathetic smile but remained quiet.

It was Hester who finally spoke. "Valentino's behavior is suspect, but if you take out the Zonks and the magical leeching doesn't stop, we could extend the investigation."

Adler huffed. "I really don't think that will be necessary. We'll get to that after Ms. Beaufont completes her case." He looked down at her sharply. "In the future, you shouldn't need to convene with us so often, but rather complete your case based on the information we've provided you. Take out the Zonks, and I'm sure we will be done with this."

Liv let out a breath, wishing Clark would look at her directly. Feeling defeated, Liv's shoulders slumped. "Yeah, okay. I'll go exterminate some ugly fairies if that's what you all want."

CHAPTER THIRTY-FIVE

L iv's first day off all week, and she was planning how to kill a horde of fairies.

"Remember back in the day when we used to catch a matinee on Sundays and not plot the destruction of innocent creatures?" Liv asked Plato as they waited for Rory by the entrance to the underground.

Plato shrugged. "I always snoozed through the movies. I prefer adventure."

Liv tossed the ShimVen into the air. "Yeah, I guess so. I do miss Netflixing and having a moment to sleep in, though."

"You're a Beaufont," Plato stated. "You're not someone who gets to be lazy on weekends and goof off."

"No, not anymore." Liv looked at the cat sideways. "By the way—"

"No one says 'by the way' casually. The phrase should be, 'I've been working up to ask you something.'"

"Okay, fine," Liv continued. "I've been working up to

ask you how you found me the day I left the House of Seven five years ago."

"How?" Plato questioned.

"Well, and 'why' would be good to know too."

Plato looked up as Rory approached. "Liv, I could sense you a hundred miles away."

"Because of my magic?"

He shook his head. "Because of your pain. I sensed you needed a friend."

Liv nodded. "That I did."

She didn't completely buy that her oldest friend had made her acquaintance simply because he sensed she needed him, but she wanted to believe it with all her being. Deep down, Liv knew that Plato had had a very important reason for joining her that fateful day and never leaving her side since. However, she didn't want to spoil this moment, or maybe she didn't want to know the truth.

Rory dashed forward, catching the ShimVen before it dropped back into Liv's palm. "What are you doing?"

Liv gave him a strange look. "It's a ball of wax. I'm playing with it."

Rory shook his head. "The ball of wax is encasing the ShimVens, which are meat-eating beetles."

Liv shivered. "That's how they expect me to deal with the Zonks?"

Rory wore a similar expression of repulsion as he shoved the ball back into her hand. "Yeah. What a horrible way to take out magical creatures!"

Liv shook her head, carefully pushing the ball into her pocket. "Don't worry, I don't plan to use it on the Zonks."

"So you're going against the council's orders?" Rory asked.

"Of course I am," Liv stated. "The Zonks aren't the problem, but I was thinking that maybe they could help us."

Rory nodded proudly. "I was thinking the same thing." He pulled out a jar of purple liquid. "I brought you a bartering gift."

"What is that? Some sort of juice?" Liv asked.

He handed it to her. "Oh, no, it's the Zonk's favorite food. Mushed eggplant spiced with crushed rolly-pollies."

"Man, is it any a wonder those things are so ugly?"

At the entrance to the room where Liv had first met the Zonks, she paused, watching the little fairies stick bits of green into the cracks. They were, as Rory had mentioned, not concerned by her presence. She wasn't sure if they even knew she was there.

After a full minute of watching them work, she cleared her throat. The fairies halted in unison, turning around like a coordinated dance. Liv kept her expression neutral as she regarded the many ugly faces. The green glow of the substance they were holding making their features seem more sinister.

"Hey, there, lovely fairies," Liv began, holding up the jar of purple paste. "So, I brought you a gift."

She unscrewed the lid and held it out.

The fairies made collective noises of excitement and formed a large heart.

Good start, Liv thought.

She pulled the jar back. "I know you're trying to stop Valentino, but it's not enough."

The Zonks' heart dissolved and they scattered, buzzing with sudden irritation.

Liv set the jar down and backed away. "I think that if we work together, we could be successful. You don't want Valentino trapping ghosts, and neither do I. You're trying to fix the problem by stopping him, but he's finding ways to get around the blocks you create." She pointed to the glowing green filling most of the room's cracks, obviously barricading the room on the other side where Valentino was working.

"I know that you're fixers, but I was wondering if, in this instance, you could try to be distractors?" Liv said, trying to ignore the buzzing as it grew louder. "I need you to create a diversion so that I can get into the room and disable whatever device he's got going."

The fairies exchanged looks and then formed a question mark.

"How?" Liv asked. "Good question. I was thinking that you should become a nuisance—"

The buzzing became almost deafening.

Liv waved her arms. "I'm not saying you *are* a nuisance; quite the opposite. But for this plan to work, you'd have to do something to draw Valentino and his men away from the ghost collector. Maybe you even break something in the tunnels that draws them out."

The fairies formed an angry face.

"If you know how to fix things, you know how to break them," Liv rushed on. "I should know. It's called reverse engineering in my business. I don't care what you do; I just need you to buy some time. Do you think you can help?"

The angry face dissolved as the fairies broke formation, looking at each other as if having a silent caucus. "Yes. Yes. Yes," they sang in unison.

Liv let out a sigh of relief. "Perfect. Let's get started."

The fairies formed a giant hand.

Liv didn't know what to make of that.

"I think they are saying to stop," Plato said.

"Then why don't they just say it?" Liv asked. "They are apparently capable of speech, even if only in chanting form."

A single Zonk flew forward, making Liv lean back, prepared to attack if needed.

The other fairies formed a large model of Liv, making her head look a little bigger than she thought it was. A few other fairies bound together, creating a larger Zonk who flew next to the model of Liv.

"You want me to take one of you with me?" Liv asked.

"Yes. Yes. Yes," they sang again.

Liv looked down at Plato. "I guess it couldn't hurt."

"They appear to communicate telepathically with each other, so having one of them with you will put you in contact with all of them," Plato reasoned.

"Good idea," Liv stated, holding out a finger for the single Zonk to shake. "I'm looking forward to working with you."

The fairy buzzed loudly and smiled, and somehow the positive gesture made the creature uglier.

If looks could kill, the Zonks could just look at Valentino and smile.

CHAPTER THIRTY-SIX

W aiting was a virtue that giants held in high esteem. However, being forced to hang out in the tunnels and not help Liv was incredibly difficult for Rory Laurens.

He'd liked the magician from the beginning, before he was even certain that she had magic. Something about the honest purity in her eyes endeared her to him. She also had John's favor, and there was no one whose judgment Rory trusted more. John was a good man, who did right by people, even if that meant he lost out. It was people like him who Rory went above and beyond to help.

"We got the Zonks' cooperation," Liv said over the phone.

Rory held it up, looking at her face on the screen. "Is that one with you now?"

"Yeah, he's like my walkie-talkie to the pack," Liv answered and glanced at the fairy flying next to her head. "Wait, are you a he? Or a she? Or a—"

"Would you shut your trap before you say something that gets you eaten?" Rory warned.

She rolled her eyes. "Those are reasonable questions. How am I supposed to use the right pronoun without the correct information?"

"Try talking less and doing more," Rory stated.

"Fine, until then you can talk to my butt," Liv said, and the phone went dark because she'd stuck it back in her pocket.

Rory heard footsteps in the tunnel, so he closed his eyes and activated a camouflage spell. They were a specialty of giants. That was how they'd gone relatively unnoticed for centuries. Most humans didn't even know that giants were all around them because so many preferred to operate fully camouflaged all the time. Rory had once been like that, but being invisible also gave him a real look into people. When they didn't know you were watching them, they didn't hide their suffering. Rory dropped his camouflage, the first of his family to do so in a century, and worked to integrate himself into society as a strangely tall person. No one had suspected him of being anything more than a freak all these years. Well, until Liv Beaufont came along.

Rory slipped back another inch, hoping he was leaving enough room for the men to pass without noticing him.

"I've already unplugged the first store," Valentino said over the phone he was holding. "And I've gone ahead and activated the second round. They want two to three sources of energy."

They? Rory wondered. *Who was Valentino working for?*

"Yeah, I know we don't have much time remaining," Valentino said, hiking up his long suit jacket. It was a pale shade of green, like something a Leprechaun would wear, made from a special fabric. "Apparently someone is onto us, so I've ordered double security as the source powers up. Anyone who tries to intervene now will have a rude awakening. I have the power of a hundred ghosts in the store I'm carrying with me."

Valentino climbed through the hole, his voice less distinct as he got farther away. "I'm coming that way. Let's turn the conduit on high. We need to get this done and get out of here."

Waiting was something Liv was horrible at. She knew that the Zonks had to do their job first, but hanging out in the dark tunnel waiting for the signal was excruciatingly frustrating. She'd put Rory on mute and parked her butt in a dark corner as the Zonks charged off to do whatever it was they were going to do. Beside her the single fairy bobbed up and down in the air, its bulging eyes visible in the dark. She noticed that up close the Zonk was...well, still super-ugly, but its features were also kind of interesting, as if a bat had gotten mixed with a rat and then bred with a moth.

Ahead Liv heard the charging of feet. She stiffened, listening for the direction. The sound dissipated. The Zonk looked at her and nodded.

Okay, here we go, Liv thought, tightness seizing in her chest. She started for the main room where the leeched energy was stored.

CHAPTER THIRTY-SEVEN

Three times Rory had tried to reach Liv with no luck. Valentino was onto them, or someone else was. He was accelerating the process. Worst of all, he already had a source of magic stored and was carrying it around with him, headed straight for Liv.

She didn't stand a chance if she faced off with someone with that much magic. He would crush her before she released a single spell.

Rory's heart raced in his chest. He had to help Liv but getting to her wasn't going to be easy. This option had always been there, but using it was dangerous. Rory removed a smooth, round stone from the pocket of his jeans. It had been passed down from his grandfather to his father and then to him. Transport stones were rare and most giants didn't have one, but his family had preserved theirs, taking care to only use it in emergencies. It had been many years since he'd chanced using it, knowing that its power would be diminished until it had time to recharge. Not only that, because its power was tied to the

Earth, there were certain risks when using the stone—ones his father had learned about the hard way. Each experience was different, and Rory had no idea what might happen this time.

He rubbed his thumb on the top of the stone and his index and middle fingers over the bottom. The rock instantly grew hotter in his hands as he thought of the location he needed to travel to. When the stone was almost too hot to touch, Rory squeezed his eyes shut, knowing that the flash that would come next would be close to blinding.

Liv was unsurprised that ghosts were filing into the room ahead. What she hadn't expected was the sheer volume of ghosts crowding into the space. They dropped from the ceiling or walked through the walls. None of them seemed concerned about her, their focus directed ahead of them.

An icy chill ran through her core as ghosts passed through her. Liv jumped to the side, but it didn't matter. There were ghosts everywhere.

When she looked around the room, she couldn't make out anything besides the shimmering white figures of the ghosts all marching forward. Then Liv noticed they were all entering a large prism in the middle of the chamber. As they approached it, the prism would blur and suck them in, making the ghosts look like they were being drawn in by a vacuum cleaner.

Liv blinked at the strange scene, noticing how shadows

moved around inside of the prism. Those had to be the trapped ghosts.

Connected to the prism were multiple hoses. One led to a huge machine which had several lights flashing. On the other side of the prism was a similar machine, but stuck into the middle was a large canister with a glass cylinder suspended in the middle. A bluish substance was rising in the cylinder.

"Is that…" Liv asked Plato.

"The converted magical energy," he answered.

"Gross. It's like he's boiling down ghosts and making them into a magical broth," Liv observed.

Plato's ear twitched. "I think someone is coming. You better hurry."

Liv looked at the Zonk, who hadn't left her side. "Your friends? Aren't they causing a diversion?"

"Yes. Yes. Yes," the fairy answered.

"Then who is coming?" Liv asked.

"I don't know, but we better get to work shutting this down," Plato answered.

In the center of a dark tunnel, Rory landed, his head hitting the ceiling with a thud.

"Ouch," he growled, rubbing his scalp. Even though he'd transported in a crouch, the stone always delivered him as it saw fit. That was part of the risk.

A low rumble rocked the ground under his feet.

There was the other risk. Earthquakes.

Dust rained from overhead. There couldn't be a worse

place to be when an earthquake struck. Rory ducked, covering his face as he raced after Liv. Not only did he need to warn her about Valentino, but he also had to get her out of this mess before she was buried because of him.

Sprinting to the first piece of machinery, Liv tried to take a quick read. This was the one that attracted the ghosts, she'd guessed. The other one converted and condensed their magical energy. She had to shut this one down first and then release the ghosts. That much she knew. Anything beyond that was still a mystery.

The ground suddenly shook under her feet and Liv spun, looking for Plato. He'd disappeared. The timing couldn't be worse.

Beside her, she heard the buzzing she'd recently come to associate with her Zonk friend. "Hey, do you know how we can disable this machine? We need the ghosts to stop coming."

"We fix. We fix. We fix," the little fairy assured her.

"Yes, I get that," Liv said as dust and rock sprinkled from overhead. She looked around, trying to figure out what was causing the commotion. Maybe Rory was stomping around somewhere.

"To fix the problem, we need to disable this machine." Liv pointed to the giant box. "Do you think you can figure out a way to jam the sensors? I could pull the wires, but I'm afraid of what that would do. I'm going to try to figure out the prism. There's got to be a way to release the trapped ghosts."

The Zonk thought for a moment and then zipped over to the machine. "Fix. Fix, Fix," the fairy chanted, almost blurring in the air as it flew.

Another tremor and Liv nearly lost her balance, falling close to the prism. Her hand went through the glass, to her surprise. As it did, she felt a sucking sensation, like the prism was trying to draw her into it. She yanked her hand back but it resisted, making her pull harder. She threw herself back and tumbled onto her bottom, rolling behind the other machine.

Liv was about to get up when two figures rushed into the room. She sank back into the shadows, watching.

CHAPTER THIRTY-EIGHT

Moving through the crumbling tunnel wasn't easy for Rory, but he tried to slide through without causing further damage. The ground shook more violently with each new earthquake. Ahead, he could hear men shouting. He had planned it so he landed only a few dozen yards from the main room. He watched as two men ran into the room, charging through ghosts. Behind them were two others.

Rory yelled, making them halt. As if they were reluctant to see what had howled, they spun around slowly.

At the sight of Rory crouched in the tunnel, they shot each other anxious looks and ran in the opposite direction. They hurried past the room and kept running.

That was easy, Rory thought.

Behind him, he heard more sounds. He turned to find two men holding weapons. Not the kind of weapons he could respect, like swords or mallets. These mortals were holding guns: a coward's weapon.

"What's going on here?" one of the men yelled as he charged into the room, looking at the conduit.

"What's one of those gross-looking insects doing in here?" the other man yelled, running over and swatting at the Zonk.

Liv had faith that the fairy could do its job, but only if given a chance.

"Hey, ugly," Liv said, jumping out of her hiding place. "Watch who you're calling gross. That's my friend."

The men spun to face her, vengeance springing to their faces at once.

"We heard a pest might be coming down here to intervene," the first man said, striding over, not at all intimidated by the sight of Liv.

"Pest?" she questioned, puffing out her chest. "I'm not the one who leeched energy off the innocent and made a mess for others to clean up." She pointed at the balding man and then his friend, who had pulled out a knife. "You two look like the pests, if I'm honest."

The man without a weapon held out his hand to the other man. "Don't worry about this one. Just looks like some newbie magician got lost. The boss said these types aren't an issue. We just detain her and he'll deal with her."

The other man laughed. "But we could tire her out before he arrives."

Liv was relieved to see the Zonk had gone back to shutting down the conduit. She just had to ensure it had time to finish. Liv didn't know how combat magic worked entirely, but it felt as though it responded to her needs. She held up her hand and muttered a phrase she'd never heard before. It literally sprang to her lips from nowhere.

"*Hel-E-Hi-Cha*," she said in a deep voice.

The first man rose off his feet, suspended in midair. The other flew back and knocked into the far wall, his knife clattering to the ground.

Liv watched as the first man kicked in the air and the other shook his head, discombobulated by the sudden assault.

"Save your energy," Plato said from a far corner or overhead or behind Liv. She spun, thinking she'd find him, but he was nowhere in sight and yet he seemed so close.

Liv nodded when she'd made a full circle. The feline was right. She didn't need to waste her precious energy on these goons. She leaned down and grabbed the knife the man had dropped.

"You boys have five seconds to get out of here before I chop you up for dinner," Liv said. "Newbie magicians are the worst because we don't know our own strength or when to stop using it."

Liv spun the knife in her hand, surprised when it stopped with perfect timing and she hadn't cut her fingers off in the process. The first man returned to the ground and the second jumped up, and they both sprinted out the door and away.

CHAPTER THIRTY-NINE

Rory ground his fingers into his palm, heat building in his head, making his eyes red. The floor shook violently under them, nearly knocking the two men off-balance.

Usually, Rory would rely on his brute strength to take these men down, but in the narrow tunnel, he was at a disadvantage. Moving was tricky, and getting anywhere fast was impossible. With the ground shaking more with each passing minute, it complicated the whole situation. Rory had to deal with these meatheads fast and get to Liv.

He heard the click of the gun and narrowed his eyes at the man closest to him. With a simple brush of Rory's hand, the man flew back through the tunnel, landing fifteen feet away, his gun clattering out of his hand.

The other man fired, the bullet hitting Rory square in the chest. He looked down, annoyance on his face.

"Seriously? This is one of my favorite shirts," he growled, looking at the hole the bullet had made in his flannel button-up. He picked the bullet out and flicked it away, shaking his head.

The man backed away, realizing at once that he was absolutely screwed. Giant skin was incredibly tough, and when their magic was activated, as Rory's was now, they were nearly unstoppable. Nearly. Magicians, the experienced ones, knew how to break through a giant's defenses, but Rory didn't have to worry about that with a single mortal staring up at him.

The giant pushed his hand through the air in a quick movement. Although it didn't touch the man, he flew back, landing in a heap next to his associate.

Rory turned in Liv's direction, but it was too late. The tunnel ahead was in the process of collapsing, dust and debris falling in a rush.

The Zonk buzzed loudly, pulling several wires free from the big machine. The humming Liv didn't even realize monopolized the room ceased. The prism paled for an instant, then grew brighter, and then went out completely.

The ghost who was about to walk straight into the prism halted and looked around, confused. Behind him, others did the same, as if they were waking from a daze.

"Go away!" Liv commanded, ushering them out the way they'd come. "Get out of here. This was a trap."

The ghosts looked at her, many of them tilting their heads to the side as though trying to understand her better from a different angle.

"Seriously, get out of here!" Liv yelled, trying to push

the closest ghost away, her hands going straight through the old man.

He blinked at her impassively, and a moment later receded like he had just remembered something he needed to do. One by one, the ghosts dropped through the floor or floated up through the ceiling as the room shook furiously.

Outside in the tunnel, there was a loud crash, followed by a cloud of dust. Liv covered her mouth and coughed, her eyes burning from the debris in the air.

She looked around. "Good work, Zonk. Now we need to figure out how to reverse the prism so that we can get the ghosts in there out."

Inside the prism, shadows danced. Sometimes a form came close to the surface, its features crisp, then faded again. How many ghosts were trapped in there? It was hard to tell.

Liv glanced at the container on the other machine. It wasn't even half full. She wasn't sure how much magic was stored in it, but she couldn't chance it getting into the wrong hands. She tugged at the cylinder, trying to work it free. She heard the Zonk tinkering with the other machine.

The cylinder was stuck in tight, making Liv's fingers cramp from the effort of trying to get it loose. She jerked, and when it finally came free, she stumbled back with the container in tow. The force sent her straight into the prism; she couldn't stop the momentum. She was going to fall directly into it. The sucking feeling took her over. There was no way to resist it.

And then something lurched out of the shadows: a lion the size of a pony. It rammed into her with its paws, knocking her the other way as it leapt over the prism and disappeared.

"Pl-Pl-Pl..." Liv stuttered, suddenly disoriented. She couldn't process what had happened since everything had occurred so fast. She would have thought she'd imagined the whole thing but then Liv looked down and saw the rip in her shirt, the giant lion's claw marks on her shoulder, and the blood oozing down her arm.

CHAPTER FORTY

The men Rory had thrown had fled, which was the smart thing to do with the tunnels collapsing, but he needed to be on the other side of a mound of rubble. He couldn't chance teleporting again. It was because he had done that in the first place that he was in this position, putting Liv in danger. Not Plato, though. That lynx, wherever he was, would live out his nine lives or however many he had left. But Liv—she could still be crushed. A magician could live a few hundred years, but it was never guaranteed. Nothing was, Rory had found.

He hesitated, gazing at the heap of rocks. Magic would be the easiest way to clear it, but that was also the cause of the problem. Rory knew it would take more time, but he set to work clearing the tunnel by hand. That felt like the right approach, and feelings were as good as gold to him. Logic was the downfall of most men because it took the most important factor out of the equation: emotion.

Liv dropped the canister, and it rolled away. Her attention was stolen by the wound on her arm. It didn't hurt yet, but she knew that was only due to shock.

To her surprise, the Zonk quit what it was doing and raced over to her, that strange green substance suddenly in its hands.

"I'm okay," Liv said as it tried to get closer, shoving the glowing green stuff in her direction.

"Hurt. Hurt. Hurt," it sang. "I fix."

Liv nodded. What else was she supposed to say as the room shook from a strange earthquake and then also spun from her lightheadedness.

She was incredibly grateful that Plato or whatever that was had saved her from falling into the prism, and she was only a little miffed that the creature had mauled her arm in the process. She looked away as the Zonk worked, not able to stand the sight of her ripped flesh a moment longer.

Running footsteps stole Liv's attention, and she looked up as a man in a dark green suit, the tails hanging past his knees, ran into the room. He wore a bowler hat, and his expression was full of fury.

Valentino halted as he looked around. He stared first at the prism, pale and dark, the foreboding figures lurking at the surfaces. Then he glanced at Liv, undeniable rage simmering in his eyes.

"*You*," he said, the one word carrying with it conviction and resentment. "How dare you come into my area and try to stop things? Who do you think you are?"

Liv waved the Zonk away, straightening up. "I'm Liv Beaufont, a Warrior for the House of Seven and your worst damn nightmare."

Valentino laughed, a splintered sound carrying no joy. "You're nothing but an untrained magician with no respect for authority."

How did he know that? Liv wondered.

"Like I said, your worst nightmare," Liv repeated.

From the pocket of his long jacket, Valentino pulled out another canister, this one filled to the brim with the bluish liquid. "I was told not to kill you, but I'm known for not being a very good listener."

"Who told you not to kill me?" she questioned.

Another laugh. "People more powerful than you or me." Valentino looked at the canister smugly. "Well, they used to be. Do you know that with what I'm holding right now, I have power you can't even contemplate?"

Liv rolled her eyes. "Come on, give me some credit. I wasn't born yesterday. And also, why do you have to sound so villainous? Like, seriously? You sound like every bad guy who ever met his demise because of greed and deceit."

Liv rose from the ground suddenly and was flung into the machine behind her by a force unlike anything she'd ever experienced. There had been no warning. Valentino didn't flick his wrist or mutter a spell or even twitch. He simply looked at her and she was thrown several feet.

Her head rammed into the machine hard. She thought the ground rumbled under her again, but realized that it was only parts falling around her. The earthquake appeared to have stopped for the moment.

Liv rolled to the side as Valentino floated through the air, landing at her feet. She looked up at the man, not knowing how to proceed. Before she could even consider her options, he yanked her up so she was standing like a statue. Although she tried to move her hands, they felt like they were tied to her body.

"Let me go," Liv said through tight lips.

"Gladly," Valentino answered, and she rose off the ground, hovering just above the prism. "Adding you to this batch will get me to my goal much quicker than using ghosts. It's actually quite nice that you showed up when you did."

Liv half expected the giant lion to jump out of the shadows again to push her out of the way. She tensed, not looking forward to the sharp nails slicing through her arms again.

"Where is the canister?" Valentino asked, his attention suddenly on the machine he'd just thrown her into. "What did you do with it?"

"I released all the magic," Liv lied.

He gave her a skeptical sideways look. "It doesn't matter." A moment later an empty canister appeared where the other one had been. "I think you have enough magic to nearly fill this one all the way, and then... Well, I'll be unstoppable."

"Not if the House locks your magic," Liv fired at him.

This seemed to stall Valentino for a moment. "Yes, I suppose you're right. On second thought, I shouldn't harm you."

He shook her rapidly before setting Liv down dangerously close to the prism. "Yes, on second thought, I think we can help each other."

Something fell out of Liv's pocket as her feet touched the ground, but she was too preoccupied with the Zonk who was following her to try to repair her new injuries to notice.

"I'm not in the business of helping men like you," Liv stated, barely allowed to move her jaw because Valentino had her mostly paralyzed.

He smiled, dragging in a breath. "Oh, but that's the thing; you don't have a choice." He slipped the cylinder of magic into the inside pocket of his jacket. "You, Liv Beaufont, are going to report to the House that you destroyed my area trying to stop my operation. Although I got away, you wrecked all the canisters that I had. Is that understood?"

Liv knew that was wrong. At her core, she knew she hadn't done what Valentino had said or destroyed the magic. However, she found herself nodding. "That's right," she heard someone say, and realized it was her voice.

"Good," Valentino said. "Now, what happened to the canisters of magic?"

"They were all destroyed," Liv stated in a robotic voice. In her head, she was screaming, "No, that's wrong," but it didn't reach her lips.

"And now, I think we should ensure the proof is real." Valentino swiped his hand through the air like a ringmaster opening a show at the circus and the conduit machine cracked, steam issuing from it.

Liv watched but her thoughts muddied. The longer she stood motionless, the harder it was for her to sort reality from the false memories. Maybe all the canisters *had* been destroyed, although for some reason that felt wrong.

Valentino pointed to the machine closest to them and it

exploded, sending sparks all over the place. They hit the floor by Liv's feet, but she remained frozen. Fire broke out from the various machines, taking over the space. Liv knew she needed to run. She needed to get to clean air, but she stood paralyzed.

The Zonk squealed, zipping down to her legs which had been hit by sparks and assaulted when she flew through the air. It was trying to fix her, but it was useless. Her real issue couldn't be fixed, namely that she didn't remember what had happened. Valentino had gotten away, but he was still standing in front of her.

The Zonk let out a high-pitched screech and flew straight up to the ceiling before fleeing. Liv couldn't understand why it had abandoned her until she looked down and saw the ball of wax that must have dropped from her pocket. It had broken open, and hordes of black beetles were crawling out of it. She didn't think much of it until she noticed that they were growing as they progressed across the floor, brandishing their menacing pincers in the air as they made a terrible hissing sound.

As Valentino pointed at the prism, he noticed the Shim-Vens—the man-eating bugs. "What the hell?"

He sent spells at the horde, turning them over and destroying one after another.

Liv suddenly realized she could move. Her fingers flexed, and she backed up several feet.

Valentino caught this movement from his peripheral vision and she was suddenly zooming through the room, then she hit the back wall. "I'm not done with you yet. You'll leave here and report back to the House of Seven, but not until I say. We must make this look like you really botched everything."

Liv slumped, her shoulder felt like it had been dislocated. She grabbed it with her other hand and jerked, trying to put it back into place. A scream ripped from her mouth, and she thought she'd pass out from the pain. Instead, she fell to her side, her cheek pressed hard into the concrete.

And she saw it.

The blue canister. It was only half full, but still... Inches from her face, hidden behind broken equipment, was the other canister. That made no sense to her, because they had both been destroyed—or that was what she remembered, anyway.

Liv reached for the partially full canister as she pushed herself up. Valentino's hand was extended toward the prism, his focus on destroying it, when Liv drew the energy out of the canister. She wasn't sure how it would work, but the task came naturally to her, as if she were using it as a wand or staff. Possession of the cylinder of magic gave her access to it. She felt the magic pulse through every fiber of her being, overwhelming her synapses.

"No!" Liv yelled, her voice seeming to shake the entire room.

Valentino looked up in alarm, his eyes darting to the canister in Liv's grasp. She held her hand out toward him, but he was quick, throwing up an invisible shield. Liv could feel the fight between their magics. As she sought to overpower Valentino, he did the same, his force challenging her on every level.

Liv grunted as sweat poured down her forehead. She inched back, Valentino's magic pushing her away.

The room was quickly filling with fire. She should either run or extinguish it. She had to use her magic for good, but she needed every ounce to combat the magician in front of her.

He was forced back several feet, colliding with the wall.

Liv didn't know how this would end, since it seemed impossible that either of them could win. He wasn't a match for her, not anymore, but she wasn't quite powerful enough with only half the canister of magic to fuel her efforts.

The veins in Valentino's head looked close to bursting as her power pushed him to the side a few more inches.

Liv stood her ground but didn't know how much longer it would last, and then from somewhere she heard a voice she recognized. "Don't push. Pull," it said.

Of course, Liv thought and immediately changed the direction of her magic, yanking Valentino toward her. His eyes bulged at the realization of what was about to happen. He rose into the air and his feet grazed the ground as he sped forward, sucked straight into the prism in a blur. It had happened fast and was over fast. Liv couldn't believe any of it had been real.

She looked around at the fire and smoke. The prism was a prison one could enter but not escape. The room was wrecked, but she was alive.

Light shone from the prism suddenly, glowing brighter by the second. It was like staring at the sun. Liv knew instinctively that the prism was overly full, holding both the ghost magic and now Valentino's, and there was no way to release the power. Liv had stopped Valentino, but she couldn't prevent what was going to happen next. The prism was about to explode, and there was no escaping it.

CHAPTER FORTY-ONE

Rory threw the last large rock out of the way, making an opening that was big enough for him to fit through. Magic would have cleared the tunnel faster, but clearing the rubble by hand had been safer.

On the other side, a light so bright Rory couldn't stand to look at it shone from the room ahead. He shielded his eyes as he charged. "Liv!" he yelled, speeding toward her.

When he reached the entrance to the room, it was hard to make out what was happening. Two large machines were totally destroyed. In the center of the space, a prism the size of a car glowed brightly, vibrating intensely like a volcano about to erupt. And on the far side of the room was Liv, her face red and a blue canister of magic in her hands.

"Come on," Rory yelled.

"I can't," she screamed, her voice nearly drowned out by the fires circling her.

Rory understood at once. She was stuck, and by the looks of it, injured. Liv raised her hands to quell the fires streaming from the prism and machines, but her efforts were futile; the fire would disappear for seconds and then reignite. The magic in the prism couldn't be contained, and it would soon erupt.

"Fly over here," Rory suggested.

Liv hovered a few inches off the ground but fell back down with a thud. Flying took practice and was not easy to pull off when everything around seemed close to exploding.

Rory knew what he must do in that instant, and he didn't hesitate. He strode straight into the fire that surrounded Liv.

Her mouth was gaping open when he crossed the space and snatched her up like a ragdoll. Gently he tossed her onto his back, and she grabbed him around the neck as he charged back the way he'd come.

Liv kept her feet high as they traversed the fire.

The prism hovered a few inches off the ground, and it sounded like glass was shattering inside it over and over. They didn't have much time, or maybe none at all.

Rory had never imagined dying like this. He wouldn't survive the explosion; nothing in the tunnels would. Everything above the surface would feel the repercussions too.

He ran, holding Liv high on his back, careful to pick the path that had the fewest flames.

When they had made it to the other side of the room, Liv slid to the ground, landing on her feet. She streaked around Rory as the noise became deafening. The floor was like lava, melting their shoes as they walked, and the air was thick with smoke. The prism was seconds away from detonating and unleashing all the magic it had stored.

Liv closed her eyes and opened a portal at the entrance to the room. The archway shone with pale light, the blues and greens not quite intense enough.

"Come on, Liv," Rory encouraged, his voice booming. "You've got to believe in yourself. Confidence is the key to portal magic."

She held her hand out in front of her and yelled, voice full of guttural desires. The portal intensified, now looking like an actual door, not an indistinct image.

Rory grabbed Liv by the shoulder and pushed her through the portal, stepping through after her, unconcerned with where they were going. As he crossed the threshold, the prism exploded, sending magic everywhere like shards of glass.

On the other side, he was unsurprised to find Liv doubled over next to John's Repair shop and Plato sitting casually next to her, licking his paw.

CHAPTER FORTY-TWO

"You realize that you put yourself and many mortals in danger," Adler said, looking down at Liv from the bench.

She rolled her shoulder back and forth several times. Hester Devries had helped Liv when she'd shown up at the house, her arm still badly injured. She'd also treated the other cuts and bruises she'd incurred while fighting Valentino. Apparently, the magician had a unique brand of healing magic, which was rare and ran in families although it often skipped several generations.

Hester had been impressed when she'd seen the bandage of sorts the Zonk had put on Liv's shoulder to try to heal the scratches. "It used a substance known as smoglite, which is incredibly versatile," Hester had explained as Trudy had brought Liv a new black t-shirt and jeans.

"I thought you might like this," Trudy had said, giving Liv the clothes since hers were mostly burned and in shreds.

Liv looked at the clothes and Trudy, wondering if they were her way of saying, "I accept you as you are."

Liv thanked her as she hissed from a sudden stinging sensation wrapping around her arm.

"I'm sorry," Hester stated. "There's no way to lessen the pain. I'm pulling the poison out of the wound."

"Poison?" Liv questioned.

"Oh, yes, lynxes have a powerful poison that renders their opponent's unable to move," Hester explained.

Liv remembered trying to fly or even traverse the fires. It had felt impossible. If Rory hadn't shown up...well, she'd be dead. Even the portal would have been impossible if she hadn't drawn from the canister of magic, which was now in the care of the Councilors, who had taken it when she had shown up alone, bleeding, and exhausted.

"He didn't mean to hurt me," Liv said after the stinging died away.

"Who is that, dear?" Hester asked, dressing the wound.

"The lynx," Liv replied.

Hester looked at her uncertainly. "If you battled a lynx and came away alive, you are fortunate indeed. They almost never lose."

"It wasn't like that..." Liv began, but then let her words fade. There were certain things she couldn't tell the Councilors about what had happened in the underground tunnels. Plato, for instance. And Rory. She worried that what she could report wouldn't make any sense.

Liv looked Adler straight in the eye. "I know that, but Valentino was out of control. He was the problem. He was hungry for power. If I hadn't stopped him, who knows what he would have done with the magic?"

"Where is Valentino now?" Adler asked, tapping his long fingers on the bench.

"Well, he's dead, or whatever that prism did to him," Liv stated. She looked at Clark for backup, but he appeared as impassive as ever.

"And you said he tried to brainwash you into believing he'd gotten away?" Raina asked.

"Yes," Liv answered.

"Are you quite certain that he *didn't* get away?" Raina questioned. "He was in control of a great deal of magic, and brainwashing is hard to overcome."

Adler leaned forward. "Yes, how do we know the events you've told are as they really happened?"

"That's not what I mean," Raina stated. "I'm simply pointing out that the events might be muddled in Liv's head. She needs rest."

Adler shook his head. "Most Warriors won't rest tonight since they have to clean up this mess. She shouldn't either."

The other Warriors who had been present when Liv arrived had been sent to the underground tunnels to cover up the commotion the explosion had created. Stefan and Akio had left at once, not looking at all put out by having to put their cases aside for this one.

"How many canisters remained, Ms. Beaufont?" Haro asked.

Liv trembled inside. She knew the answer, but she still questioned it. "There was one; the one I gave to you all."

"But you said there were two," Lorenzo stated.

Liv nodded. "There were two more, but they exploded

with Valentino—or rather, they were the cause of the explosion."

"Are you quite certain?" Adler pressed.

Liv made to nod but then shook her head. "I don't know. I mean, I think both canisters were destroyed."

"Let the record show that the Warrior is unsure of what happened to the canisters of magic and might need to undergo a reverse brainwashing procedure," Adler said at once.

"I-I-I..." Liv stuttered. She glanced at Clark again, but he was unwilling to acknowledge her. She didn't understand it. She'd completed her second case, and she'd survived. She'd brought down an evil man, and he didn't seem the least bit proud of her. But then, she didn't know why it mattered. She hadn't done any of this for him. It had been for their mother and father. For Ian and Reese. For the Beaufont family.

"Ms. Beaufont, you were told to dispel the Zonks," Adler stated.

"But they weren't the problem, as I've proven," Liv shot back.

"Regardless, going against the orders of the Councilors is grounds for punishment and—"

"Liv risked her life to protect magic," Raina said, cutting Adler off.

"And that's the true job of a Warrior," Hester said proudly.

Haro nodded, almost smiling. "I agree. I commend you, young Warrior, on how you handled this case. It might not have been as we, the Councilors, advised, but a little improvising is important in your role."

Adler's light eyes dropped as a scowl took over his face. "I think it's important that we maintain order, is all."

"And thanks to Liv, we have," Raina said joyfully. "I daresay we have more to celebrate tonight than we could have dreamed."

"Celebrate?" Liv asked, perplexed and suddenly wondering where the white tiger was.

"Oh, you must have been too busy with your case," Hester said with a smile. "Tonight is a grand event. It's All Hallow's Eve."

CHAPTER FORTY-THREE

"I don't have anything to wear," Liv argued.

Sophia tapped her small chin and thought for a moment. "Do you want to be a mermaid or a unicorn?"

"I think I want to be a girl who is asleep," Liv answered.

"You have to come to the celebration," Sophia insisted. "Everyone is so excited about you completing this case. I've overheard a lot of people talking about it."

"That's the thing; I don't *have* to do anything," Liv stated, admiring Sophia's dragon costume. She made one of the most beautiful blue dragons Liv had ever set eyes on, with her shimmering scales and long tail.

"So, mermaid or unicorn?" Sophia asked again.

"How about something that isn't real, like a humble vegan or an unpretentious hipster?" Liv asked snidely.

Sophia nodded and pointed. "I've got it."

A moment later, Liv was wearing a ballerina costume, complete with tutu and tiara.

"I didn't realize you wanted me to throw up, dear sister," Liv said, looking down at her pink tights.

Sophia giggled and changed Liv back. "Okay, fine. I think everyone will overlook it if you're not dressed up this year, but next year I want us to do a group costume. Clark, too."

Liv grumbled to herself at the thought of Clark. If he was going to be a part of their costume, it would have something to do with being a traitor.

Music echoed from the hallway outside, making Liv nearly jump. Her nerves were shot after the underground. The shaking of the ground made her think it was another earthquake. She'd had to tell the council those had been the result of Valentino's magic, although Rory had admitted he'd caused the cave-in. She hadn't gotten the details, and he'd pretty much said she didn't need to know.

"You go on ahead," Liv said to Sophia, whose face was brimming with excitement.

"Does that mean you're going to disappear and not show up?"

Liv rolled her eyes. "No, it means that I need a moment to myself before I have to pretend to be nice to people."

"Okay, that's fair," Sophia stated. "I'm going to go save you a spot by the chocolate fountain. They transform the one in the garden so that it flows with chocolate. It's big enough to bathe in."

Liv sighed. "Why can't it be a ranch dressing fountain? I'd be all over that."

"Who doesn't like chocolate?" Sophia asked.

"The soulless," Liv answered. "So, me and vampires."

Sophia offered Liv one last smile, which was almost not visible under the large headdress she was wearing, before going out the door.

Liv looked around the living room of Sophia and Clark's suite. "Okay, come on out."

The room remained quite still. She was about to call out again when from the shadows, Plato materialized, his head hanging as he crossed the space to her.

"Are you sulking?" she asked him when he took a seat before her.

"Are you angry?" he asked.

"If I remember correctly, and I'm not absolutely sure I do," Liv began, "you were trying to save my life. That *was* you, right?"

"You would have fallen into the prism and been lost forever," Plato said, looking up at her, his green eyes shining brightly. "But no, that wasn't me. Let's say it was a friend and I'm just relaying their message."

"Oh, right," Liv said, squatting and looking at Plato. "Will you please tell your friend that I appreciate him saving my life, even if he mauled me in the process?"

"Do you believe what they tell you about me?" Plato asked boldly.

Liv thought about it for a moment. He had heard what Rory and others had been saying about lynxes. Plato had pretended not to care, but the truth was evident on his face. "I believe only that which I see with my own eyes and hear with my own ears and feel with my own heart."

"What does that mean?" Plato questioned.

"It means that as long as you are by my side, I'll never question your loyalty, even if I don't know all the secrets you keep."

"You are both a wise and naïve magician, Liv Beaufont."

Plato bowed his head to her in a show of respect. "Never, ever change."

CHAPTER FORTY-FOUR

The music that filled the House of Seven was eerie, full of haunting notes as Liv descended the stairs to the main floor. Old memories of All Hallow's Eve washed over her with each step. It felt like coming home as she neared the atrium and dining hall that led to the ballroom and the outside gardens. She had never wanted to return home after leaving, which was why she had made one that she loved. However, looking at the decorations and guests dressed in costumes made her lonely for something she had never thought she'd want again: a family.

When she reached the bottom of the grand staircase, she hesitated, thinking she should race down the opposite hallway and leave. However, it would upset Sophia, and nothing was worth that. The little girl was all that was right about the world. She used her magic for good, smiled and made everything better for it and inspired those around her with her light. If magic had ever been worth protecting, it was now, in the world where Sophia Beaufont lived.

"Let me guess," a voice said at Liv's back. "You're dressed as a magician."

Liv spun to find Stefan Ludwig wearing a cunning smile and a tweed jacket, his hair parted smartly down the middle. "And who are you supposed to be, a college professor?"

He tightened his tie and slipped his hands into his pocket. "Actually, I'm F. Scott Fitzgerald."

Liv lifted an eyebrow. "So, when you're not slaughtering innocent magicians, you're reading torturous literature? That sounds about right."

"So you're not a Fitzgerald fan?"

"*Au contraire*. I love all torturous literature, especially if it has a beautiful flow. I just never took you as the...type."

Stefan offered her his arm and smiled. "You know, Liv, in my younger and more vulnerable years, my father gave me some advice that I've been turning over in my head ever since."

"Floss in the back?" Liv asked.

"Never judge a man by how he looks, but always judge him by how he treats others."

Liv looked at the arm he still held out and walked past him. "Well, I guess I'll withhold judgment." She halted, thinking of something. "Your family? Are they new to the House of Seven? I don't remember the Ludwigs."

He nodded, striding up next to her. "Yes, most in the House were replaced in recent years for different reasons. It is only the Beaufonts, Sinclairs, and Takahashis who remain from the Founders."

"Yes, and I remember the Mantovani family. I mean, I grew up with them, although Bianca apparently didn't grow up," Liv stated, looking at the feast in the next room, which seemed to go on for miles.

Stefan laughed. "Oh, I don't think ten more lifetimes will mature *that* magician. She's a product of elitism, which does no one any good."

Liv agreed with a nod, not feeling underdressed at all as she looked out at the sea of elaborate costumes. "But yes, the Ludwigs, De Vries, and Rosarios are all new to the Seven, aren't they?"

He nodded. "They are, and most of us are good, even if you see us as pretentious snobs you'd rather not share a house with."

"How did your family get chosen?" Liv inquired. "Was it because of bountiful donations or centuries of doing the Seven's bidding."

Stefan scanned the room, looking unimpressed. "My grandparents freed an entire village of creatures who were slaves to magicians a few centuries ago. Since then, our name has been on the list and recently came up, giving Raina and me a chance to carry on their legacy."

Liv yawned loudly. "Nice try. I've heard that story a hundred times, though."

Stefan winked at her. "No, you haven't, but if you want the complete tale, do look us up in the history books. It is quite a fascinating period, although not one magicians can be proud of."

Liv excused herself with a nod and strode around the room, hugging the perimeter. She didn't know many in the crowded space and most had their faces covered, making it impossible to discern who they were. That was why she was shocked when a knight in armor walked straight up to her, grabbed her arm, and tugged her away from the crush.

"Hey, what do you think you're doing?" Liv asked, tugging out from the man's grip.

He spun and said, "Don't ask questions. Simply follow me."

She didn't know why she did it, but Liv allowed the man to lead her to the gardens.

The lights twinkling in the topiaries were a magical sight that complimented the fire light of the torches stationed around the garden, and the cool, night air was a welcome sensation on her face after the crowded ballroom.

The knight halted when they were between a brick wall and row of shrubs. He twirled his finger in a circle, and all the noises around them faded away. Liv thought she had gone deaf until Clark lifted the knight's visor to fully reveal his face.

"I put a cloaking spell on us so we can't be heard or seen," he explained.

"Well, damn it," Liv complained. "I wanted everyone to watch while I kicked your ass for being a jerk-face."

Clark scanned the gardens before meeting Liv's eyes. "I know I've been distant."

"Distant?" she questioned. "You treat me like I'm a goblin. You won't even look at me during the Councilors' interrogations. I could have used your help today, and you—"

"I know," Clark said in a hush. "I'm sorry. It's just that I thought...well, I've been trying to remain close to the others."

"Right," Liv said, rolling her eyes. "Because if you scratch their backs, they'll—"

"No, Liv," Clark cut her off. "Because if I can stay close and learn more, I can figure out what's going on."

"What?" Liv asked, suddenly confused.

A loud clanging noise arose as Clark reached into his armor. The gesture wasn't at all graceful. A moment later he withdrew a strip of paper. "Reese left me something, but I only just found it in my stuff. I don't know how or when she put it there, but I know it's from her. It has her mark."

Liv took the piece of paper and opened it, seeing the mark of the butterfly with three antennas, the symbol their sister always put on her correspondence. "Someone could have forged it."

Clark shook his head. "No, it's her handwriting. And the way it showed up on my desk? Well, it reminded me of a spell Reese had been working on. She called it 'the living will' spell. The idea was that if anything should happen to someone, upon their death, the message or token or whatever they left for someone would be delivered on the seventh day following their death."

"And this note?" Liv asked, although she knew the answer.

"It appeared on the morning of the seventh day after her and Ian's deaths."

Liv opened the parchment all the way and read through it three times, but it didn't make any sense to her.

Olivia has the key. You have the heart. Together you must finish what we started.

Love,

Reese.

Liv looked up, not sure what to make of the three sentences. "I have the key to what?"

Clark took the paper back. "That I don't know. I don't even know what she meant by the heart, but I know that Ian and Reese were trying to tell us something. We can't ignore this message."

For a moment, Liv wanted to pull out the ring in her pocket and show it to Clark, but she still didn't trust him. "What do you mean, we can't ignore it?"

Clark looked around for a moment before focusing on her again, his movements tense. "I'm not sure what's going on. I think Ian and Reese were onto something. Maybe even our parents, too—"

"Oh, so you're finally admitting that their deaths were suspect?" Liv asked, cutting him off.

He waved his metal gauntlets at her. "I'm not sure that's what I'm saying. All I know is that we should stick together and try to learn more. We need evidence and more information."

"Four people we love have died, and we have nothing to prove that it was suspect except a lot of circumstantial evidence that doesn't add up. Like, why did they die together? Mom and Dad, and Ian and Reese? Why were their deaths unexplained? And—"

Ian nodded, interrupting her. "I know. It *is* weird, and I think you're overly paranoid. I'm probably overly dismissive."

"Well, as long as you're finally owning that."

Clark leaned closer. "There's something else."

Liv simply stared at her brother, waiting for his next words.

"I went and checked for the canister in the storage locker after the fact, and it's missing."

"What?" Liv asked.

"Yeah, and then I checked the record you provided, and it claims that you said both canisters were destroyed in the explosion," Clark explained.

"But I brought back one of them," Liv said and hesitated. "Wait, I did, didn't I?" Suddenly she couldn't remember what the reality was: this, or the one Valentino had planted in her head. It was all muddled.

"I think someone was hoping that you'd confuse things, and they're relying on that now," Clark said.

The truth dawned on Liv, and she felt a loud ticking in her chest. "Do you think that Adler—"

The look on Clark's face silenced her. "I don't know what to believe yet. You shouldn't either. We need to investigate, but carefully. It feels as though Ian and Reese might have left us clues, but we need to proceed with great caution."

"Yes, because if someone killed them for what they knew, the exact same thing could happen to us."

Clark agreed with a nod. "I promise to stick by your side, even if that doesn't appear to be what I'm doing."

"You're creating a façade, so as to not draw attention," Liv realized.

"Yes, because you're drawing enough attention," he said with a laugh.

"Should I stop?" she questioned. Getting closer to the truth was the only thing Liv had wanted for a long time, but she'd given up, and then she'd forgotten.

"No, keep doing what you're doing," Clark told her. "I

wasn't able to tell you this publicly, but what you did with this case was brilliant. Mom and Dad would have been extremely proud of your bravery."

Liv didn't know what to say to that, and the tension in her throat was so tight it was hard to breathe through it.

"Liv, going forward, I want us to work together," Clark said, holding out a hand. "But that means you're going to have to be upfront with me. Trust me, and also listen to me when I give you advice. Do we have a deal?"

Liv eyed his armored hand. He was offering a true partnership. That was how the Warriors and Councilors were supposed to operate, but they hadn't been acting in that way since the beginning. She thought of the House of Seven and how it had been set up to create balance. Warriors and Councilors, working together to protect magic. Her parents had loved and honored those roles. They had risked everything for them because that was what they believed in.

And although Liv had doubted the honor of the House of Seven for so long, deep in her core, she felt that its original mission was still true. The partnerships the Founders had set up were a beautiful thing, meant to preserve one of the most powerful forces in the world: magic.

Liv took Clark's hand and shook it, looking him directly in the eyes. She felt invisible energy bind their hands, as if creating a pact. "Yes. To working together, brother, so that we can find the truth and also protect magic."

Clark smiled back at his sister. "Actually, do you remember what Dad used to say about truth and magic?"

Liv thought for a moment and was about to tell him

that she didn't recall, but then a voice she hadn't heard in ages and had sorely missed echoed in her head. She spoke the words as they sounded in her mind. "The truth that binds all things is the ultimate way to protect magic, but first it must be discovered."

FINIS

Returning to my fantasy roots after a stint in science fiction and chick lit, has been majorly awesome. I still had to put some scifi elements in this series though, because that's my thing. The magic tech was a lot of fun and hopefully will complicate things (in a good way) as the books progress.

When Michael and I were crafting this universe, I remember sitting on the floor of my office and writing notes as he spouted off ideas. Those notes are pretty much unreadable. I've decided that I'm going to start recording our conversations, since then I can actually go back and review everything he said. Seriously, Michael, do you take speed talking classes?

Michael was pretty adamant, early on, that there be a giant on Liv's team. He kept calling him George, which totally made my notes hilarious when reviewing: "George throws her into a bar fight." "George is secretly nice." "George wants a tall girlfriend." The reason this is especially funny is "George" is the fake name I call my ex-husband in books and on social media to protect his identity. George *is* secretly nice. Very secretly.

At one point, we were trying to figure out a companion for Liv. Dogs are great, but that's been done a lot. Then there are trolls and fairies and whatnot. I threw out there that Liv's sidekick was a cat. To which Michael asked, "Why a cat?"

I looked up at my office chair at that moment to find my own cat sitting in my spot. That's why I'd taken a seat on the floor. Damn animal runs the show at my house. That's when Plato was created.

The next morning, I randomly opened these chaotic notes to a page. It read, "Dogs are hookers."

Seriously, I need to record our conversations. Piecing together the notes and trying to figure out all the awesome ideas we wanted included in this first book took some time. I'm pretty sure I had to turn the notebook upside down, at one point, to read the words that went around the paper. Still, I think it all worked out. Michael got his giant and I got the cat and many of the best moments in the book came out of that first conversation.

Michael randomly throws out ideas when we're talking. They always get me thinking and bring a freshness to the book. One such idea was when Liv got drunk. Michael was talking about Liv being a rebel and said, "And so this guy says, 'Are you drunk?' and Liv answers, 'Are you ugly?' Then later she can be like, 'Well, you're still ugly.'"

And that's how the magic happens. I believe that I've become a better writer working with Michael. He helps me to innovate my own writing. And has taught me that sometimes the best chapters are where the characters just chill and explore and bond. Oh, and the banter.

I loved crafting this series as a team and look forward to many more.

Without further ado, I'll turn the mic over to MA. I'm sure he can't wait to tell you about why he *didn't* go down the slide in Bali. Everyone else was doing it...

MICHAEL'S AUTHOR NOTES
JANUARY 31, 2019

THANK YOU for not only reading this story but these *Author Notes* as well.

(I think I've been good with always opening with "thank you." If not, I need to edit the other *Author Notes*!)

RANDOM (*sometimes*) THOUGHTS?

DOGS ARE HOOKERS

I wonder if Sarah is going to look at all the items she mentioned in her *Author Notes* and say, "Really? Dogs are hookers is the piece you took out of that?'

First, she does mention the whole "I'm going to record our conversations" part in our talks. However, that comment has been made multiple times, and it hasn't yet occurred, so I'm lumping it in there with "the check's in the mail," "words are on the page," and "the sequel will be done soon." That isn't a comment about Sarah, she writes FAST.

Ok, back to dogs.

If you follow Sarah on social media, she mentions this

…"cat" (for lack of a better term, since that is the physical form the conniving jester sent to punish humankind is walking around in at the moment.)

Don't believe me? Why is a grown-ass adult woman who wouldn't let a man move her from her desk allowing a one-foot-tall meowing monstrosity do it? Hmmm? See…

It's true.

Now, back to dogs.

Wait, back to the cat. I didn't finish that thought.

Anyway, she mentions her cat and ALL the issues she has with it, and I believe has tried to sell or give away said cat multiple times. She has a dysfunctional relationship with her cat. Then again, most (but not all) cat owners have a master-slave relationship with their cat.

I guess we know who is prepared for the alien overlord future.

Anyway, I'm giving Sarah grief about her cat challenge, laughing at her as she TRIES to defend her position (can't, it's objectively a problem) and she mentions that cats give their love to precious few. The chosen. The chosen few of the cats that receive their benevolent love.

"So, dogs are hookers, then?" I asked.

And BAM! We have an *Author's Note*.

AROUND THE WORLD IN 80 DAYS

One of the interesting (at least to me) aspects of my life is the ability to work from anywhere and at any time. In the future, I hope to re-read my own *Author Notes* and remember my life as a diary entry.

This will be short—I'm in my dark(er) office. Power was shot to hell when the "neighbors" up a couple of floors had a contractor flood their unit, the unit beneath them, and one over (ours) right before the Christmas holidays.

We were leaving for six weeks.

Ok, so fans installed, holes drilled in walls, and vents cut out to dry the walls. I'm told I will have electricity in my office when everything dries.

We were gone for six weeks, practically. Fans were finished, we arrive back (to a messy office because of moving stuff around for the fans) and electricity…

Is still not working.

People come back over, go to the jack in the floor. "Yup, water is probably in the floor. It hasn't evaporated because of the PVC pipe, and that's why it won't work."

It would have been nice for someone to have thought about that BEFORE we left on vacation. So, right now I'm sitting in the dark office, typing on the laptop with light streaming in from the nearby bathroom.

With another fan blowing air into a 4" hole to dry out the long pipe.

Just for giggles, they hooked up the lights in the other bedroom to the same circuit. So, there is no electricity in that room either.

I recognize that we are blessed to have electricity at all, and no electricity in two locations isn't the biggest problem.

But, have you counted how many things you plug in to charge up in your life?

It's a lot.

FAN PRICING

$0.99 Saturdays (new LMBPN stuff) and $0.99

Wednesday (both LMBPN books and friends of LMBPN books.) Get great stuff from us and others at tantalizing prices.

Go ahead. I bet you can't read just one.

Sign up here: http://lmbpn.com/email/.

HOW TO MARKET FOR BOOKS YOU LOVE
Review them so others have your thoughts, and tell friends and the dogs of your enemies (because who wants to talk to enemies?)… *Enough said ;-)*

Ad Aeternitatem,

Michael Anderle

ACKNOWLEDGMENTS
SARAH NOFFKE

My favorite part of writing any book is creating the acknowledgements page. It reminds me that writing a book is not a solo task. I might sit alone and write, but the finished product is a result of the support and encouragement of a tribe of people.

Thank you to the readers who buy the books, read them, review and recommend. YOU are the one who keeps us writing. I'm always inspired by the messages I receive from readers. Thank you supporting the books and offering so much richness to my life.

Thank you to my LBMPN family for all the support. Steve, Michael, Lynne, Moonchild, Jennifer and so many others who help champion the book to publication and beyond.

Thank you to the beta readers who offered so many valuable insights early on. Thank you to John, Chrisa, Kelly, Martin and Larry.

Thank you to the JIT team for all the awesome feedback. A new series is always exciting and nerve-wracking.

Michael and I thought we had a great idea for a new world, but we don't really know until we get objective feedback. What would I do without all you awesome readers?

Thank you to my friends and family. Writing is a strange profession. I work weird hours, talk to myself, have a strange diet, get antsy about deadlines. But the wonderful people in my life continue to show their encouragement and thoughtfulness no matter what. It is never lost on me because I know that I wouldn't be doing what I love without all you amazing people, cheering me on.

And as with all my books, the final thank you goes to my muse, Lydia. I wrote my first book so that I could make my daughter proud, and it's never stopped. I write every book for you, my love.

Check out Sarah Noffke's YA Dystopian Fantasy:

What if everything you knew was a lie?

Em is a Defect, one of the unfortunate Dream Travelers not gifted with a psychic power. Desperate to do whatever it takes to earn her gift, she endures painful injections. But they aren't working.

The truth is hiding.

A long-kept secret begins to unravel when Em Fuller starts looking for the truth. Her seemingly perfect town is not at all what she thought it was.

What she finds doesn't make sense.

While searching for clues, someone grabs Em, pulling her into a closet to hide from the authorities. But it's not a stranger. For years, Em thought that Rogue Vider was dead.

Some things are worse than death.

Rogue reveals a shocking, unforgivable truth.

She has a choice: Run or hide.

Em's society has been betraying her, but she has no idea how to break away from its authority without hurting everyone she loves.

Get Defects here.

CONNECT WITH THE AUTHORS

Connect with Sarah and sign up for her email list here:

http://www.sarahnoffke.com/connect/

You can catch her podcast, LA Chicks, here:

http://lachicks.libsyn.com/

Connect with Michael Anderle and sign up for his email list here:

Website: http://lmbpn.com

Email List: http://lmbpn.com/email/

Facebook:
www.facebook.com/TheKurtherianGambitBooks

BOOKS BY MICHAEL ANDERLE

For a complete list of books by Michael Anderle, please visit:

www.lmbpn.com/ma-books/

All LMBPN Audiobooks are Available at Audible.com and iTunes

To see all LMBPN audiobooks, including those written by
Michael Anderle please visit:

www.lmbpn.com/audible

www.ingramcontent.com/pod-product-compliance
Lightning Source LLC
Chambersburg PA
CBHW031613100726
47898CB00006B/1775